Entice

Also by Carrie Jones
Need
Captivate

Entice

Carrie Jones

BLOOMSBURY

NEW YORK BERLIN LONDON SYDNEY

First published in the United States of America in December 2010
by Bloomsbury Books for Young Readers
www.bloomsburyteens.com

For information about permission to reproduce selections from this book, write to
Permissions, Bloomsbury BFYR, 175 Fifth Avenue, New York, New York 10010

Library of Congress Cataloging-in-Publication Data
Jones, Carrie.
Entice / Carrie Jones. — 1st U.S. ed.
p. cm.
Summary: When evil pixies invade Bedford, capturing more teens every day, sixteen-year-
old Zara's quest to bring Nick back from Valhalla becomes more urgent, but she fears he will
not return with her since she has been pixie kissed and become Astley's queen.
ISBN 978-1-59990-553-2
[1. Supernatural—Fiction. 2. Pixies—Fiction. 3. Metamorphosis—Fiction.
4. Missing persons—Fiction. 5. Kings, queens, rulers, etc.—Fiction.
6. Maine—Fiction.] I. Title.
PZ7.J6817Ent 2010   [Fic]—dc22   2010027655

Book design by Nicole Gastonguay
Typeset by Westchester Book Composition
Printed in the U.S.A. by Quad/Graphics, Fairfield, Pennsylvania
2 4 6 8 10 9 7 5 3 1

All papers used by Bloomsbury Publishing, Inc., are natural, recyclable products
made from wood grown in well-managed forests. The manufacturing processes
conform to the environmental regulations of the country of origin.

To Emily—the most awesome and glorious person ever! Drink water!

Law enforcement authorities are still investigating the strange bus accident that recently killed several Sumner High School students. Meanwhile, Bedford police advise that another boy has been reported missing from that town, bringing the total up to eight. —NEWS CHANNEL 8

"Am I really not allowed to complain about being here?" I ask as we enter Bedford High School about an hour late for the winter ball. In an attempt to make it more ball and less high school, the lights are dimmed in the front foyer and giant white snowflakes and twinkly lights dangle from the ceiling. They are supposed to look festive, but they are dingy from years of use. The white is sort of an off-yellow that looks like old tea-stained teeth more than snow.

Cassidy, my tall, braided, partially elf friend, puts her arm around me. "If we aren't allowed to complain about your new pixie status, you aren't allowed to complain about the dance."

Issie stomps the real snow off of her pink and gold heels and chirps, "Actually, I think you are allowed to complain a couple times, but not—"

"Not excessively?" Devyn suggests, pulling his birdlike body up to its full height. It's like he's posturing, showing me that he's protecting Issie. He keeps looking at me out of the corner of his eye like I might attack any second. But I won't—I mean, I don't think I will.

"Exactly. Not excessively." Issie beams up at him, smiling, and it's so sweet how she does it and how he smiles back that something inside me breaks a tiny bit. Nick and I used to be like that. Then he died. Sort of. A pixie king killed him. He died in my arms and then a winged woman took him away to some mystical place that only warriors who have died in battle can go. My breath stops, just remembering it—the blood, the way he was just gone.

"Zara?" Cassidy's arm tightens around my shoulders as we march forward. I guess since she's a bit psychic and can "see into my soul," she's the only one who seems to trust me a hundred percent when *I* don't even trust me a hundred percent. "You okay?"

I nod. I am not going to ruin the night for them. But then I smell it . . . Dove soap, the copper metal tang of blood. "Something's wrong."

Issie sidles up to me. "I know you miss Nick, but we'll find a way to get him—"

I shake my head, listening. "That's not it. Something's wrong in the school. I can smell blood . . . blood and fear."

Issie drops my arm as Devyn stills and says, "I smell it too."

Dev and I exchange a look and start running down the hallway. I yell behind to where Issie and Cass are. "Hide, guys. Okay?"

We burst into the dark, decorated cafeteria. White Christmas-style trees with blue lights are splayed along the walls. Hip-hop music pumps through the air. People are moving frantically, but they're dancing mostly, not running for their lives. Devyn and I stand there, surveying all the gowns and suits, smelling the sweat and way-too-intense cologne.

"Do you see anything?" I ask.

He starts to say no, but then he points to the darkest corner, where fake Christmas trees half hide movement in the soda machine alcove. Two girls in bizarre gowns are yanking at a guy I don't recognize, pulling on his tie, hustling him out the emergency exit door. He's bleeding from the nose and the wrist. That's the blood I'm smelling, and even though it's pretty obvious he's been drinking alcohol, I can smell his fear too. It rolls off him almost solid, like a color of air around him—yellow and dark brown.

"Dev—," I start.

He interrupts me. "I can't change here. People will see."

Devyn is a were. He can shift into an eagle.

"Just back me up," I tell him, which is a total role reversal. I'm usually the one who backs other people up. Still, I say it and mean it as I bump through dancing groups and couples who are so into themselves that they don't notice anything at all.

Devyn murmurs in my ear, "There are two of them."

"Devyn . . . let me go first," I say again, trying to hurry without being too obvious. The girls are hustling the guy toward a door marked FIRE EXIT. They're moving pretty fast and I know if they get him out of here he's a goner, because they aren't regular girls. They are pixies. They're going to bite at him and torture him and basically drain his soul until he goes insane or dies.

How do I know this? I know because now I'm a pixie too.

I bang toward them and position myself between them and the door. Just like me, they appear human, hiding their blue skin and their freaky sharp teeth with a glamour. One wears a red dress that looks and smells like it's been hanging out in a Goodwill since the 1980s. Puffy sleeves with shoulder pads give her football uniform shoulders, and monster ruffles along the bottom hem do not help things. The other one wears a black cutout dress that only supermodels should even look at. She's got her hair in a French twist.

"Stop," I say.

Eighties Dress raises an eyebrow. "We are having far too much fun to stop."

Oh, that's original.

The second pixie, who looks like a red-haired Barbie, snarls at me while batting her eyelashes, which would be weird enough even if she didn't have blood on her teeth.

I try to make myself as tough seeming as possible. "I said stop."

They laugh.

I admit that I am not the most intimidating-looking person— pixie? whatever—but laughing at me is *so* not cool. This horrible, *horrible* primal rush of anger surges through me as I take a step forward and the guy in between the pixies staggers backward, hitting the wall. His suit coat rumples up behind his butt as he starts sliding down. Devyn lunges forward to help him, but Evil Red-Haired Barbie shoves Devyn backward into me. I catch him at the waist and leap around him.

"You need to calm down," I say, pointing my finger at her like some kind of angry teacher-person, "*and* you need to leave. This is my school, and you are not messing with the people here."

"You and Mr. Skinny are going to stop us?" Barbie tucks her hair behind her ears, obviously not impressed.

"Eww. Why would you even want to claim this school? It smells like a strip mall," the other one says.

I don't answer either of them, just stare the first one down as Drunk Boy flops onto the floor and starts crawling away.

"I don't want to hurt you," I say, stepping forward, "so this is your last chance."

"She's a pacifist," Devyn says behind me, standing up again. I wonder why he's saying this. Is it to remind me of who I used to be or to remind himself? "Do you know what that means?" he adds.

They look at us blankly.

"It means I don't believe in fighting," I explain, taking another step closer. The tension fills the air. I know they're both ready to strike, to tear and rip with teeth and hands. But I have no idea if I can fight them. I know I'm stronger now that I'm a pixie, but all the emotions rushing through me . . . I don't know if I can control them.

Nick would take the stronger one down first, make a statement. So that's what I decide to do. My arm snatches out and grabs Barbie by the wrist. I squeeze and sweep my legs underneath her to try to trip her. She doesn't fall for it, jumping back. Her free hand smashes into my stomach. I *oomph* but don't fall either. Instead, I do the first thing I can think of, which is kick at her again—and this time it's like something has switched on. I'm way faster than I should be. The kick connects with her shin. I send another one to her thigh as she staggers.

Then I grab her hair. My fingers smoosh into the twist. Yanking her head to my ear, I say, "Get out of here before I ruin your heels *and* your dress *and* your face."

She snarls menacingly at me, but there's no way she can move.

"Devyn, is anyone looking?" I ask.

"Nope," he answers.

The other pixie harrumphs. "Fine. We'll go. Can we take the meat?"

She gestures toward the drunk boy, who is trying to crawl back toward the punch table.

"No," I answer. "This is me in my warning phase. This is *me* telling *you* to get out before I really lose my pacifist ways and kill you. So tell your little king— Who is your king?"

"Frank," Barbie answers.

"Frank," I repeat, taking it in. Not my biological father. Frank, the one who released all my dad's pixies from where we'd trapped them in an old Victorian house in the woods. Frank, the one who killed my boyfriend, Nick. "Well, tell Frank that he has a ridiculous name for an evil pixie king and also tell him that I will not stand for any of his little minions attacking people at my school. Got it?"

"And to return the people who are missing," Devyn adds.

Something clutches my stomach. It's dread. I look at Devyn. What's happened since I've turned? "How many people?"

"Too many to count," Eighties Dress says. "The people here are so easy to take. And to kill. And scaring them? It's delicious."

Anger scrapes my throat. "No more. Tell him no more. The people here are not toys."

Even I can hear the threat in my voice, hard and even, a drum pounding war beats into the air.

Eighties doesn't answer. Her friend does. "Who are you to tell Frank what to do?"

Good question. I shove Barbie toward the fire door and try to come up with a snappy answer worthy of cult movies and TV shows. But before I say anything, Devyn answers for me, almost like he's proud of me rather than horrified that I've just turned into one of them. "She is Zara White, a pixie queen."

*L*ife goes on as usual in this small coastal Maine town. Even though eight boys are missing, local teens celebrated at the high school's annual winter dance tonight. —NEWS CHANNEL 8

After the pixies are safely disposed of outside, Devyn and I find Issie and Cassidy waiting by the bathrooms. Devyn continues the looking-at-me-out-of-the-corner-of-his-eyes routine, but I'm hoping the fact that I dispatched the pixies will make him trust me a bit more. That I managed to do it without going blue and feral makes me feel just the tiniest bit more confident about my new species, but the truth is I really don't know what it means to be a pixie. I don't know if it's changed my insides, that soul part of me, the pacifist part.

"Was there an apocalypse in there?" Is asks when she and Cassidy and I enter the empty bathroom. "Is everyone dead? Please don't tell me everyone is dead."

"Nobody died," I say, sighing and reaching up. "Except maybe my hair."

They usher me toward the bathroom mirrors, where I tell them what happened. Cassidy twists my hair into a messy knot.

Issie tries to wipe a bloodstain off my arm. I stare into the mirror, take in the crazy circles under my eyes, the whole blah look of me. "I look horrible."

"Naw," Issie lies. I know she's lying because her bottom lip trembles.

Cassidy grabs me by the shoulders, stands behind me, and rests her head on top of mine. "You look like a warrior."

"Yeah!" Issie agrees. "A slightly short warrior. A pixie warrior."

There's an awkward pause.

"Do you feel different?" she asks in a much gentler voice. "Now that you're all . . . you know . . ."

"Yeah." I nod. "Stronger. I feel . . . I smell things more. It's like my senses are sharper but I feel more volatile, you know? Like anything will make me cranky."

"Especially evil pixies trying to steal away members of our male student population?" Issie suggests.

"Especially," I agree as I borrow Cassidy's mascara, which you're not supposed to do because of bacteria, but considering the rest of my crazy life, I'm willing to take this particular health risk. "I can't believe there are so many people missing. Eight? That's just horrible, Is. We have to get Nick back and stop this."

Cierra slams into the bathroom with Callie, who is sporting ribbons in her bright blue Mohawk. They smile hello and everyone compliments one another's dresses, and then they go into the stalls. Issie leans down and whispers, "What do you want to do? Should we all go home?"

I want to, but that would be selfish. "Nah, I want to see you and the Devster dance. And stuff."

She goes up on tiptoes. "Really?"

"Swear." I put up my hand like a Girl Scout promise. "And we will all just pretend everything is normal and supernatural threats don't hover outside the fire exit door."

"So we go into denial," Cassidy says, smiling, as she scratches her waist.

"Yep." I reach up and wipe some mascara that's clotted near her eye. "But only for the rest of the dance. Then we go into action."

All around us people are dancing, laughing, spinning, having fun in the kind of corny, cheese ball way that people do when they know the dance is beyond lame but somehow that ultra-geekiness almost makes it cool. Along the wall and in little clumps are the dateless girls who are eyeing the dateless guys. I am one of those dateless girls now, because Nick is gone, really gone.

Issie stops dancing with Devyn long enough to wrap an arm around my shoulders. She leans in and yells in my ear because that's the only way her tiny voice can be heard over the raging music. "You miss him, huh?"

My stomach clenches up. "Yeah."

"We'll find him," she insists. "We'll bring him back."

I give her a half smile and nod, because the truth is I have to believe what she says. I have to believe that Nick is alive in Valhalla and that somehow we can bring him back here, where he belongs.

"We'll get him," I yell back, trying to sound as determined and positive as I can. My lips hit her dangling pink flamingo earrings. She smells like coconuts.

She does one of her super-vigorous nods. "That's right. We will!"

Devyn looks back and forth between us. His mouth presses into a line and I know—I *know*—that he has doubts.

Just then the music changes from loud and awesome and frenetic to slow-dance time. I groan. Devyn pulls Issie into his arms. He looks tired from all the exercise. I can see it in the crinkles around his eyes, the tightness of his lips, like he's holding the pain in so Issie can have fun and not worry. He's only just started walking again. He'd been injured and was stuck in a wheelchair, paralyzed in a pixie attack, actually.

Cassidy and I stand together while Issie and Devyn sort of sway side to side and press into each other. They both look fragile and bird boned, easily broken.

"They are so sweet," Cassidy says into my ear.

I nod. She smells like lavender and herbs.

"You doing okay?" she asks again. Her voice flits down to me. I nod again.

This time she doesn't let me get away with it. She bumps me with her hip. "Liar."

I kneel down and fidget with the anklet Nick gave me. It's thin and silver, a reminder of him flush against my skin. I check the clasp, make sure it won't break, and say, "To say this sucks is an understatement."

She pets my head like I'm a puppy. "I know, honey. I know. Your misery is pretty obvious."

Callie and Paul, who have matching Mohawks and have been going out forever, tango past us even though this song is totally not a tango. They both smile and Callie waves, just lifts her hand up a tiny bit.

Jay Dahlberg scoots closer to us and fake bows. When he stands up straight again, his thick blond hair ruffles into his eyes. He reaches out his hand like some sort of eighteenth-century duke. "Miss Cassidy, may I please have this dance?"

She scratches at her neck while simultaneously saying in this super-fake pretentious voice, "I would be honored, Mr. Dahlberg."

He pulls her into his arms and she looks at me over her shoulder as if to ask if it's okay. I give her the thumbs-up sign and start toward the wall.

Nick and I slow-danced once, late at night after we'd gone to a really awful movie about a girl ghost kid who didn't actually say anything, just looked pale and walked around while people screamed when they saw her. After that had happened for the twenty-seventh time in the movie, Nick remarked, "No wonder she wants to kill people. They're giving that girl a complex."

After the movie Nick pulled me out of his red MINI Cooper and stood me under the stars. Our feet crunched on the snow.

"What are you doing?" I laughed as he put his arms around me.

"Salvaging our date." He cuddled me close to him so that I could breathe his pine scent and the leather of his jacket. He was warm. He was always so warm.

The music on his iPod in the MINI changed to a slow U2 song. He was not into U2. I am, but only old U2 from the eighties and nineties. This was one of those—a haunting heartbeat of a song all about love and war.

"You hate this song," I murmured into his sweater. He is so much taller than I am. I went up on tiptoes to get closer.

He bent his head toward me and smiled. "But you love it."

He must have downloaded it for me, which was so sweet. I snuggled in closer, as close as I could. "You know it's about the Polish Solidarity movement?"

"Really?" He acted mock surprised. And then we kissed. His lips fit perfectly.

"Zara," a male voice by my ear makes me jump. The clean smell of Dove soap mixed with mushrooms seems to overwhelm my nose. It is how I smell now too. It is the specific smell of pixie kings and queens.

Astley stands in front of me, dark blond and tall and much more rugged looking than when he was half dead and bound to a tree just a few weeks ago. My skin bristles. So much has happened so quickly. I lost Nick. I lost my humanity. And what did I gain? I became a pixie.

I grab Astley by the impeccably dressed elbow and fast-walk him to the side of the room by the vending machines, scanning the crowd. People have noticed he's here. Devyn makes to come over, as does Cassidy, but I shoo them away with my hand and loud-whisper to Astley, "What are you doing here? I already had to deal with enough pixies tonight, thank you. No offense."

He doesn't answer my question. Instead he appraises my outfit. "You look lovely. I am used to you in those jeans with the holes and peace signs inked onto them. They have that homeless look, but—"

He pauses for a second, awkwardly, and I can tell that he's remembering me when I turned pixie, after he'd kissed me when I was a bloody, awful mess, feral and barely conscious. I can feel my face flush with heat that comes from embarrassment. I don't know how I know he's thinking about this, but I do.

"Yeah . . . well . . . Issie and Cassidy dressed me, so no homeless look tonight," I explain, feeling pretty self-conscious. Letting go of his elbow, I yank on the bodice of my dress so I don't show too much skin; then I realize how silly this is since he pretty much saw me naked when he turned me. I lean my shoulders against the wall. *Do not think about it. Do NOT think about it . . .*

He shifts closer to me, puts an arm up on the wall, hand next to my head, and asks, "How did they take the news that you had changed?"

"They were suspicious at first," I say, putting it pretty mildly. I don't explain how they didn't want to let me in Issie's house at all or how Devyn basically threatened me. "But they've accepted it—I think."

For a second I contemplate telling him that they only trusted me because Cassidy checked me out for evil intentions, which she could do because, unlike me, she has an elf ancestor a long way back. But I don't quite trust him a hundred percent yet even though I trusted him enough to dehumanize me and turn me into a pixie. Strange but true, like pretty much everything in my life.

"Did you hear what I said before about pixies? Devyn and I had to bounce two pixie girls who were munching on a drunk guy," I tell him.

"Bounce?" He lifts an eyebrow. His voice gets lower when he's confused. I never noticed that before.

I tell him the story. He doesn't say anything for a minute, and then he touches my arm lightly, just brushing it with his fingers almost like he's afraid to startle me. It's the quickest of movements, and then he uses that same hand to gesture toward the dancers. "They are all so innocent, are they not?"

"Innocent?" It's hard to think of Cierra and her current boy toy, Jake, as all that innocent since they are basically dry-humping in the corner. One of the teachers, Mr. Burns, heads straight over there. He's power-walking like a pro.

"They are so unaware of all the magic in their midst. Here we are, pixies. Your friend Devyn is a were. Outside, in the woods, scores of pixies lurk, regrouping, hungry, filled with needs."

I whirl on him. "We have to protect them."

He cocks his head just the tiniest of bits. His hair shakes out over his eyes and then falls back into place. He is standing so close to me. I step backward as he says, in his super-calm voice, "Of course. And you have to meet our people, Zara. They need to meet their queen. They will fight beside you."

"And we have to find Nick," I insist. "We have to get started."

He doesn't answer, just puts out his hands. The music switches to another ballad about love and loss. "Dance with me, Zara?"

"Oh . . ." I stumble for words. "I don't—ah Nick—"

He swoops me into his arms before I finish my sentence. He dances formally, gracefully, not like a high school guy at all, but I guess that's the pixie king in him. He's more like a professional dancer on one of those dance competition reality shows. His posture is straight and his movements are fluid. He is nothing like Nick, who dances like a big goofy dog, really. Dancing with Astley is easy. It feels like I've been doing it forever.

"It's not so bad, is it?" Astley whispers near my ear.

I pull away, a little jarred. "Yes. Yes. No— I mean—"

He smiles at my confusion but doesn't let go. His hand moves slightly against my back. It's like I'm hyperattuned to every move he makes. I don't know if it's just normal pixie senses or because he's my king.

Their clothes are different too. Nick dresses like a guy from Maine, massive boots or running shoes, jeans, clothes from one of the nicer stores at the mall, while Astley's clothes are textured and expensive, richly made. The fabrics are deeper and more rugged somehow. They make me think of Scotland.

I decide to use the moment to ask him some of the questions

that circle round and round inside my mind. "Did you find out anything? Did you talk to your mother?"

His mother is supposed to know how to get to Valhalla, this ungettable place of myth that supposedly has Nick. Astley frowns and then pulls me all the way into his chest. It moves with each of his breaths. "She is missing at the moment."

"Missing!" This time I pull all the way away. "How convenient."

His hand reaches out and grabs mine before I can react. "I am not lying to you, Zara. She does this a lot."

"Right," I say as he tries to draw me closer. That's not going to happen. I pull against him. Frustration rattles my teeth. "I refuse to dance with you."

"I could force you."

"But you won't." I say this like I'm certain of it, like I'm certain of who he is, but really I'm not certain of anything.

We stand there for a moment, staring down each other as the rest of the people in the cafeteria swirl and swoon and fall in love. We are at a stalemate. His eyes soften. He lets me go, dropping his arms away, and I feel suddenly, terribly alone. I almost kind of want to dance with him again, which is so wrong, I know.

For a moment his face is sad, but he covers it quickly with a smile. "I apologize. I have confused you somehow. I am going to patrol outside, make sure it is safe for the students as they leave."

He bows and backs away, leaving me in the middle of the dance floor. He cuts through the throngs of people easily, bumping and jostling no one, as if he could do it blindfolded.

I reach down and check the clasp of my anklet. It's still tight, still secure. I am not alone, not while there is still hope of finding

Nick, not while I still have my friends. My will seems to solid up. There is so much to do and so little time to waste.

Despite my total dread over the big Grandma Betty confrontation that's waiting for me, after forty-five minutes of dance hell I go outside and patrol around for pixies, just to make sure all the happy-dancing humans are safe when they leave to go home.

This is the world of a pixie—my world now, I guess—pacing and hunting, sniffing the air and looking for threats. I look for threats because I need to keep people safe. I look for threats because I do not want to *be* the threat. It's a fine line, I guess—a fine line between good and bad, between savior and predator, between hero and villain. I do not want to be the villain and I do not want people dead, not on my watch, not ever. I have to believe that every step I take is a step toward good, because if I don't—if I don't believe that—then everything, absolutely everything, is lost.

Something thuds onto the snow. I dart toward it even as my fists start shaking again, imagining Frank.

"It's just sludge," I tell myself, and I'm right. It is only snow and ice packed behind the tire of a truck. It's come loose and fallen to the ground.

Every noise I hear is a potential problem. Every smell I take inside me is a potential warning. Every squirrel leaping from one tree branch to another could be not a squirrel but a pixie. Now that I am pixie I hear so much better and I smell so much better—not me personally smelling good, but my sense of smell has improved— and so I sniff in. It's not a sniff. A sniff is an involuntary action; this is an actual intentional sniffing in.

The whole time I'm thinking: How will we get to Valhalla? How will we find Nick?

I pace back and forth in the parking lot, listening for pixies, and then—the smell wafts through my nostrils. My muscles tense and I'm pacing right by Issie's car when Astley jumps off a big streetlamp right in front of me. He stands beneath the light, which makes his hair seem more gold than ever. A fine coating of pixie dust mingles with the snow.

"I thought you left," I said.

"Why?" he asks roughly. "I said I would be patrolling. You didn't believe it?" He squares his shoulders and looks away from me.

"I thought maybe you'd given up. Too many evil pixies. Too many humans to keep safe."

"I am not the sort who gives up." He gives a half shrug. His shoulders seem to stretch out the hard fabric of his jacket. With all that blond hair and golden-tinted skin, he looks almost like he could glow, but he doesn't quite. Instead he leaves tiny traces of glitter wherever he goes. It's the sign of a pixie king. He squints his eyes, looking in the distance, and adds, "I decided I should stay and be assured that you'd manage to make it safely home. Are you leaving now without your friends?"

I squat down, drag my finger through the thin layer of snow. "No. I'm just patrolling too. I don't want anyone to get hurt by—" I break off and don't know how to say it without being rude.

"Pixies like us?" He half asks, half finishes after a slight pause.

I don't answer and instead look down. I've been writing the letter N in the snow, N for Nick, tracing and retracing the three solid lines of it, and I hadn't even noticed what I was doing. Standing up, I ask, "Have you seen any?"

"Quite a few. Amelie is out there patrolling about a half mile away. Between the two of us, we have pushed off a good number." He rubs at the side of his face like he's checking for stubble or something. "She loves a decent fight. It frightens me sometimes how much she loves it."

Amelie is one of his subjects. She is tall and has dreadlocks. She is a lot older than us. She's maybe around thirty. I don't know much about her. I don't know much about anything pixie, actually—things like how their society is set up or how they began. There are so many secrets, floating around me like the snowflakes. I try to catch them in my hand, discern their shape and identity, but they melt into tiny pools of water. It's just long enough for me to know they existed but not enough to let me examine them.

"Zara? What is wrong?" Astley reaches out. His finger touches the bottom of my chin and he lifts my head so that I meet his eyes. I step backward to put some distance between us, but I don't look away.

"I'm worried."

"About?" he prods.

"That we won't find Valhalla and Nick." I make a rough motion to indicate myself. "That this will be for nothing and that my grandmother will kill me or kick me out of the house for going all pixie on her."

I cross my arms over my chest. He nods. People start coming out of the school.

"That I can understand. She is fierce." He pauses like he's weighing his words, or maybe he has to burp. I don't know. A clump of snow falls off a tree and onto the hood of a Subaru. He tenses and then continues. "But if she loves you, she will still love you despite your species."

Right. I cringe. "Weres don't like pixies."

"Not everywhere. We aren't always enemies."

"Around here you are."

"Around here things are not the way they should be. Your father was a weak king. He was a weak man. We are not all like that."

I don't want to hear it. I've already heard that my pixie father is weak so many times already.

"It's just . . ." Struggling to find the words, I pull in my lips for a second and then start again. "I just . . . I want to be the same person I was before. I don't want to be beholden to you because you're my king—no offense. I don't want to think that it's cool to torture people. I want to be good. I want to have a soul."

I kick at the snow around my N. Some of it ruins one of the lines. "I know that sounds stupid," I mumble. I start to squat down to fix the N, but before I can he grabs me by the shoulders.

"Listen to me, Zara. I do not know what you believe. I believe each of us is a replica. Similar to the way Christians believe Adam was made in the image of God, replicated." He pulls in a deep breath as car doors start to open. I can tell he's trying to search for danger. I search too, but I can't find any except right here with Astley, my king, the guy I kissed, the guy I let turn me. He continues on, placated, I guess, by sensing no immediate threats. "So too do pixies believe that we are replicated from Odin—"

"The Norse god?" I feel one of my eyebrows creep up. "You're telling me there are other gods? I don't believe in other gods."

"'Gods' might be the wrong word for them. They are creatures like us, but not like us, maybe not like your God either." He crams his hands into his pockets. "My point is that we believe we are made in Odin's image—as pixies, not humans. We are made in his image and he is not evil, Zara. He is supposed to be wise and good and kind."

"Supposed to be?"

"Well, I have not met him." Astley smiles. "He is also one of the keys to finding Valhalla, because it is his home."

"So we just have to find him—and that's basically as difficult as finding heaven?" I say as hope pretty much deserts me. "And how do we do that, since you can't even find your own mom, our one big lead?"

His lips flatten into a hard line that matches his eyes.

"I'm sorry. I sound so harsh. I'm just scared that we won't find him." I hide my head in my hands for a second. "I appreciate your help. Please don't think that I don't."

He gently moves my hands away from my face and says, "This is not easy for you, Zara. I am aware of that. You have lost your wolf. You have lost your humanity. Your reality has shifted and your town is under siege. It is unprecedented what is happening here."

A car engine starts, then another. Someone yells, "It is *so* freaking cold!"

This kid, Sam Cambridge, shouts, "Crap! It's snowing again."

And I hear other voices: talking about ugly dresses, how this Stephanie girl totally hit on this other girl's date, people who were flirted with . . .

"I cannot believe her," someone shrills. "She was totally all over him."

I feel the air change. My muscles tense.

Astley cocks his head. "What?"

Reaching out to grab his arm, I feel dizzy with the enormity of everything that has happened, that is happening. "You're right. They are all so innocent. I used to be like that. Now I don't fit in." He opens his mouth but I stop him. "Do not say that I fit in with you, because that would be super cheesy."

He nods and I let go of his leather sleeve. We stand there for a second, and then I ask, "Can you patrol in the air? Glamour yourself so nobody sees you and circle around? I'll stay on the ground. Man, I wish I could fly."

"Occasionally a queen is capable of flying. My mother is capable. We shall talk to her about Valhalla as soon as I can locate her, and I *shall* locate her," he insists. He gives me a probing look, but I can't tell what it is about. "I have already asked Vander, one of my top lieutenants, to look into it."

After just a heartbeat, he lifts into the sky and blinks out, glamoured.

"Thank you!" I yell after him, staring into the darkness and all the tiny flecks of snow tumbling down toward me. My tongue darts out and I catch one. It melts instantly, cold and wet in my mouth.

Then I smell them. Two pixies. One is coming from the woods at the right edge of the parking lot. The other is simply walking up the access road to the high school.

"Astley!" I yell.

Some freshman kid looks at me. His eyebrows lift up.

"Sorry," I mutter as he walks by. "Looking for a friend."

Astley appears above me for the briefest of seconds and whispers, "You incapacitate the one from the woods; I shall get the other."

He's gone before I have a chance to respond. Wow, though. He thinks I can handle one. That's kind of a flattering big deal. Nick never let me fight alone. He always thought I'd get hurt, and I wasn't good at it, really. But now I can, right? I just handled those two in the high school. I quickly walk toward the woods, trying not to draw attention to myself and following the scent while simultaneously waving bye to the people leaving the dance. In my head, I've got a ridiculous monologue going on, like a voice-over in a movie . . .

My name is Zara White and I'm almost seventeen years old. I'm a pixie, and my boyfriend was killed by a pixie king with the ludicrous name of Frank.

Sometimes I worry about my mental health.

There's a line of parked cars in front of the woods and a slight narrow incline with grass that separates those cars from the trees. I stare into the darkness, trying to isolate the pixie. It isn't easy.

People talk behind me, distracting me. I don't want them to get hurt. I'm trying to magically will them away when the pixie emerges from the dark, slipping between two trees. He doesn't seem to smell me and starts toward a girl from the volleyball team who is skipping through the parking lot with a friend while their dates straggle behind. The pixie is wearing jeans, a winter coat, a red wool hat pulled low over his ears—human clothes—but he's not glamoured, so he looks like some sort of blue humanoid devil. His teeth glint under the parking lot lights. He smiles slowly and it's obvious that his attention has turned to the guys. Pixies prefer to torture and drain guys. I am not sure why—it's another one of those secrets.

I race up the little hill in two quick steps and rush him, tackling him at the knees. His entire body makes an *oomph* sound, like all the air has just been knocked out of him, but he quickly whirls around. His hands go toward my throat. My hands go toward his and I try to pin him down. He flips me over and I smash his face with my elbow, which feels super violent and horrible. Crunching bone sound fills the night air. His hands loosen. I take the opportunity to grab his throat and apply just enough pressure to hurt his vocal cords, to cut off air but not to kill him. He tries to snarl at me, but it comes out more like a whimper.

Bringing my face just a few centimeters from his, I whisper, "Do not touch the humans. Got it? No killing. No bleeding. No torture. Or you die."

I can't believe I've just said that. I squeeze a tiny bit more and then let go, shoving his head into the snow. He growls at me, but his eyes are defeated and he scrambles to his feet, then runs off. I wipe my hands against the side of my dress, turn around, and look behind me. Callie and Paul—Mohawks covered by matching orange hats—are standing there, mouths wide open. Their eyes are large and confused, a bit panicked. Crud.

"What the hell?" Paul manages to say. His hand is clutching Callie's arm like he's holding her back, and she's one step ahead of him like she is protecting him or was going to intervene or something. Tiny snowflakes swirl around them.

"Just, um— Hey, guys! He just got—he just—he just gave me an opportunity to show off my fine wrestling skills . . . WWF domination for me! Um, yeah . . . boys . . ." I stumble for an explanation. I am obviously not doing well, because they keep staring.

Callie's mouth closes and opens again like she wants to say something, but no actual words come out. The silence is beyond awkward.

I keep trying. "You have a good time at the dance? Need me to show you any wrestling moves? Oh! There's Issie. Got to go."

I race off toward Issie's car before they can ask any questions. I'm not sure how long I've officially been a pixie, but it's less than a couple days and I'm already outing myself. Great. I rush up to the group and stop. I stand still and try to sense pixies. All I get is Astley.

Is grabs my arm. "Where were you? Do *not* make me go all nagging mother on you. You can't just disappear like that. The last time you did you were gone—"

"Issie, she was out patrolling. I told you that," Cassidy says, pulling her wrap around her shoulders. It starts to fall off. Devyn catches it and fixes it.

Issie lets go of my arm and opens the door to her Toyota. "My heart can't take all this patrolling, disappearing, dying, morphing into new beings—"

"Callie and Paul just saw me take down a pixie," I interrupt as we pile into the car. Cassidy and I get in the back together.

"Shut up!" Issie shouts as she gets in behind the steering wheel. She accidentally honks the horn and starts babbling like she always does when she's nervous. "Oh my gosh! What are we going to do . . . ? What are we going to— This is like that time on *Buffy* when—"

"Is . . ." Devyn tries to comfort her and make her stop talking, I think. His hand rubs circles on her back.

"I told them he hit on me and that I was showing him my wrestling moves. I think they maybe believed it." I pull on my seat belt and roll down the window even though it's cold. I need to be able to smell for pixies. "We can't leave until everyone's out. I want to be sure nothing happens."

"Did they really believe you?" Devyn asks.

My breath whooshes out with the reality of it and I adjust my previous statement. "I don't think so."

"Well, there's another lovely complication." Devyn groans. "You have to try to be more careful."

"Devyn!" I yell back. "I am not making quote-unquote complications. He was going after someone in the parking lot. I couldn't ignore that."

"True," he admits.

Issie cringes. "Guys. No fighting. We are all on the same side here. Dude, it's cold. I'm turning up the heat."

Issie hates conflict, and out of respect for that we shut up and wait. Devyn and I sniff out our windows for threats as the stragglers head to their cars in their dress-up clothes and fancy shoes. It breaks my heart with worry to watch everyone, even the people I don't like very much. Like Brittney, who has tormented me since I moved here. She's always mocking my peace jeans and my love for Amnesty International, the human rights organization.

Eventually everyone, except the maintenance guy, is gone. Their trucks and cars roll out on the roads, heading to distant points in Bedford and neighboring towns.

I sigh as Issie pulls onto the access road to the high school.

"What is it, Zara?" Devyn asks. He puts up our windows with some buttons up front. Heat blasts through the little fan thingies, struggling to make the car warmer than subzero.

"I just can't keep them all safe," I explain. "That kills me."

I see the kindness in Cassidy's eyes, and my words trail off because there really is no point in continuing this discussion. How can I keep everyone in town safe? I couldn't even keep Nick safe. My heart feels dizzy in my chest.

"You mean 'we,'" Devyn says stiffly.

I push away the image of Nick bleeding on the snow and lean forward. "What?"

"You should say 'we,' as in 'we can't keep them all safe,'" Devyn explains. He opens up his window a crack again. Cold air rushes in.

"What he's saying is that you are not in this alone, that we are a gang of four like in *Buffy* or in *Scooby-Doo* or in *Heroes* or

25

something," Issie says as she rounds a corner a little too sharply. The car swerves. Cassidy bangs into me. Devyn holds on to the door frame as he pulls himself out to get a better look.

"He's following the car," Devyn says.

"*He* would," Issie snorts. "Wait. Who is 'he'?"

"The pixie king." Devyn pulls back inside the car, pushes up the window, and sits forward. "What an imbecile. How dare he follow—"

"Guys, he's letting us see him," I explain. "He could glamour himself if he didn't want us to. He's not being sneaky."

Devyn twists around to look at me. Even in the darkness his eyes flash. "What? They can make themselves invisible? All pixies or just kings?"

"Just kings, I think." I'm not sure. "They all hide pretty well in the woods, though."

"And why didn't you tell us this?" he demands. I feel like all the progress I've made with him up to now is in danger of being erased.

"I only just found out, Devyn."

He doesn't say anything. Nobody does. I pluck at the fraying edge of the seat belt and try to imagine that I'm in their shoes dealing with me—a newly formed pixie. How would I feel? I'd feel worried and nauseated. I'd want to trust myself, but I'd hold back a bit, right? I'd be worried and looking for any tiny sign of deception, because I would have to in order to stay safe. These aren't simple problems with simple solutions. It's not like I borrowed Issie's dress and forgot to give it back, or cheated off Devyn's test paper. I've turned pixie. I could kill them pretty easily if I wanted to—not that I ever would want to, I don't think. Would I?

"I am not hiding things from you," I say, trying to convince them. "I am still me. I am still Zara in love with Nick, friend of you guys, part of the gang. Okay?"

Cassidy sighs heavily into the car air. "They're just nervous because—"

"Because I turned. I know." My voice is soft. "I thought you guys trusted me."

"We do, sweetie. We do," Issie simpers. "We just don't know how much influence he has on you." She lifts one hand off the wheel and gestures back toward Astley.

"None," I say. "He has none."

But I don't know if this is actually true. Who am I really? Am I still the same person if I'm not even technically a person anymore? Does being stronger make me different? Will it? I mean, I've always thought tall people had a totally different perspective on the world than short people, and that culture and circumstances and choices make you who you are. So by being pixie rather than human, I have changed who I am, or at least who I will become. My head rests against the seat back and I close my eyes.

"Uh-oh, Zara's having an existential moment," Cassidy says.

I snap my eyes open. "How would you know that?"

"Elf blood." She smiles and taps her temple with one of her long fingernails.

"Excuse me? What does 'existential' mean?" Issie asks.

"Well, according to Kierkegaard," Devyn begins in this totally pompous teacher tone, "a person is solely accountable for creating meaning in his or her life. And she/he should live that life with passion and sincerity despite all the horrifying roadblocks that confront him or her, such as despair, boredom, angst, pixies . . ."

"I hate when Devyn says 'she/he,'" I mutter to Cassidy. She snorts.

"So, what does that have to do with Zara?" Issie asks.

"I just mean that Zara is focused on herself and her place in the world right this second," Cassidy explains. She puts an arm around me. "Which is absolutely understandable given the circumstances."

"True," Issie agrees. "Plus, you've missed a few days of school and you are so behind on AP Bio. And the whole track team is floundering. Now that Ian and Megan are gone and Nick is gone and you . . ."

We are all silent. We drive through the darkness on crazy roads, bumping from potholes and frost heaves. Roads are meant to be smooth paths, straight lanes to destinations, but they aren't like that at all, are they? Life isn't like that either. I rest my head on Cassidy's shoulder and let Issie drive us the rest of the bumpy way to my grandmother's house.

"We have to find Astley's mother," I announce. "She knows how to get to Valhalla."

Cassidy pets the side of my head. "Awesome. We'll do a Web search."

"A name would help," Devyn suggests.

A name. Of course. We need a name.

They were monsters. We were attacked by monsters. All I can remember is blue and teeth.
—STATUS UPDATE, SUMNER STUDENT

We spend most of the car ride home talking about the escalation of violence, about how FBI agents have shown up in town to help the local police, how people still don't realize that it's not a serial killer but a group of paranormal creatures that's hurting everyone. And because we spend all that time talking about how we can stop them, how we have to do something, but how we feel almost powerless, I kind of repress the fact that I'm about to see Betty.

"Should I call first?" I ask as Issie pulls into my driveway. Panic edges into my voice, shrilling it. Betty is not an easy woman. She is tough and awesome and blunt, but not . . . *easy*. And she was really anti me turning pixie. "Maybe I should call first and warn her."

"Zare, you are already here. Calling is pointless," Issie says as she puts her car in park.

"Agreed," Cassidy declares. She pats me on the leg. The dress fabric makes slithery noises as I stare at my grandmother's shingled

Cape with its cute porch and woods all around it. It looks so calm and happy, not like a weretiger lives there, not like a pixie king once ransacked it.

"She's going to kill me," I say.

Issie turns off the car while murmuring supportive things, and Devyn says, all matter-of-factly, "Absolutely. Do you want us to come in with you?"

I think about it for a second. "I do but I don't. I don't want you all to witness her yelling at me, but I also don't want her to tear me apart. You know, literally tear me apart. She does that to pixies."

"Witnessed it." Issie shudders.

I open the car door. Cassidy grabs my wrist, stopping me before I get too far. "You sure, Zara?"

I nod. "I'm sure. You guys be safe going home, okay?"

"We will," Issie chirps, all confident and proud. "I'm driving."

I'm about to say something about being extra careful when I smell Astley. He lands on the snow in front of me, tall and steady. If Issie wants to learn how to be confident, she should study him. He's a textbook case. He cocks his head as I stare and then says, "I expect this might be difficult for you, Zara. Would you like me to accompany you?"

"We already offered," Devyn says out the window, which he's opened again. His voice is snippy. "Why don't you leave before you do any more harm? And what's your mother's name?"

Astley doesn't even acknowledge that Devyn has spoken. He just keeps his eyes locked on my face. I shake my head.

"I've got to face her myself," I say. I lower my voice so the others don't hear. "Can you follow them? Make sure they stay safe, especially Issie after she drops off the others. Hide, though, so they don't know, okay?"

He pulls his lips in toward his teeth and then slowly nods in agreement.

I wave to Issie. "I'm good, guys. You can go."

She turns the car back on and Devyn yells out the window, "Do not do anything stupid, pixie."

"His name is Astley," I shout back, but Devyn merely raises an eyebrow as the passenger-side window goes up. Just then the front door of the house opens. Betty stands there. Her dark blue plaid flannel pajamas from L.L.Bean hang off her wide shoulders; her close-cropped gray hair is all askew. My heart whooshes into my spleen. Astley puts out a hand to steady me.

"You sure you don't want me to stay with you?" he asks. His voice is low, husky.

"No. Take care of the others, please. I have to do this myself." I swallow hard and take a step forward. "But thank you."

He lifts up into the sky and disappears into the white snow-flakes and darkness. The night seems to have gotten even colder somehow as I trudge through the snow toward our porch. Betty stands there under the yellow light, simply staring. She doesn't say a word, which makes it even worse, you know? Because Betty is always saying something, imparting wisdom, cracking dirty jokes, whatever.

That's when I realize what I've done to her. I've made her wait, helpless, while I went off and became a pixie, and then even went to a freaking dance. All that time she had to wait, knowing I could have died and that there was nothing she could do about it. I've done this to her because I was so dead-set on not being help-less about Nick, about being proactive, about finally being a hero.

Everything inside me seems to freeze and then break into tiny shards of ice. My breath hitches in my chest, but I manage to take one step forward and then another. My foot hits the wood of the porch. Betty swallows so loudly that I can actually hear it, although that might be because of my new, improved pixie hearing. The snowflakes are wet and sloshy as they fall.

"Gram," I start as I step fully onto the porch, planting both feet. "I'm so sorry. I'm so—"

She opens her arms and leaps toward me, crossing the porch in one long, springy step. Right now she is still human, totally human, and clutches me to her—not with weretiger anger, but with love. My face smooshes against the soft flannel. Her hand goes up to my hair and she says, "No words, Zara. Just let me be happy you're home."

She invites me inside without hesitating and sits me gently on the sofa before slouching next to me. Our legs touch. We talk for a long time. I tell her everything and she growls every once in a while. I know she's disappointed in me, but she's proud in a weird way too.

After a couple hours we head upstairs to our bedrooms. She kisses me good night and says, "You are just like your father."

I back into the wall, hitting my head on a picture of me when I was three, dressed in a princess ballerina costume. "That's mean."

"Not your biological father, that pixie." She spits out the word "pixie" and wipes her hands on her pajama legs like they have cooties on them. Her eyes flash. "You are like your real father, my son. Stubborn. Kind. Always wanting to save everyone. Foolish. Sweet."

"Oh . . ." My stepdad, the dad who raised me, died less than a year ago from a heart attack—maybe brought on by a pixie sighting. That's part of how I ended up here in Maine, living with his mom, my grandmother Betty, while my mom fills out the rest of her employment contract in Charleston.

Betty straightens the picture I knocked with my head and clucks. "I like it when you smile."

"Even though I'm a pixie." I regret saying it the moment the words are out of my mouth.

She grabs me by the shoulders, suddenly intense and strong. "You will never be a pixie. You will always be my granddaughter, Zara. That is who you are, damn it. Don't forget it. We are not defined by our species any more than our nationality or our gender. What we do, our choices, that's what defines us."

I have a hard time meeting her eyes. That's what I've always believed too, but somehow I keep forgetting it now that I've turned. It's like I don't get the benefit of the life rules I make for everyone else.

"Okay," I whisper.

Her breath comes out in tiny spurts as she leans in and kisses my forehead again. I don't think she's ever kissed me so much. "You get a good night's sleep," she says, "and then in the morning we're going to get started figuring out how to get the bad pixies out of this town of ours."

The clock chimes the end of an hour and a shudder breaks through me.

"What if he's dead, really dead?" I suck in the air, trying not to give in and cry. "Gone-forever dead, you know? And I changed for nothing."

She raises an eyebrow, probably startled by my big change of topic. The clock downstairs keeps chiming midnight. "You don't believe that, do you?"

I shake my head hard, the way a little kid does when she's

trying to convince herself of something important. Cassidy used her elf powers to show me Nick alive. He was in a bed and not moving, but he was alive. We all saw that. He was real.

Betty's voice is solid in the air. "Then don't say it. Saying it gives it power. Good night."

Betty must be annoyed at me, I think, because that's abrupt even for her. I go into my room and change out of the silly dress-up clothes Issie and Cass made me wear and put on some flannel boxers and a Luka Bloom T-shirt. I pull the covers up to my chin and stare up at the Amnesty International poster on the ceiling. I can hear Betty sniffling downstairs. She's crying softly, trying not to let me hear it, but I'm a pixie now and I do. I do hear her. I hear and know so many things I'd rather not hear and know . . . the weakness inside people, the soft squish of snowflakes hitting the roof, the ache in my grandmother's heart, and the ache in my own.

Law enforcement officers have imposed a curfew on all Bedford residents under the age of eighteen. At a press conference held at Bedford City Hall today, Sheriff J. Farrar explained, "The majority of the disappearances have occurred after dark. We are advising that everyone only travel in groups. Do not go into wooded areas alone. Do not accept rides from strangers."
—NEWS CHANNEL 8

I spend the day planning out strategy with Devyn, who comes over after lunch. He insists I catch up with AP Lit and AP Bio first, and a couple other of my harder classes. It all gives me a headache. Schoolwork is not at the top of my list right now, even though it has to be, because if I survive all this, I do want to go to college someday. I can't imagine going into the interview and explaining that I failed out of high school because of a pixie invasion. *Right*. We set up camp in the living room. Devyn moves stiffly because of his old pixie injury, but it makes me so happy to see him walking without help in front of the woodstove and pacing past the couch and coffee table as he pontificates and goes into professor mode. Betty is still at some craft fair with Mrs. Nix, her best friend and our school secretary.

We spend some time trying to figure out the anagram my dad once wrote in the margin of his Lovecraft book until Astley texts me his mom's name and we start to type it obsessively into various search engines. We come up with some mentions of her at antique shows and clock symposiums throughout the world, but nothing that pins her down, let alone an address.

While Dev surfs the Web, we talk and I keep walking toward the windows, looking out, searching the woods for signs of pixies. It's like I can't keep still. I wonder if this is some sort of pixie-change side effect.

"They aren't attacking in the daylight anymore," Devyn says. "Not after the Sumner bus incident and a couple after that."

"What are people saying?"

"That there's a serial killer." He groans. "There was a news crew from Boston up here when you were off changing. Some federal agents have been sniffing around too. People think Nick's parents sent for him to get out of danger. Some people think there's an alien apocalypse coming. You missed a lot, Zara."

I am silent. I can tell by how he says the word "changing" that he's still having a hard time dealing with it. I can't blame him. I'm having a hard time dealing with it too. I touch my fingertips to the cold pane of the glass. "The world is so white. It hurts my eyes, you know?"

He doesn't answer, just stands up again, moaning a little bit as he does.

"You feeling okay?" I leave the window and scoot over to him. "Does it hurt much to stand?"

"It hurts. It's worth it, though, to be able to do it." He sneezes. "Sorry. Allergies."

"Allergic to pixies?" I joke.

"Ha-ha," he says sarcastically. "I have to go soon. My parents are geeking out with the experiments now. They want me to help. They said thank you for offering to give more blood for them to use. It's good of you."

That makes me turn away from the window. "Good of me? I'm hardly good, Devyn. We trapped people in a house. That's illegal. It's technically kidnapping. We fight them. That's assault. I beat one guy up after the dance. Plus those two girls . . ."

"Pixies, not people. Pixies, not girls," he corrects.

Pixies, not people.

"I still feel like a person, and I don't feel good. Fighting makes me feel evil," I mumble.

Devyn gathers his stuff up to leave.

"Seriously, though," I continue, more forcefully. "Do I have fewer rights, less importance because I'm not a human? Do the laws suddenly not apply to me?"

"Animals don't have rights," Devyn snaps. "And that's what I am half the time. I can't even begin to imagine what would happen if regular people suddenly knew that people like me were out there."

"How would you like it if people called you a shifter or a were instead of a guy?"

He cracks his knuckles and slugs on his backpack. He grimaces as he straightens his back. "I would hate that."

"So you understand why I hate it?"

"I do." Rubbing a hand across his face, he steps toward the door. "I'm sorry, Zara. It's just so much to get used to, and with Nick gone . . . I know I haven't been fair."

"Yeah, well, it's complicated, I know. And I can't blame you. I just miss you. I mean, you are right here, but when you don't totally trust me, it feels like we're . . ." I struggle for the words. "Disconnected?"

He pats my shoulder and steps into the cold. I follow him out because I don't want to be alone just yet. He says, "You know, Nick is out here somewhere."

The thought of it makes me squee. I jump up and hit my head on the porch roof. Snow tumbles down around me and suddenly the tension is broken. I can't believe I can jump so high. I roll on the snow giggling, and Devyn just cracks up watching me. I chuck a snowball at him. I swear if Nick could see me now, he would crack up too, and fall down next to me and probably smoosh snow in my face. Or maybe not.

Dev wipes the snow off his face and reaches a hand down to help me up. "You are such a goofball, Zara."

"I know."

He studies my face, squinting at me. "What happened? Your expression just changed."

Swallowing hard, I decide to just say it. Maybe if I can say what worries me, Devyn will really see that I'm still Zara. Maybe I'll see it too. "Nick hated pixies. I'm not sure he'd ever believe they could be good, not after seeing the evil some have done. I'm not sure if he could ever love me now."

"Zara . . ." Dev's hand tightens around mine, but there's no comfort he can offer here.

Charging on, I say, "I changed so I could save him, but that change could ruin us. I know he'll think it's ruined me."

My lungs seem to crumple into tiny tight balls just thinking about it, about how maybe I made a mistake.

"He'll figure it out eventually."

"Figure what out?"

"That you're still you." Dev squeezes my hand and lets go. "I mean, if I can catch on . . ."

"It's taken you forever," I kid, because I don't want this to be some greeting-card kind of moment.

"Less than seventy-two hours since the initial transformation, give or take twelve hours either way."

"Wow. That's longer than I thought." I nudge him with my elbow. "And seriously, Dev, *I'm* not even sure who I am anymore. How can I expect other people to just be okay with everything?"

We say good-bye. He drives away in his parents' big ol' Buick. Once he's gone, I step outside and sniff the air. It's cold. I can't smell any pixies, but I know there are some out there, hiding, waiting, just outside the realm of my senses. I wonder if they are Astley's pixies keeping watch or bad ones waiting to attack. Not that I've really met any of Astley's pixies except Amelie.

Eventually, I stand up and go in the house and do a little more research and planning. Betty comes home before her shift. She turns tiger and patrols the area, then scratches at the door to come inside. I let her in and step back as she enters. I know *she* still loves me when she's human, but I'm not so sure about her tiger self.

The cold air rushes in, so I reach around her to shut the door. At over four hundred pounds, she fills up the space between the door and the stairway. All ten feet of her bends and faces me. She opens her mouth. There is blood on her teeth and her breath reeks like copper and Dove soap. She has killed.

"Got one, huh?" I say, trying to sound flip. "Right outside?"

She bobs her head up and down and brushes past me into the living room. Her massive paws trail snow inside.

Something in my stomach feels sick. "How do you know it was a bad one? And, um, not a good one?"

She doesn't answer, just plops down in the middle of the room and lifts her right front paw. There's a piece of wood splintered in it.

"You want me to take it out now? Before you turn?"

She just looks at me with those massive amber eyes. Her head is so huge.

I breathe in deeply and sit on the floor in front of her. "Do not bite me."

She rolls her eyes.

"What? You're all tiger now . . . I don't know." I smile at her so she knows that I'm teasing—kind of.

I take her paw in my hands. It's so huge, easily as big as my entire face. The claws are about three inches long. Examining it better, I can tell that the splinter is a piece of branch slanted in. It's lodged in pretty deep from the pressure of her walking on it.

"You've pushed it in pretty good. I think I need both hands." I lift my knees up and rest her paw on them for stability. With both hands I grip the branch. "On three. One . . . two . . ."

I yank. She yowls, but the wood pops right out. I slam my hand against the wound and apply pressure. Her fur is cold and wet and thick.

"There. That wasn't so bad, was it?" I give her a smile. "Does it hurt much?"

She purrs and then pushes her paw through my hand into my chest, knocking me down on the floor. She stands above me, all four hundred pounds of her.

"Gram?" My voice is embarrassingly high-pitched.

Her head comes down to mine and her tongue darts out, licking the entire length of my face. She bats her paw against my hip and purrs again.

"Eww. Wet." I laugh and she leaps over me, heading into her bedroom, where she'll change back into human. I watch her fine tiger self go. She wiggles her tail.

"Grandmothers." I grunt loud enough for her to hear me, but she doesn't respond.

When she comes back into the living room, I'm still cruising the Web on her computer looking for clues about Astley's mom.

"Any luck?" she asks. She's wearing her uniform.

"What's the cliché Mom is always saying?" I ask.

"Needle in a haystack." She sits down next to me and leans forward to peruse the screen. Then she turns and examines my face. "Thanks for the help with my paw."

"Glad to see you brushed your teeth."

She laughs. "Had to. Pixies taste horrible, like soap."

"Good to know. And you're sure it was a bad pixie and not one of Astley's? Because—"

"It was stalking Devyn."

"Oh. Not protecting Devyn? Like trailing him to keep him safe?" I offer.

She grunts and crosses her arms over her chest. "Zara, I could smell the need on it."

"Okay." Shuddering, I stare at her wrinkled face, those bright, active eyes, her soft, short gray hair. "You're so beautiful as a tiger."

"Not as a human, huh?" she teases and slaps my thigh.

"Shut up."

"Did you just tell your grandmother to shut up? Brat," she jokes back and stands up, stretching as if her human form is just too confining. She grunts. "I should have been a cop."

I have no idea where this comes from, but I go with it. "Why?"

"Because then I could be out patrolling instead of stuck at the station waiting for an ambulance call."

"Can't you just take out the ambulance?"

"Keith is on duty tonight. He's the driver. You know we can't go out alone."

"Can't you just tell Keith?"

She sighs. "I don't know. How do you tell a guy like Keith that you're a weretiger and that you need him to drive the ambulance around so you can hunt for pixies?"

"You just tell him," I suggest, pushing myself away from the computer and giving her my full attention. "And then you show him."

Her face closes up and she looks suddenly fragile and old— and very human.

"You are very human, Gram."

She smiles. "You say that even after seeing my paws and my teeth?"

"Yeah." I fake shudder and mock the lines from Little Red Riding Hood: "What very big teeth you have, Grandmother."

"All the better to eat pixies with," she plays along and smiles.

I grab the throw pillow on the couch and hug it.

She reaches over and kisses the top of my head, then whispers so faintly that I can barely hear her, "You are very human too."

"I hope so."

She harrumphs and stands up. "How about I burn us some dinner before my shift starts."

End of conversation.

One missing Maine boy has been found alive but with amnesia and serious injuries after having disappeared for more than two weeks. Parents hold out hope that their missing youngsters will see the same outcome. —NEWS CHANNEL 8

A noise startles me out of my super-long couch nap. I groan and stretch. Someone knocks on the door. The sun has set and the clock says it's seven. Even early in the evening our town seems deserted and haunted. The roads wander around dark corners. Trees crowd the edges. Snow reflects the moonlight like a silent white mirror. I peek out the window, and for a moment I think it's Nick, but that is impossible.

When I open the door, Astley simply holds out his hand in the darkness. I take it and step outside almost hypnotized, not really even caring that I'm wearing this extra-large gray L.L.Bean sweatshirt and the bunny pj bottoms that Is gave me. I just go with him into the snowy cold. Something about the dark trees beyond our lawn makes me twitch a little. My foot slips on the snow. Anything could be out there.

"Betty's in the shower," I whisper. "What are you doing here? Did you see the Frank guy? Or my father? Are they lurking out there?"

"No. I have not." He clears his throat awkwardly. "There has been no sign of your father."

I guess I'd been holding my breath, because it all comes out of my mouth in a big rush. I don't know if I'm upset that he's missing and maybe dead, or relieved, or scared, or what. My feelings about him are so jumbled. He was manipulative and weak, but he tried so hard to be good. He let my mom go free, without turning her. I know he did.

Astley waits for a second before he speaks. Maybe he can tell that I'm trying to get a handle on my emotions or something. He glances toward the house and takes a step away from the door. "I want to show you our people."

"Our people?" I say as his fingers tighten around mine. The world seems to shift on its axis, tilting me into a more confused state than I'm already in. "I'm not sure I really want—"

"You are our queen, Zara. It is time you met your pixies." His other arm wraps around my waist. "We shall fly."

"We have to be quick. Betty will—"

He nods. "I know."

Flying is cold and swift. We swoop over the tops of trees and through the snowflakes. It has been snowing lightly for days and it still hasn't stopped. I honestly don't think it ever will. I long for the warm streets and bright sun of Charleston, my old home. I can almost smell the flowers, see the poinsettias that everyone along the Battery puts out for Christmas, the bright white lights along the porticoes. Life was so much easier then. I push the longing away. Below us the roads cut through trees. Town snowplows hustle as quickly as they can, clearing the way for cars and people. I hang on to Astley as he brings me to a clearing in the woods that's not too far away from the high school. When we get closer, I can spot headstones of varying heights, in white, black, and gray. It's a cemetery. The pixies are gathered in between headstones. Some even stand on monuments. They each seem to have some sort of light source. It's a dizzying array of shadows and fabric, movement against the stark white snow. Fear pushes into my throat. As we start losing altitude, everyone turns away from us as if refusing to acknowledge our presence.

"They know I have difficulties with landing," Astley explains, clearing his throat. He smells embarrassed somehow.

I remember those difficult landings, but it's still weird seeing this mass respect for him, saving him from humiliation. If it were me, my friends would tease me endlessly about it and pointedly stare while I fell, for full laugh effects. "They respect you, so they turn around?" I ask.

"They are kind. Hold on." He drives into the snow hard, feet first, and then plops over backward. I land half on top of him, half to the side, and the look on his face is so frustrated and embarrassed that I can't help laughing. I give Astley my hand and help haul him up. Once he lets go, I start brushing the snow off my pajama bottoms and sweatshirt. He does the same. Oh, man . . . I'm in bunny pajamas meeting pixies. This is so not right. A soft laugh echoes under my breath at the absurdity of it.

The pixies surround us. Most are in regular clothes. None have bunnies on them. They wear jeans and cords and a couple have on those rugged brown construction pants with a lot of pockets. They wear leather and down jackets. One woman has a long royal purple coat. There are a couple dresses and a kilt, all of which look crazily inappropriate. They are glamoured in all skin colors and ages, except none are younger than high school. Many of them hold flashlights pointed down, making cones of light on the snow. Some have candles.

I touch Astley's arm, overwhelmed. "There are so many."

"These are only the ones who are here with me. There are hundreds more." He stops brushing at the snow on his thighs and instead reaches out as if to touch my cheek. I step away. His hand stays in the air and then he makes a grand sweeping motion. "Turn around, my people, and meet your queen."

As one they spin. There are so many eyes staring at me. I suck in my breath as my stomach wobbles.

"They are your people now," he says, running a finger along the line of his jaw.

My people. *My* pixies. *My* responsibility. The wobble in my stomach becomes a full-fledged knot of fear.

I reach out and touch a tombstone. JOSEPH THOMPSON. 1971–1990. So much death here and everywhere. I do not want to put up a tombstone for Nick or Astley or anyone else I love or am responsible for.

Astley takes my hand in his and leaps to the top of a flattened tombstone that resembles a giant granite box. He pulls me up with him. The pixies move through the snow, closer and closer to us. He gives me a look that's meant to be reassuring, but it's hard to be reassured when you're surrounded by pixies, even if they are supposed to be *your* pixies and therefore on the side of good. A cloud crosses the moon, but there is still enough light for me to see the faces staring up at me. Almost against my will, I grip his hand a little harder.

He stands taller. He seems regal, terribly regal, and I must look so puny and pathetic next to him. But I am not puny and pathetic. I was a princess and now I am supposed to be a warrior, even if I am wearing pink bunny pajama bottoms.

"Pixies of the Stars," he announces. His voice is warm and loud across the graveyard. "Pixies of the Birch. I present to you your queen."

One by one they bow.

I stand there for a second, and then I can't help it. I start shaking. I start shaking because it's absurd, like some weird circus of the dark. Their movements are too solid, too regal, too *everything*, really. How can I be one of them? How can I be their queen? I bend over and hold my stomach over the craziness of it all. The pixies' breaths draw in. Astley stiffens beside me and drops my hand, and I know I need to get it together. It's like being stuck in a dream where you're in class stark naked, and you are aware that you're stark naked but you can't figure out how to get out of the dream. Everything is in slow motion.

"I'm sorry." I raise up one hand. "I'm so sorry."

I straighten up, biting my lip for a second. The snow tumbles down and I brave myself up enough to say what I'm thinking: "I'm sorry. I can't do this. I just . . ."

I hop off the grave and rush toward the exit, race through the gates. I'm not one of them. I'm just . . . *not*. Somebody could catch me in a second, I'm sure. Somebody could stop me, but nobody does. So I run and run and run.

I am walking on the Bangor road for about ten minutes before Astley catches up with me. He lands in front of me the moment a pickup truck trundles by. He manages to only half fall and recovers quickly before putting his hands on his hips. The wind blows his hair in blond waves around his head. He pulls a hat out of his pocket and hands it to me before going back into the same belligerent posture.

"Are you okay?" he asks.

That's not what I expected. "You looked mad," I say.

"I am not mad, Zara." He runs his hand through his hair. "I am concerned."

Concerned. "That you made the wrong choice? I'm sorry. I'm so sorry, Astley, but I'm not meant to be a pixie. I'm not meant to be a queen. It's too much."

His nose crinkles up and he looks up at the sky like he's searching for some kind of help dealing with me. Finally he says, "You are meant to be my queen."

"How can you know that? And don't say, 'I just know.' My mom always says that. I hate that."

His face softens. "I forget how young you are sometimes."

"You aren't much older than me."

"Well, being king ages you."

When I look at him, I can tell that it has. All that responsibility and I'm supposed to be strong enough to share in it now.

"How?" My voice is so soft I wonder if he can hear it. I make it a little louder. "Have bad things happened to you? Are you okay? Do you want to talk about it?"

He stiffens and then smiles a soft, sad smile. "I do not—not yet—but thank you, and I am much better now that you are my queen. Thank you for being my queen, Zara."

"You're welcome," I say, because I don't know what else to say, don't know the words to get him to explain the sadness in his eyes. "I'm so embarrassed."

"It will be okay," he says, putting my arm through his as we walk. It feels nice and comfortable, solid and warm. "It is easy to be overwhelmed."

Some evangelical groups are claiming that the events in Bedford, Maine—the site of all those missing boys and the site of the school bus attack—are a sign of an upcoming apocalypse. Some teens have even made T-shirts saying BEDFORD, MAINE: THE END OF THE WORLD STARTS HERE. —CARL FLECK REPORT ON FNN NIGHTLY WORLD NEWS

There are certain signs that your town is totally messed up:

1. Snow that lasts forever.
2. Evil pixies torturing and/or maiming people.
3. You are a regular nightly segment on cable news networks.
4. FBI agents patrol the streets.
5. Half the school population has to stay home because their parents are too freaked to let them out of the house.

Issie, Devyn, Cassidy, and I have discussed this all day, hunkered down in the Maine Grind, our town's one coffee shop. While we were there, Cassidy figured out the old anagram A BAA EBBED FLY TIGHT VIGOR TROLLS, which we found in one of my dad's old Lovecraft books. It means, GET TO VALHALLA BY BIFORST BRIDGE. The BiForst Bridge is mentioned on a lot of the Web sites Devyn found. It's a rainbow bridge, which we thought had to be too hokey to be real, but I guess not.

"So we have to find a rainbow we can step on?" Issie asked, only half kidding. "Do we have to find a leprechaun too?"

As the sun sets, we head out to patrol, minus Cassidy, who has a French test tomorrow. Pixies are stronger at night. Their senses and powers heighten, and they usually use the cover of darkness to attack. Ever since Frank came to town and my father ran away, they've been attacking a lot, to gain strength and control. They themselves are out of control.

We park the car in the back lot of a big-box store. Issie turns around and says, "You're looking for him, aren't you?"

I unbuckle my seat belt and lean forward. "Nick?"

"No, not Nick. The pixie king who killed him. Frank." She shudders saying his name.

"I am."

But we do not find him or any bad pixies tonight, and when we finally get home, Betty acts like some specially trained government interrogator. Issie sends me a text saying she is grounded because of all the violence and abductions. She has to go home right after school every day now. Her mother flipped, I guess.

`That is sooo horrible,` I text.

`*SOB*,` she responds. `She is carrying round a pizza cutter 4 protection she's so freaked. She wants me to carry a steak knife.`

At least Betty doesn't try to ground me. I basically spend the night finishing my ridiculously awful homework and worrying about what would happen if Astley was gone, since I don't really feel like I'm destined to be some ruling pixie queen. Eventually I give up and write Urgent Action letters about the abuse of priests in Myanmar. Then I surf the Net looking for clues about Astley's mom or Valhalla, pretty much anything. I fail again and again.

There's a picture of Nick and me taped to my mirror. We got it at a picture-taking machine at the movie place in Bangor. We're both sticking out our tongues. He's pretending to lick me. It's all I can do to not get all drama queen and kiss it and murmur that I'm trying to get him back, that I refuse to give up.

I don't see Astley until Monday, when he shows up at the door of my Spanish class and nods at me. Even through the glass, I can tell that he's pale and almost sweating. He's holding a piece of gauze to his head. My heart bumps around in my chest, worried and scared all at once.

Paul hits my chair and whispers, "Do you know him?"

"Yeah," I whisper back.

"It looks like he's been in a fight."

I raise my hand for the Spanish teacher. "May I go to the restroom, please?"

She raises one dark eyebrow. "*¿En español?*"

You'd think with all the craziness around here that teachers would give us a little slack, but no. It's like they think by being hardasses they are helping us somehow. *In freaking Spanish.* Grrr. If pixies were attacking, would she expect me to yell "Run!" in Spanish?

"*¿Puedo utilizar el baño, por favor?*" I ask.

She nods yes, and I scoot my chair back and fly out the door.

"Whew. She must have to go. Maybe she's pregnant," Brittney says like she's a character in some mean-girl movie.

"*¿En español?*"

I shut the door gently behind me before I can hear Brittney's response. If she can say that in Spanish, she has way more brain cells than I do.

"In Norwegian that would be '*Hun må dra. Kanskje er hun gravid.*'" Astley attempts to smile.

I can't help teasing him. "Which? Asking to go to the bathroom or dissing me because I'm pregnant."

"You are with child?" His eyes open wide, all mock terrified.

"No! Shut up. You know I'm not." I punch him in the arm and then lead him into the stairwell, shutting the door behind us. "Okay. Seriously, Astley, what happened to you? Why is your head bleeding?"

The long light tube hanging slightly from the drop ceiling begins to flicker. It makes a tiny hissing noise that human ears wouldn't be able to hear. The light will fizzle out completely soon if the janitor doesn't fix it.

"Sometimes," Astley says, his voice a sad, tired stretch into the air, "I get a little tired of being Mr. Perfect, you know?"

A vein in his temple pulses so hard I can see it. He leans against the wall.

"And that's what made your head bleed?" I lift the gauze away from his face to check out the wound. He doesn't pay any attention. Doesn't even flinch.

He continues talking. "Do you know how hard it is to be king? To always have to try to be good, to be perfect? Do you have any idea how hard it is to help you go after your stupid idiot of a were, all the time thinking you should just be satisfied with me, because that is how it is supposed to—"

"Astley, I— 'Stupid idiot' is not—"

He raises a hand up to silence me and I press my lips hard together, because what can I say, really? What can I say that won't hurt him more than he already hurts? I may not have anything to do with the cut on his head, but he hurts inside because of me. He's even being mean about Nick because of me.

"I'm sorry," I whisper.

"Do not say that." His voice cracks and his eyes flash with embarrassment. His arms cross in front of his chest and he looks down at the floor—Astley *never* looks down—and scuffs a shoe across the linoleum. The light fizzles again. The hum of it breaking gets a couple decibels louder.

I grab his face in my hands. Stubble grazes my palms. "But I am so sorry. I am sorry you hurt and that you think you have to be perfect, and I'm sorry I freaked out at the cemetery . . . I'll try harder."

I close my eyes.

"I know you will." He makes a muffled noise and I open my eyes again. His eyes burn blue, cold like a winter sky when it isn't snowing. They seem endless. "I have no doubts about you, Zara."

Swallowing hard, I steady myself and recover. "Are you going to tell me what happened to your forehead?"

"I had a fight."

"With who?"

"Amelie."

"Amelie! That's ridiculous. She would never fight with you."

"She would and she did."

Stepping back from him, I ask, "Why?"

He grasps my wrist. The radiator pops to life. The bell is going to ring soon.

"I want you to come with me," he says, abruptly changing the topic.

"Where? I have to go back to Spanish before the bell rings." I think I have maybe three minutes left.

"Iceland."

"Iceland?" My voice squeaks. I try to maintain my composure. "You want to go to Iceland? In the winter? In the middle of all this pixie craziness? We can't do that. We have to keep people safe. We can't just up and leave and go to freaking Iceland."

He sighs. "You sound like Amelie. Only she never says the word 'freaking.'"

His voice is so heartbroken that my anger and shock sort of dissipate. His fingers still hold my wrist, surrounding it with his.

"You feel like none of us have faith in you anymore, is that it?" I guess. "Like you're losing control?"

"Exactly." He puts a hand on my back, then gently steers me toward the door leading to the hall heading to class, away from him.

I stop walking, think about how behind with my work I already am, how I haven't had an Amnesty meeting in ages, how I've already missed so many indoor track practices . . . But I half turn to face him and say, "I have faith in you, Astley, and I'll go with you to Iceland. When do we go?"

"Would you like to know why?"

I bite my lip and wait for the reason. A tiny spark of hope expands in my heart as he smiles.

"I have a lead," he says. He lifts his hands up when he says it, all excited. "Vander found some evidence that points to the BiForst Bridge being in Iceland."

I digest that, then ask, "Seriously?"

"Seriously. Asgard is where it is located, and we have a tip that the way to get there involves a geyser in Iceland. It is an amazing lead." He bounces on the tips of his toes and his smile reaches his eyes. "We are one step closer, Zara. I told you we would find your wolf."

I launch myself into his arms squeeing. He laughs and swings me around in a circle, my feet lightly bumping the walls. The bell rings. I need to get back to class to get my books. I need to go home and get my passport. I need to tell Issie and Dev and Betty, although she will probably flip. But all I can do right now is hug Astley and say the same thing over and over again: "Thank you. Thank you. Thank you!"

It's not till lunch that I get the chance to tell Dev, Issie, and Cassidy.

"Okay, okay! This is totally exciting," Issie says. We're sitting in the library instead of eating lunch, googling "Valhalla" and "Iceland" and "geyser." "But what if he just wants to whisk you away out of the country for a romantic rendezvous?"

"It's not like that." I rock back in my chair and stamp my feet on the floor. This is so awesome. "He doesn't like me that way."

She just points a finger at me, which in Issie speak means, "I am so totally right, you idiot, but I am too nice to argue with you."

I really don't think she is. Right, I mean—I know she's nice. She even promises to bring a note to my track coach for me and collect all my schoolwork. Again. And Cassidy volunteers to run the Amnesty meeting that is supposed to be tomorrow. I have the best friends. Ever.

Even Devyn is excited. He points to the computer screen. "Look at this! There are links to Valhalla and Iceland. How amazing is that? I'm so embarrassed we never found it."

Is jumps up, stands behind Dev, and kisses the top of his head. "You can't be perfect all the time, Mr. Man. It's okay."

He scrolls down the page. His eyes are lit up because he's so pumped. Cassidy yanks in her breath and points at a picture of a giant wolf. "What's that?"

"Fenrir," Devyn says. "It's part of the mythology. He's chained by the gods, but when he gets free, it's supposed to portend the coming of the apocalypse, basically, an all-out war between good and evil."

"Lovely," Cassidy says. "Can you scroll down more so I don't have to look at it?"

Farther down we see a picture of the BiForst rainbow bridge.

"Much better." Cassidy sighs and stretches her hands out to me to grab. "Can you believe you're going to get Nick?"

"I can," I say, smiling. "I really can."

At home I gather up my suitcase and passport, and then I call Betty at work. She does not react well. She's all, "You are *trusting* him!" Enough said.

The Bangor airport is small, with only two main gates plus an extra one off to one side for international passengers. Because its runway is so long and because of where Maine is located, this is where planes land if they are having trouble (drunk passengers biting flight attendants, engine issues) before or after they head across the Atlantic. It's also where U.S. military planes land to gas up on their way to Afghanistan or Kuwait or wherever the country is fighting. There are troops here right now, lounging around in camouflage, talking on cell phones to people at home. In the gift shop, one soldier is telling a younger one to buy lighters. "It's like gold over there," he says. The younger soldier snatches up about twenty of them, thanking him. It's heartbreaking, really, how young some of them are. We're at war too, I guess, and I guess *we're* young, but I don't actually feel young as Astley and I make it through airport screening, smile at the TSA agents, and then hunker down in vinyl chairs right across from the gate agents' desk.

I stare up at the giant number 2 at our gate. An airplane rolls down the runway toward Gate 1. A few people mill about. I breathe in the smell of people and metal and forced air. "I can't believe we're in an airport," I say.

Astley runs a hand through his thick hair and pulls his laptop out of his dark leather backpack. "Most other pixies can't fly on planes, you know. They can't handle the iron."

"Why don't you share the magic iron pills then? Wouldn't that be a good thing to do?"

He rubs the skin behind his ear and explains, "It gives our people an advantage."

Our people. He calls them "our people," but to me, my people are in Bedford, fighting, being threatened. The guilt drives me against the dark blue vinyl seat. I tuck my legs up under me, push my thumbs against the top of my eyes.

"Do you have a pain?" Astley asks me. His voice is right at my ear, worried, deeper than normal.

"I think my feet smell. My feet never smell except when I go on airplanes. Why is that?"

His hand goes against my forehead. "Are you ill? You are not making sense."

I open my eyes, look at him. He's worried and scruffy looking under the fluorescent airport terminal lights. "I'm fine," I respond.

He lifts an eyebrow.

"Okay . . . I'm feeling super excited but kind of guilty about leaving," I admit, rubbing at my forehead.

"Zara, I could travel myself. Are you sure you want to come?"

In front of me a little girl in white leggings with major visible panty lines and dark brown boots twirls around in a circle as her baseball-hat-wearing dad talks to the ticket agent. She pulls on her hair.

"Yep." I watch the girl tug on her long brown hair, studying the strands as if she can't believe they belong to her head. "Tell me when we'll hear from your pixie friend again?"

"He said he would call me again once we arrived."

The little girl crouches down, balancing on the tips of her feet. She manages this a moment before giving up and plopping on the carpet, dingy alternating squares of bluish gray.

"I'm so nervous," I announce.

All of a sudden, for no reason at all, the little girl's face scrunches up and she starts crying sad toddler cries, just giving in to the sorrow. Her voice is deep and pained. Her dad doesn't even turn around. My stepdad would have scooped me up in his arms. My pixie father? Who knows . . .

"Sometimes I almost wonder if humans are worth saving," Astley murmurs.

"Pixies are just as bad," I say.

"True. Do not listen to me. I am just tired."

I swallow hard. "Do you think we have the capacity for good?"

"Pixies or living creatures in general?"

"Both."

"I have to believe that."

"Why?"

Before he can answer, the gate attendant leans toward the microphone and says, "We are now boarding Priority Pass passengers for Flight 5781 to Iceland. Again, only Priority Pass passengers."

"That is us." Astley stretches his arms over his head.

"Really?" I've never flown first class before, and as much as I think this is materialistic of me, I am kind of psyched.

"Really. We are royalty after all." Astley rolls his eyes before I can get all upset. He stands up, offering me his hand, which is solid and clean. I take it and we stand there for a minute, just staring at each other, and then he slowly lets go of my hand. One finger, then another. "I shall tell you why I believe this on the plane, and perhaps it will help you feel more comfortable about your own change, all right?"

I nod. "All right."

Stretching and gathering my carry-on, I watch the people mill about. The flight attendant has dandruff. Flakes fall as she scratches her hair. The little girl stops crying, her dad never seeming to notice. A woman with super-huge noise-reduction headphones reads a *Glamour* magazine. A man in a tie wearing a wedding band holds a John Grisham novel in one hand. They are all so innocent, so unaware that they are sitting here with pixies. They have no idea that the entire world could change if we fail. And I am glad that they don't, since sometimes not knowing is so much safer, so much saner.

The woman puts down her magazine. I lean forward and ask, "Are you done with that? Would you mind if I read it on the plane?"

For a second she looks shocked, but then she says, "Of course not. It's good and mindless."

"That is exactly what I need," I say, taking it from the seat. "Thank you."

Astley and I sit next to each other. After we're buckled, I start to pull the armrest down, but he stops me. "There's a lot of metal in that."

"But we took the pills."

"It would be better to leave it up." His voice holds an apology in it. It's not an order; it's a suggestion, so I nudge the armrest back up between the seats with my elbow.

"Better?"

"Much." He smiles and hands me a little white airplane pillow and a deep blue blanket. "Thank you."

People keep boarding, pushing their carry-ons in front of them or pulling them behind. A woman cradles a baby close to her body. A man expels some gas. Astley looks at me and presses his lips together, trying not to laugh. I cover my nose and mouth with my hand.

"There are a lot of people in a plane," I whisper, "and a lot of smells."

I touch the wall by my right. It's plastic and it seems plain beige at first glance, but there are actually tiny little swirling circles on it. I wonder if I would have noticed that if I were still human. I wonder if everything is like that: if things just seem shallow and pale, but then if you stare closer, you can see the hidden aspects. Astley leans back in his chair, stretches his legs underneath the seat in front of him. His hair is darkish blond, but if you look closely there are red strands mixed in. They flash in the sun, the shades running from copper to strawberry blond. Looking away, I run my finger along the ridge by the oblong window. Some airport workers in orange vests and jumpsuits drive food trucks and scurry around. I wonder what they look like beneath their surfaces, what sort of lives they lead, if they have swirling circles in them as well.

Once everyone boards, the flight attendant checks that the cabin is ready for departure. She demonstrates how to buckle a seat belt (I can't believe people don't know how to do that), shows how our seat cushions are floatation devices, and explains how to use the oxygen masks if there is a sudden drop in cabin pressure. As she talks, Astley grows paler and paler. We taxi down the runway and he just keeps swallowing way more than a normal person would.

"Are you okay?"

"I am afraid of flying," he admits, fidgeting in his seat. He keeps crossing and uncrossing his legs like a little antsy kid.

"Um, you do know you fly all the time."

"But that is without the airplane."

"Oh, flying on a plane is a totally normal fear. That's called aerophobia, aviatophobia, aviophobia, or pteromechanophobia."

He laughs. "What is one supposed to do when faced with aerophobia, aviatophobia, aviophobia, or pteromechanophobia?"

"Do not mock my excessive knowledge of phobias," I kid and punch him in the arm. "I always think it's good to name your fear, face it head-on, and you're doing that. I mean, you're in a plane—that's facing your fear."

His lips press together. I can literally see the tension running off him, like blasts of orange swirls. After a moment he says, "That does not make me feel better."

"Give me your hand," I say as we start taxiing, building up speed. He doesn't ask why. He just gives it to me. It's large and sweaty and clammy. I slide my fingers between his, clamp my other hand over it, and squeeze tightly. "Sometimes, when you are scared, it just helps knowing that someone else is here."

The plane tilts upward as the nose pokes toward the sky and the front wheels leave the ground.

"You are right," he says, his voice deep and serious. "It does."

It isn't until we're safely cruising at the highest altitude that he stops shaking. I pretend like I haven't noticed a thing and resist the urge to wipe the sweat off my hands when he finally lets go.

Once the flight attendant has poured us both some cranapple juice and given us our packets of cookies, Astley clears his throat and starts to tell me the story. I know right away that it's the story he mentioned at the airport because his already formal voice gets even more regulated, more regal somehow.

"When I was twelve years of age, my father died. Someday, perhaps, you will tell me how your father died, if you like," he begins. I guess until he says it like this I've never realized that we both have fathers who died. "But for now I will tell you my story."

They'd taken a cruise ship, the *Queen Mary* 2, across the Atlantic to Spain, which seems romantic to me. Astley had been excited about the trip, about being able to hang out with his father for a while, without his mother.

"She was not . . ." He stumbles to find the right words, which is something he rarely does. "She was not like she is now. She loved my father deeply. She loved him more than anything else, more than clocks or jewels or me or herself."

The trip had gone well. Neither became seasick. Nobody got on anyone's nerves. Then they arrived in Spain and made their way overland to Madrid.

"We were in a train station. It was incredibly crowded. The earth seemed to shake. I was excited because I thought that was just the train coming closer. However, it was much more than that. My father cursed and took me by the arm, just above the elbow." He touched his elbow as if remembering. His voice grew softer. "When I looked at him I realized that something was horribly wrong.

"The rumbling grew louder and it brought the smell of fire, burning bodies.

"Only a few moments before it reached us, people started

screaming, running madly away from the tunnel and back up toward the stairs," he said.

I remember seeing something about this on CNN. There were bombings, a terrorist attack. Almost two hundred people died.

"We were stuck in this massive wave of humanity. The heat coming from the tunnel was immense, and then came the cloud of fire. 'Cloud' is not the correct word truly. It was a massive rolling beast."

Everything inside of me tightens up and I grab Astley's hand again. He doesn't seem to notice. "Couldn't he fly?" I ask.

"No. He was one of the few kings who could not. He never taught me, which is probably part of the reason why I utterly fail at landing, but I digress." He hauls in a huge breath as a starchy man in a suit unbuckles and heads to the restroom. "He saw what was coming and he grabbed me by the other arm; then he lifted me above his head and threw me. Instead of saving himself, he threw me, Zara. He threw me all the way up the stairs."

His voice breaks with emotion, raw and jagged, an ache so huge and real that I cannot believe he is sharing it with me. I think about Nick and how he's never trusted me enough to tell me about his parents.

"Is it hard to tell me this?" I ask.

"Quite."

I wait. "Then why are you telling me? I don't mean that meanly. I just—I just want to know why you are if it hurts you to do it, you know? I'm not making sense, am I?"

"You are. You usually make sense, Zara. Honestly. I am telling you because you are my queen and I count you as my friend and because you deserve to know." He takes a sip of his cranapple juice. I wonder what I haven't told Astley, what he should know about me, what I haven't told Nick. Astley's hand shakes and he finishes his story. He had landed on a sea of people, knocked his head a bit, and passed out. When he woke up, he was in a Spanish hospital; Bentley, their butler, was hovering over him, his mother had gone mad with grief, and his father was just gone.

"He saved me, Zara."

I nod and grip his hand tighter. He squeezes back and then lets go. He uses that same hand to tuck my hair behind my ear as he says, "He saved me. He had an instant to choose my life or his and he chose mine to save. That's how I know that pixies can be good. I have seen it with my own eyes. I know what my father was. He was good. And that's what I want to be, what I want my people to be."

I pull my lips in toward my mouth. Tears threaten. "You are," I say, and I believe it without a doubt. "You are good, Astley."

He leans back in his chair and closes his eyes. "I hope so."

Astley suddenly sits up all intense. "Do you smell that?"

"What?"

"Pixie. A powerful pixie."

I focus. "Maybe. There's that Dove soap smell. I just thought it was the restroom and you."

"Lovely." He unbuckles his seat belt. The flight attendant scoots right over. "Sir, I need you to sit down."

He stares at her like she's asked him to eat a truckful of Twinkies. His frustration slams into me like a fist. It's not intentional. I just *feel* it.

"The captain has turned the seat belt sign back on," she insists.

We hit some turbulence just as she says, "Sir, I must—"

"He has diarrhea!" I interrupt.

Astley gasps and his whole face and even the tips of his ears redden. I feel a little bad about it, but it's *so* going to work and, seriously, it was the only thing I could think of.

"Oh!" She is at a loss for a second and staggers back a step as Astley rushes past her toward the bathroom. I don't know how he'll sneak out of there to check out the plane, but it was the best I could do on the spot. The flight attendant and I make eyes at each other.

"He's horribly embarrassed about it," I whisper. "He had bratwurst. Or maybe it was the baked beans. Either way you might want to get some deodorizing air spray."

Ten minutes later Astley appears beside me again.

"Were you in the bathroom this whole time?" I ask, fiddling with my anklet.

He rolls his eyes and tells me he used a glamour to hide himself. He walked up and down the aisle but couldn't locate the source of the smell.

"I don't like that," I say as he clicks the seat belt back in place.

He is still. His whole body is tense, as if waiting for an attack. After a moment he says, "Neither do I."

"Did you recognize it? Who did it smell like?"

"Your father."

I canNOT even tell you how creepy it is here. Seriously. I swear I hear people whispering my name every time we go outside, and sometimes it's like there's someone scratching on my window. I swear I am not crazy. It's just Bedford, man. LOL.
—Blog post

"Everything looks like an IKEA store," I say, grabbing Astley's elbow as we walk through the airport in Iceland.

He laughs and smiles. His happiness and purpose seem infectious, almost like the air is full of pink bubble gum, only not sticky.

"It has so many windows," I say, looking out into the darkness where the airplanes taxi and the luggage trains roll around. "And look at the chairs. They're all posh."

"Keflavik is known for being an amazing airport." He points at all the shops: Burberry, Calvin Klein, Gucci. "Would you like to buy anything? I know you are a bit lacking for stores in Bedford."

"No, no . . . I'm good." My feet almost feel like happy-dancing across the sleek light wood floor. "When do you think your pixie friend will contact us? What should we do while we wait?"

He reaches over and grabs my carry-on. "I do not know exactly when. He said he'd call sometime today, and he's arranged for a car to take us to Reykjavik."

"The capital?"

"You have been reading up," he says as we get to baggage claim. He looks down at me like he's all proud for a second. My whole body tingles in some strange, wild way and my heartbeat jumps to five hundred beats a minute. I almost think he's going to kiss me, but he'd never do that. He only did it that once just to turn me. His lips part a little, but he just says, "You stay here; I shall get the bags."

I packed heavy because I didn't know what to bring on a rescue mission to a mythological land or to Iceland.

I check my clock. It's ten a.m. and it's still dark outside. The sun won't rise for another ninety minutes, and then it'll set four hours after that, which is totally wild. I thought Maine was bad, but this country is so close to the north pole that it's even darker.

Astley returns with our bags. "You're shuddering. Are you cold?"

I shrug and make to grab my suitcase, but he nods toward a man in a dark suit, who must be our driver. The man hurries over, bows at Astley, doesn't actually say anything, and takes our stuff.

By the time we're done with customs and the bags and getting settled in the car, the sun has started to rise. The sky is gray and overcast. Snow melds into the ground and there aren't forests, just occasional clumps of big Christmas-type trees. It's Maine cold. Squat buildings sprawl up out of the ground as if they sprouted there.

"It seems so unreal to be here," I say to Astley. We're sitting together in the back of the car. It's all cushy even though it's small. He looks healthy again. The cut on his face is gone. His color is good. "It's like the world is suddenly shifted and this place couldn't possibly be on it."

"I know." He crosses his legs.

I turn my cell phone on and stare at its blankness. "I don't have a signal."

"Did you have them turn it on so you can get calls internationally?" he asks.

Of course not. I didn't know you had to. As we drive toward Reykjavik, I can't even begin to count all the things I should have done but I didn't. I begin to list them in my head and give up.

He smiles and settles back into his seat. "Excited?"

"Ridiculously."

His smile gets even bigger. "It is nice to see you happy."

"Well, thanks for making me happy," I respond, adjusting my seat belt. There's an awkward silence except for the rumbling of the car's engine. We just stare out the windows, not touching each other, but I feel really close to him somehow anyway. Maybe it's the bond between king and queen. Or maybe it's because the car zooms closer to the city of Reykjavik, one mile, then another. We're one mile closer to Nick.

Nobody calls Astley on our ride in. We get no tips. We get no advice. Nothing. I try to be patient and not disappointed as we check into the Hotel 1302, which is this boutique hotel that's totally monochromatic, just whites and blacks and grays—stark elegance. The oak floors are actually heated and there's funky art and sculptures everywhere. Astley and I have suites next to each other. An adjoining door attaches our rooms. When we say good-bye, I crash on the big white bed, stare at the black walls, and grab my phone. But there's nobody to call, thanks to my failure to get an international calling plan. I haul myself off the bed and yank off my shoes before padding over to the bathroom, which doesn't even have a wall separating it from the rest of the suite, which is just weird. Still, it's just as starkly beautiful as everything else—a huge glass shower waits at the end of granite walls. Fluffy towels in white and black sit on black shelves, with a modern white sink above them. There's even a white claw-foot tub, but it's the shower that calls to me. And I listen.

After my shower I read the city guidebook and stare out the windows at the ridiculously early setting sun and the beautiful white buildings that house the theater and the cultural center. My hands press against the glass, making marks. The glass chills against my skin, unlike the wood beneath my feet. I should make Betty install heated floors—it makes the cold much more bearable. Just the thought of Betty makes me feel more lonely. I close my eyes, wonder what she and Issie and Devyn are doing; Cassidy too. I wish I could call my mom and check up on her. It really wasn't easy leaving Bedford. I made Astley dispatch extra pixies to watch over everyone because I was so nervous about it.

A knock comes from the door to Astley's suite. I shuffle over and open it. He stares down at me, eyes focused and concerned.

"Are you sad?" he asks. "More than you usually are?"

I nod but say, "I'm okay."

His hand reaches out like he is going to touch my face, but he pulls his arm back to his side again. "Get some sleep, Zara. You must be exhausted."

Pulling my lips in toward my mouth, I swallow hard. He notices; I can tell. This time his hand lifts up and his fingers push some hair behind my ear.

"We shall find him very soon," he whispers. "I promise you."

Then his hand falls and he closes the door.

. . .

A frantic knocking wakes me up. I fall out of the bed, bump my shin on the end table, and stagger toward the door between our two suites.

Flinging open the door, I start to say, "What?"

But Astley motions for me to be silent, pointing at his phone, which is on speaker. An accented male voice echoes into our wide-open rooms, loud and easy to understand, though I can't place the accent at all.

"It is me, your highness. Please meet me at the Blue Lagoon. Be there in one hour. In the pools."

"Where?" Astley asks as my fingers clutch his naked forearm. "Where in the pools?"

"I shall find you near the entrance. Do not worry."

"Fine," Astley says as the line goes dead.

Astley clicks off the phone. We're staring into each other's eyes for a full second before I realize what's happened. When I do, I end up shrieking and leaping into his arms, screaming about how awesome he is and how grateful I am, basically making all these noises that make no sense at all. He swings me around, and for a second everything is beautiful and hopeful even though the sun has already set outside and darkness covers the world.

The Blue Lagoon pools spread out before us, almost an acre of extraordinarily warm spa water. The lagoon is a gorgeous deep blue lit up by overhead lamps. Steam rises from it as it meets the cold air. People swim around, tiny dark silhouettes in all the steam and blue. We've both changed into swimsuits in the locker rooms and now we're standing in the outside air, looking around like we'll magically sense where to go and what to do.

Astley's arm goes around my shoulders. "Your teeth are chattering, Zara. You need to get in the water."

I don't argue. Iceland air is colder than Maine air and I'm in a bathing suit. A *bathing suit*! That I had to *rent*. Just the fact of that alone kills me, it's so skeevy.

We hurry down the steps. Warm, cozy water hits my body. It's better than a bathtub. The water feels thicker. It's easy to float. On the way over Astley told me that the lagoon was made from a natural geothermal spring, that two continents are pushing away from each other and right here is the crack. Old lava covered with delicate moss frames the pools, which seem to go on forever.

Astley sighs contentedly as he dips into water up to his neck. I bob around next to him. The bottom of the pool is all knobby, not smooth at all, but the water is amazing, like having a heated bathrobe wrapped around you.

"It is beautiful," he says, looking at everything longingly.

"It is," I agree, but I'm looking around like a crazy woman. "But where is this Vander person? Is this how we get to Valhalla? I mean, it almost makes sense if there's this crack growing here."

"That is not exactly how it works." He floats on his back.

"Whatever." I don't care how it works. I just care about finding Nick. Still, I can't resist floating on my back next to Astley, closing my eyes for a second and just letting the water hold me up. Sometimes it's so hard to hold yourself up. This is a nice change.

"Sometimes I wish my life could always be like this," he says.

I bob. "Like what?"

"Peaceful. Beautiful. No violence. No threats." He turns his head to smile at me. His eyes are soft, mushy looking, but strong. I'm not sure what that look means.

"That would be so amazing." I start to say something else, but Astley's distracted. I follow his gaze, which is on a very pale man in a horrible black Speedo. Nobody except professional swimmers should wear those.

"That is him," Astley says, waving.

The man enters the water and wades over. He bows at Astley, then takes my hand and kisses it. "Your highnesses."

If I wasn't so psyched about finding Nick, I'd freak out about being called that.

Vander smiles at me. "I am sorry to be so cryptic earlier, but the location of the home of the gods is not exactly something you want to go out on a cell phone line."

Astley smiles. "We understand."

"Thank you for being so kind, your highness." The man breathes in deeply and meets our gaze, each in turn. He looks at Astley when he says, "The bridge is at Gullfoss."

Gullfoss! I actually know where that is. It's this huge waterfall that I read about in the guidebook. I squeal and do the best I can not to faint from happiness.

"The best time is the morning," he says. "The pathway between the worlds is most accessible then. There will be a rock tied with gold ribbon that you must throw into the waterfall. I will leave instructions there as well."

"Will you come with us?" Astley asks.

"If you wish it."

Astley looks at me, but I shake my head no. I don't mean to offend the pixie guy, but I want it to just be Astley and me saving Nick. Astley relays this and thanks him for his help.

"The gods be with you," he says as he leaves.

"And also with you," Astley answers. As soon as the pixie

disappears into the mist, Astley turns to me and says, "How about that?"

I hug him as hard as I possibly can, feeling joyous, ecstatic, and so very, very grateful. "Thank you, Astley. Thank you."

He laughs and kisses the top of my head.

@cierradumont Thinking of moving out of town. Suggestions? **#Bedfordstinks**

We eat dinner at the hotel later, a crazy-fancy restaurant with modern black tables, sleek lines, and food that looks pretty on the plates. But I have the hardest time concentrating on anything. I barely even saw the cute old buildings in the middle of the city that we drove by. Even now I barely see Astley across the table from me.

He passes me some pepper for my salad and asks, "Excited?"

"Just a little," I kid. Our fingers touch on the pepper shaker. He lets go.

"You could use my phone and update your friends," he suggests.

"It's okay," I say. "I found a computer with Internet access in the lobby and I e-mailed them all."

The pepper falls in little flakes. A waiter slips by us, heading to another table. It's quiet and calm here, nothing like the crazy racing heart in my chest, nothing like how all my nerves are super adrenalized from what happened in the lagoon.

"We are going to Valhalla tomorrow!" I blurt.

"I know!" Astley laughs and then stabs some lettuce. He chews for a little bit before asking me, "What is your biggest want?"

"To keep people safe and get Nick back."

He ponders this but doesn't look surprised. "And what is your biggest fear?"

"Well, it used to be of myself, of what I could become, but that's a reality now. I mean, I'm all"—I lower my voice—"pixie, so that big fear has actually come true, but my next biggest fear is failing out of school. Well, no, not really. It's just of losing people."

His eyes meet mine. His eyes are so deep and blue. "Because you have lost your father, and your mother too in a way, and now you have lost Nick."

A lump of lettuce seems stuck in my throat. It makes my eyes water. "Yeah."

His hand reaches out and covers mine on the table. "I am so sorry for all your sadness, Zara."

I don't move my hand. "I am sorry for yours too."

In my room, I can't calm down, so I make a "Steps to Happy" list on the little hotel notepad sitting on the desk.

Steps to Happy
1. Get Nick.
2. Make Nick calm down about me being pixified.
3. Buy Astley thank-you present.
4. Get back home.
5. Kick bad pixie butt and make Bedford safe.

It's a good list.

. . .

I barely sleep because I'm so excited about heading to Valhalla. When I wake up in the morning, I look around the room, trying to find some good Valhalla travel gear, but towels and bathrobes and Reykjavik guides do not seem appropriate. So I stuff into my backpack a steak knife I took from the restaurant, some sterile gauze I snatched from home (in case of wounds), and the curtain ties from the room, which I think could double as rope. I stash my water bottle and a few granola bars in case we get hungry. By the time I'm done with packing and showering, Astley is knocking on the door.

His jeans drape off his hips. His unzipped parka hangs from his shoulders. He hands me another water bottle and then slings his own pack on his shoulder. He doesn't smile. He's all serious.

"Are you ready?" he asks.

"Yep."

He pushes open the door. "You have your room key?"

"Nope!" I hop back and grab it. "My mom always forgets those too. Do you have yours?"

For a second he pretends like he doesn't, and then he pats his wallet. "Of course. Right with our passports."

"Show-off," I tease.

He finally smiles.

That's all we have for fun. We are pretty silent for the entire car ride through the dark Icelandic landscape. I'm too psyched to talk much, and I wonder if Astley feels the same way or is just respecting the silence, because he's quiet too.

There are two falls, each over a hundred feet tall. At first because of the way the land drops off, it seems that the massive river just vanishes into the earth, but it's an illusion. We're on top of the waterfall, which rushes to a pit beneath us. The sun rises as we get there, revealing how far down into a canyon the falls actually go. Half the water is frozen while the other half thunders down through the ice. Mist rises everywhere, creating tiny rainbows all over the place.

"The way to get to Valhalla is over the rainbow bridge," I whisper as I slip on the crazy terrain.

Astley grabs my arm to steady me, smiling but surveying the scene. "I know."

We are the only ones here, probably because the sun just began to rise and it's so cold and slippery. Ice and mist encase the landscape. It's like frozen magic everywhere.

"It's so beautiful," I whisper. I reach out my fingers like I could touch a rainbow somehow, but all I touch is cold mist. I pull my gloves on, and then Astley shoves big yarn mittens over them for an extra layer of protection. The mist from our breaths joins the vapor in the air.

Then I see it: a rock tied with a golden scarf. It waits near the edge of the stream. "Look!"

We rush toward it. Astley gets there first. The rock is flat and large and has writing carved into it. He picks it up and hands it to me. My hands tremble beneath the weight. We untie the scarf together. The writing is not English. I don't understand it at all, so I look to Astley for help.

"It's old Norse." His brows knit together as he stares, obviously concentrating. "It says, 'Throw the stone to the golden falls and proclaim your intent to awaken the way.'"

The wind blows against us. I stagger, trying to maintain my balance. "What does that mean?"

"I assume what it says." His eyes are bright. "I assume that—"

Something catches his attention. He stops midsentence and yells behind me, "Do not come closer!"

Whirling around, I see him too, a tall man, with dark hair that matches my own. I lean toward Astley as my heart pounds hard and fast. "Astley, that's—"

"Your father. I know." He steps in front of me acting protective, the same way Nick always did, the same way I do with Devyn and Issie.

I clutch the stone to my chest as my father steps forward. His skin is so pale. Circles live beneath his eyes. His hands are out, palms facing us. "I offer you no harm. I have come to help."

I push around Astley and confront my father. All the wrongs he's ever done form a ball of anger in my chest.

"You? Help?"

He shakes his head, comes closer. "Yes. I followed you here."

My father, the stalker. Great. I will myself to calm down.

Astley speaks before I can. "I told you to stand back. Explain yourself."

He tells us that he followed us onto the plane, glamoured himself so we wouldn't see him, and trailed us to the hotel, then to the spa and here. He saw Vander speaking to us at the lagoon.

"I do not trust him," my father says. His eyes look infinitely weary, as if he has given up on trust, on his kingdom, on everything.

"And why not?" Astley asks, bristling. He stands with his feet shoulder width apart, bracing himself. "He is most trusted. He has been with us for ages. Whereas you, sir, have only shown yourself to be untrustworthy, a king with such a failure of strength that you often do worse than evil would. So tell me why I should not trust my man?"

"I have no words to explain why. I just do not." My father's voice is so tired.

"What do you think, Zara?" Astley touches my shoulder with his glove. It's a nice, steady hand.

My father has killed and tortured, stalked my mother, and possibly caused my stepfather's death. I'd like to say that there was no way I would trust him, because that would be logical. I'd like to say that he is just all evil, because that would be easy. But nothing is that way. Nothing is all good or all bad. Even I have killed and kidnapped, haven't I? We didn't have trials when we imprisoned all his pixies. We didn't give them a choice. Sure, our motives were about keeping people safe and my father's motives were about need, but still . . . And what about redemption? What about the chance to change your ways, to make things right, to cast aside a life of bad for a moment of pure good?

"I don't . . . I don't know what to think," I say.

"Zara, when Nick died, I ran away. I could have helped you, but I did not." My father grabs my shoulders, forces me to look at him. "I have never done anything to earn your trust, or your mother's. But you are journeying to the land of the gods, Zara, and you are so young."

"I'm not that young," I sputter out. The falls rush below us. The mist swirls around my father's hair. "And I know that you have done things before, things that are good."

Astley shifts his weight next to me and I turn my head to look at him instead of my father. It is just too hard to look at my father.

"What is it?" Astley asks. "What are you thinking?"

Another rainbow pops up in the mist, just behind Astley's head, and I am suddenly filled with confidence, that this is exactly where we're supposed to be. "He let my mother go," I whisper. "When we trapped him, he saw her escaping and he let her go. And he tried to warn me about Frank. Even though he was weak, he kept trying to help me—the way a real dad would, you know?"

"It wasn't enough," my father says, his voice breaking slightly. Turning back to look at him, I see a tear forming in the corner of his eye. "We both know that."

I don't disagree. "And how do I know that you won't betray me now? That you won't just go to Valhalla and not bring Nick back, that this isn't part of some devious plan?"

The skin by the corner of his eye twitches. "I swear to you, Zara, and you know I speak the truth. You can feel it in your skin."

It's true. I can feel it. The truth he speaks is a warmth, gold and light brushing against my cheeks.

"Let me rescue him for you. Let me do this for you," he insists. His fingers brush against the fabric of my parka.

I suck my lips in toward my teeth. It feels like tears are collecting in my eyelids. I refuse to let them out. I refuse.

The water crashes down. The rainbows bend in the mist. I count to five in my head before I look up at Astley, who nods just the slightest of bits.

"Okay," I say. "Okay, but make sure you get him, Dad, please."

When I say "Dad," he closes his eyes for just the smallest of moments, and then he says, "I will."

Letting go of my shoulders, he kisses me quickly on the cheek. Then he says, "Thank you for letting me try to be the man, the father, that I have always wanted to be."

The tears leave my eyes, and then my father turns to Astley. "If anything should happen—"

"We shall take care of each other," Astley insists. "Good luck to you, sir."

My father's shoulders lift just a tiny bit as he nods. Then he says to me, "You are a beautiful, strong queen, Zara, stronger than I could ever be. You make me proud. I'll be back soon with your wolf."

Just as the instructions told us to, my father turns toward the waterfall. What if I've made a mistake trusting him? What if he's tricking me, planning to hold Nick hostage for my mother? He treads easily despite the slippery surfaces, and once he is at the edge he hauls in the stone. Then he lifts up his arms and yells in a voice that's almost as loud as the thundering water, "Bring me to the gods."

The ground's shaking increases. It's as if the entire world is breaking apart. Astley rushes to my side just as I step toward my father. His arm holds me back as a giant wolf leaps from the falls. Gasping, I stagger back. The wolf is easily twenty feet tall. A broken chain dangles from a collar on its neck. Water darkens its fur. The mouth opens. Long canines spike into huge, monstrous spears.

"No!" I scream as my father jumps sideways, trying to get away. There is no chance of escape. The beast's mouth hinges open even wider and swallows my father whole. Gone. He is just gone.

The wolf lands flat on the ground. Its head swings toward us. Huge, evil eyes widen with malice.

Shock freezes me in place.

"A—a w-w-wolf," I stutter. "A gi-giant wolf."

"Fenrir," Astley murmurs. He clutches me around the waist, dodging up and backward, entering the sky of rainbows and mist, flying us away. I struggle against him for a second, screaming, and then I give in. My father is gone. Another father . . . gone.

The wolf leaps after us, snapping its jaws.

"Astley!" I scream.

"Hold on!" he hollers as I try to climb up his back. The frozen air streaks against us. Ice forms on our skin, but still Astley spirals toward the heavens, up and away from the wolf's claws, away from another loss, another death.

I cling to Astley. The wolf howls below us. Finally it turns away as we hover a hundred feet in the air, and then it smashes toward the car.

"Oh no!" I yell just as it lands on the hood of the car, flattening it. It howls once more, triumphant, and runs away.

It's so insane, so unreal . . .

"My father . . . ," I whisper into Astley's ear.

"Died a hero," he says. "He died on the side of good."

There is nothing else for me to do except clutch Astley's back, hide my face in the cloth of his parka, and cry.

He lands us near the car. Luckily, the driver is still alive and on his cell phone calling for a tow truck. He and Astley talk about how they will explain things, but I don't listen. Astley whispers instructions about finding Vander. I stop paying any attention at all, just keep scanning the horizon for that giant wolf. My body won't stop shaking. My father died. The monster we'd been so afraid of died for me. It makes no sense and breaks my heart all at once.

"Do you know what that was?" the driver asks. The fear in his voice breaks through my shock and I really look at him. His pants are wet all down the front.

"Fenrir," Astley says. He puts his cell back in his pocket and stands with perfect posture, scanning the mist, the falls, the rainbows. "But more importantly, it was a trap. It meant to kill us. The king sensed it. He saved us."

We were set up. Why would someone do that? Someone fed the Vander guy the wrong information? It makes no sense. I moan and plop myself down on the cold snow. Giant wolf tracks mar its perfection.

Astley comes to my side. "Are you well?"

"No," I tell him, voice hoarse. "I am not well. I am broken inside. I am broken almost all-the-way deep, and I don't know . . . I don't know if I can ever be unbroken, let alone *well* again."

He swallows so hard I can see it. He grabs my hand, places it on his heart. It thumps beneath my palm, a steady rhythm going on and on despite everything. Then he places my hand over my own heart. It beats the same rhythm, a traitorous beating. A sob erupts out of my chest and he clutches me to him, shushing me, whispering nothing words into my hair.

"Who will die next?" I whisper-sob into his parka. "Who?"

"Not one more." He rubs my back in little circles. "But especially not you."

I pull away, look up at him. "Or you?"

He cringes.

I grab his shoulders. "Promise me."

After a second he nods. "I promise, but there is no shame in dying bravely, Zara, no shame in dying for good."

"And there is no shame in living for it either," I announce. The rainbows grow and shrink before my eyes, their colors shimmering against the gray mist, bright and hopeful somehow despite all the dark, all the thundering water, all the death . . . somehow still bright.

Things are SO crazy here. Seriously. Half the people in town are heading to Florida for sudden vacations, but it's just to get away from whatever crazy person it is who is killing people. And that thing with the Sumner bus? Too weird. One of the girls in my Spanish class didn't get home after school today and now everyone's looking for her. I'm totally freaking out.
—MYSTIC EMBRY BLOG

Night arrives terribly early. The long hours of darkness and sorrow have melted into the outside world, with only the lights of cars and offices posting any reassurance that the world is not utterly, totally a pit of hell.

The air in my hotel room smells of lemons now that Astley has left. When he is with me, all I can smell is him. We spent hours rehashing everything, using his cell to call Amelie (who refrained from saying "I told you so") and Betty (who did not refrain) and Issie and Devyn and Cassidy (who mostly groaned and exclaimed). We tried to figure out why someone would want to attack us specifically. Was it just for control of Bedford and the region? Was it for bigger power issues? Was Vander in on it or had he been used? We don't know. We just know that it was a deceit created on purpose to trap us and have us killed. According to Devyn, the wolf Fenrir is a sign of a great war. It was originally tethered by the gods, but now it runs free.

Everyone is surprised by the actions of my father—everyone except Astley, who seems to have more faith in souls and in good than the rest of us. Although, according to Nick, I was always the silly one, believing the best in people and pixies. Maybe I should have given my father more credit for trying. Maybe I never gave him enough for struggling so hard for so long, for keeping away from my mother as much as he could. I don't know. All I know is that he died for me.

The ache in my heart weighs too much, so I take a shower, let the warmth fall down on me. Then I shove on some shorts and a T-shirt and wrap a bathrobe around me. I don't put socks on because the heated floors feel nice. It's the only thing good I can feel.

There's a smell coming from the bedroom area. A rustle of trouser leg moving against trouser leg.

I stop.

Someone unknown waits. More than one someone, it smells like. I start humming like I'm just combing out my hair, but my toes flatten on the floor as I look around the foggy bathroom area for a weapon. A hairbrush? Oh, man. The knife is still in my back-pack, which is flopped on the floor by the bed. For some extra pro-tection, I swallow one of the anti-iron pills from a bottle on the sink and then grab the towel holder that's been drilled into the wall. I tug. It doesn't move. Both hands grip it. With all my strength, I yank it out. The bolts clatter to the floor.

It's enough to alert the intruders.

Three large men in crisp European-fancy suits rush around the corner. They stop and stare at me. One of them is Vander. I take a second to scream, "Astley!"

Then they charge. I brandish the towel bar like it's a sword and I scream like a banshee, hoping it'll be enough to push the pause button on their attack. They just keep coming. Only two can move in front, though, because there isn't enough space between the walls. I attack the one on the left, hitting at him with the bar. The skin on his face sizzles as the iron makes contact, and he growls, losing his glamour and revealing his blue pixie self.

He swears at me and I swing again, popping him in the chest, but the other one tackles me. The bar sizzles between us. He screams but doesn't let go as Vander gets into the action and yanks me backward by the hair. His thick arms lift me up and against him. One arm holds me at the waist. Another holds something sharp at my throat. A knife? It must be. The other two haul themselves off the floor as Astley flashes into the room. His face is twisted with anger. He has a dagger in his hands.

"Let her go, Vander," he orders. "I am king of the birch and stars. You are my subject and I command you to release my queen."

Vander barks. I think it's a laugh, but I don't know. The sharp blade on my throat presses so tightly against my skin that it's actually cut me. The pain isn't so horrible, but I can smell the blood, and the sight of it seems to be making Astley twitch.

"You can't order us around, King. We belong to another," Vander says.

The wound on the other one's face is still sizzling. That will scar. He says, "Put down your weapon or Vander kills her right now."

"He will kill her either way," Astley says, as calm as anything.

I gasp. That is not a cool thing to say. My heart lurches. I trusted him. He said he needed me, and now what? He can just throw me away? I clutch at the fabric of my robe, willing the lump in my heart to vanish, but it doesn't. Then Astley's eyes meet my eyes and he looks a bit to the right. It's just the slightest of looks, but I catch it. He wants me to jump out the monstrous window.

We're five stories up. I can't fly. But he can. Will he catch me? For a second I wonder if this is all some weird setup to kill me too. Kill my dad, kill me, get rid of the bloodline. But that's so elaborate and this is Astley. I trust Astley, I tell myself. I do.

"I'm going to throw up," I whisper amid the standoff.

"What?" Vander growls the word.

"I think I'm going to throw up," I say again. I force myself to hitch at the stomach. I can't really throw up, but I can pretend I will. Betty once told me during her weekly "how to survive predators" talks that pretending to throw up can sometimes stop muggings, even rape. Let's see if it can stop pixies and murder. A choking dry heave sound erupts from my throat. It's enough to make Vander give me a little slack. The knife is not so sharp against my throat.

"What should I—?" he starts to say.

But he doesn't finish, because I've elbowed him in the gut and launched myself sideways into the window. My shoulder smashes through it. Pain prisms out and down my arm, up my neck. My body follows my shoulder through the broken glass and into the cold air. No words escape my lips as I fall through the snowflakes, rushing toward the ground.

I should close my eyes.

I don't.

My body tilts sideways. The bathrobe unties from the movement. The fabric billows above me. I lift out my arms, wonder if I look like a falling angel. The rumbling of the cars below gets louder. I'll land on one or on the hard pavement. My body will flatten and break. Hopefully, it will be quick. Hopefully.

I close my eyes.

Hands clutch at my robe, hauling me off my straight-down course. Astley. I try to grab at him. He smashes me to his chest, cursing quietly, as my fall down becomes a movement sideways and then up.

"Astley!" I sob.

"We are always saving each other," he whispers into my hair. "Hold on."

And we take off into the night sky.

I'm completely frozen by the time we get to the airport. We land in a horrible thud behind a big truck. Astley apologizes, rubs at my arms, and helps me retie my robe around my waist. I'm shuddering so horribly that I can't do it myself. He rushes inside to the duty-free shops to get me better clothes and a coat and shoes.

"I shall be as quick as I possibly can," he assures me. "Huddle down by the tire. Make your body a ball. It will help."

Our cell phones, our suitcases, our bags are still at the hotel and our flight doesn't leave until morning, but we've decided the airport is the safest possible place. It's full of people. It's warm.

"What about our passports?" I ask.

"I have them on me. I have kept them on me the entire trip. I am paranoid about passports."

"Good thing."

His eyes are so sad. "Yes. Good thing."

He leaves and a plane rumbles above me as I wait. I push my back against the tire, not wanting anything to sneak up on me. I'm so tired, but it isn't until we're inside and I'm dressed and my shoulder is bandaged that I fall asleep, in one of the airport chairs. Astley's arm is wrapped around my shoulder for warmth or reassurance or something, and I don't move it away. I don't know why. I just can't. I need it there.

Tensions rise in the small Maine town of Bedford as another of its young people goes missing. This time it's a girl. She was reportedly last seen walking out of the YMCA and entering the woods. —CNNS NEWS

The entire plane ride back I have a hard time talking or even thinking. The plane blows reconditioned air into my face, stale and ugly, the same thing over and over again, and it reminds me of my life. I try to help: people get killed. I try to be a hero: people die. Astley puts his arm around my shoulders again, and I don't object, because I know that he knows how it is too, what it's like to see people die for you, to have that burden. I reach up and try to shut off the air, but the fan is broken. It just keeps rushing out. Eventually, we both give in to exhaustion and keep still, our heads leaning against each other as we rush through the air.

When I finally get home, Betty takes me into her arms and whispers, "I knew no good would come of this."

"He died, Gram," I murmur into her shoulder. She smells of wood smoke and fur and spaghetti sauce.

"I didn't think he had it in him," she admits crossly.

That hits me wrong and she knows it, because she hugs me tighter.

"At least your mom can finally rest easy." She pets my back a couple times like she's a football coach or something, awkward and aggressive, and then tells me to go take a shower; she's going to make some cinnamon toast. But when I go upstairs, I fall into bed and sleep kidnaps me before I can even take off my shoes.

The next day, I take Nick's MINI into town, thinking about how Vander betrayed us. Astley doesn't know why or how Vander was not actually pledged to him but to another king. He had an agenda, and Astley needs to figure it out. I need to find Nick, and we both need to keep the town safe. There's so much to do. It overwhelms me.

Parking on Main Street, I get out and sniff the air for pixies. It seems clear. There are cars parallel parked up the sides of the road, smooshed near to the concrete sidewalks that border the brick buildings, all of which are three stories tall, except the bank, which tops out with a whopping fourth story. According to Betty, the entire downtown, which is basically two streets a quarter mile each, burned down right before World War II. Some crazy firefighter was bored and set the fires. They rebuilt and it's nice and everything, but it lacks that old-time colonial era feeling that most New England towns have.

I step onto the concrete sidewalk, which has patches of ice and a thin layer of snow on it. The town snow-removal crew is having a hard time keeping up with all the precipitation. A man outside the health food store sighs as he shovels. The metal of the shovel scrapes against the concrete, making a horrible noise.

"Hello!" he says.

I smile at him and his rosy cheeks. He reminds me of Santa. "Hi. You need help?"

"I got it. Thanks."

I pass Finn's, the Irish pub that all Betty's EMT friends adore, and rush up the steps to the Maine Grind, which is in another brick building that used to be the Masonic Hall. The Masons are some kind of secret society that goes back for centuries, but they've lost membership, probably because only men can join. They sold the hall and meet in the basement of the YMCA now. The Maine Grind is cute and as close to trendy as anything can get in Bedford, Maine. There are big tables made of solid wood with legs painted orange and purple. There are comfy couches everywhere. The music is usually contemporary folk, but not in a bad way. They even have chai. In Bedford this is huge.

I order a chai and head to the big brown leather couch that Devyn and Issie are already hunkered into. It sort of swallows you when you sit. Is sips hot chocolate. Devyn gulps water—I have no idea why. It's the perfect day for warm drinks full of calories and sugar, but Devyn is on this "my body is a temple" kick all of a sudden and eats only whole foods and no refined sugars.

"Cassidy's in the bathroom itching," Issie says as I adjust myself on the couch. "Her sweater is driving her crazy. People were staring 'cause she couldn't stop scratching. It was sort of sad. I always thought being fae was cool, but if all synthetic clothing makes you itch, it sort of negates the whole awesome factor. Oh my gosh, I'm babbling. I'm so glad you're back."

"It's too bad she couldn't just run around naked," Devyn says. He takes a swig of water.

Issie elbows him hard in the stomach and he makes an *oomph* noise. A little bit of water spurts out of his mouth.

"I meant too bad for her, since clothes drive her crazy." He rubs at his side and grabs a napkin to wipe at his jeans where the water fell.

"You meant too bad for the male populace's viewing pleasure," Issie insists. Her voice gets half huffy and half teasing, and it's hard to tell if she's being funny or serious. She crosses her legs. She's wearing bright yellow tights under a jean miniskirt and hot pink boots to match. Only Issie could get away with that. She regains her composure and puts up her hands in surrender. "Sorry! Sorry. Total insecure moment. I am unworthy."

Devyn just smiles and pulls his laptop out of its bag. "So, Iceland. Is there anything you'd like to go over? Any subtle clues? Any idea why the pixie set you up?"

"And are you emotionally okay? About the king sacrificing himself like that? It was so unexpected," Issie says, reaching out to pat my arm.

"Did you guys know Betty doesn't want us to look for Nick?" I blurt, not answering any of their questions.

They exchange a look and Devyn nods. "We knew. She's pretty adamant that none of us try again. She believes Nick is gone for good, Zara."

"He's not."

Issie grabs my hand in hers and squeezes. "We know. Don't worry. We haven't given up on him either."

For a second tears collect at the edges of my eyes. It takes all my will not to cry, but I don't. I won't.

"He's not gone," I whisper.

"Don't worry. We aren't giving up," Devyn says, booting up his laptop and looking embarrassed about all the emotion.

Issie admires her boots, stretching one leg out in front of her.

"How many times do you think we'll have to tell Zara we won't give up?" she teases.

"According to my calculations, five hundred and thirty-eight," Devyn answers. He eyes me. "And how are you feeling, Zara? Has the morphing into a new species bothered you, emotionally or physically? Do you have any side effects?"

I swear he actually opens up a document that has "Pixie Change Side Effects" as the subject line.

"No," I sputter.

"Any self-loathing? My parents said that would be normal, and you could go see them for a counseling session, if you'd like," he says, taps a line into his document, then adds, "For free, obviously."

"No, I'm good," I lie. "Same old Zara."

They both look at each other like they know I'm lying. Dev closes the document and opens another. "So, I've been research-ing Valhalla, obviously."

He then proceeds to give us the lowdown:

1. Valhalla is from the Old Norse *Valhöll*, for "hall of the slain."
2. Valhalla is in Asgard, which is where the gods like Odin and Thor lived in ancient myth.
3. Nobody seems to agree about where Asgard is. Some scholars say near Troy, others in Asia, others in Iceland.

"So what we have basically is a fat lot of nothing," Issie announces, then cringes. "Sorry, Zara. I know you want this to be easy. We all want it to be easy."

I swallow some chai and put the yellow mug back on the coffee table, next to a copy of *Utne Reader*. Issie starts pulling on her tights, which have started to resemble elephant skin around her ankle.

"It's okay," I say, despite the growing feeling of desperation inside me. My fingers reach for my anklet, just to touch it a little bit and think of Nick.

Devyn raises an eyebrow but doesn't look at me as I sigh. Instead he stays focused on his laptop screen. "I've got absolutely nothing on the name Astley gave me for his mother. I've run it through everything—DMV, all the search engines . . ."

"What we need is a psychic witch moment where we create a witch finder, the way Willow and Tara did in *Buffy*, or a transporter homing beacon type thing, like they have in *Star Trek*—" Issie stops herself because she must be noticing that we are all staring pretty blankly at her. "Does anyone know what I'm talking about?"

None of us do. I fiddle with the zipper of my hoodie and then get distracted by Callie, who is standing in between the coffee table and another couch, just sort of staring at us like she's remembering what she saw the other night. I swallow hard and say, as brightly as I can, "Hey, Callie."

"You guys are up to something," Callie says, folding her arms across her body. She glares at us, but it's not a mean glare, and she shakes her head so much that her green retro-1980s Mohawk waves in the air.

"You're always skulking. You're always whispering. And if Nick just went away on vacation, why do you all look so—so devastated. Plus, you danced with that hot blond guy with all the rich-boy clothes at the ball."

"Um . . ." I don't know what to say.

Issie shoots me a "don't say anything" look. I feel suddenly, terribly self-conscious.

"Talk," Callie demands. She taps her Converse-clad foot on the hard floor. I almost expect her to finger snap like they do in show choir. They are doing these old 1940s Cole Porter songs this year. There is a lot of finger snapping. "Not about the dance and the hot guy. I want you to talk about what you are hiding—and don't tell us 'nothing.' I know it's not nothing."

Cassidy trots out from her scratching spree in the bathroom just in time. She makes her voice low. "Nick's missing. The whole thing about him visiting his parents is a lie. Do not tell!"

My mouth drops open. It's not what Callie asked, but it's a good enough deflection that it makes her lose her train of thought.

"Oh no!" She gasps and clutches me to her chest.

All I can think is: I do not want to talk about this.

Callie finally lets me go and starts clucking and worrying and asking us why didn't we tell the police and what's going to happen and where did we last see him? Her questions become louder and louder, circling around as Cassidy and Devyn try to answer them. Eventually I just give up and go to the bathroom. Issie follows me. She stands behind me.

"Don't want to talk about it, huh?" she asks.

I shake my head. She stares at me for a second, and I have no idea what's going through her brain. Finally she clears her throat and says, "I am sorry I was freaked about you turning. It wasn't fair of me at all. And I love you. You're still my best friend, you know."

"Mine too," I say, pushing away the tears.

"It's okay to be sad, Zare." She pulls a brush out of her purse and hands it to me, which I guess is a hint. "You don't have to be our fearless leader all the time, you know."

I stare into the smudged-up mirror and start brushing. My hair is all staticky wild up here. "I'm not much of a fearless leader."

"Even fearless leaders get sad," she says.

"Yeah?"

"Yeah."

After we've managed to escape good-intentioned Callie, we all bundle up against the cold and walk out to our cars, where I spot Astley. He stands in the falling snow as casual as all get-out, just leaning on Nick's car, which seems wrong somehow. I think it's mostly because Nick would hate the thought of a pixie king being anywhere near his car. Astley is wearing a dark wool cargo jacket with a button-down shirt that's got these crazy lapels sticking out in white points, showing a good inch of his chest. He looks more like he's getting ready to hang out at the MTV Video Music Awards than waiting for me on a street in Bedford, Maine.

"Get off that car," Devyn growls at him. It's a low rumbling noise with the tiniest bit of a birdlike squawk.

Issie simultaneously sighs and then mutters, "Great. What's *he* doing here?"

"Maybe he has a lead on Valhalla. I mean, a better one," I say and rush over to him before anyone can stop me. He smiles when he sees me, an open-faced smile that makes him handsome despite his total pixie nature. I smile back, then check his eyes. They are obviously pained. I ask, "What is it?"

I swallow hard, terrified that it's something bad about Nick.

"I was just checking on you, seeing how you were doing," he says. He lifts his leg up, bends it at the knee, and starts fiddling with his sock. It's argyle, a grandpa kind of sock, and looks soft, like cashmere. It doesn't quite fit with the rest of his ensemble.

"Oh." I cock my head, trying to figure him out. I realize I must look like a puppy and straighten my head back up again.

"I have been worrying about you after—Iceland," he says as his gaze moves past me and toward Issie and Devyn and Cassidy, who are on their way over. He lets go of his sock and stands on two feet again.

Cassidy's lips are turned down. Her oval face seems to be even longer than normal. Devyn comes and stands next to me, giving off a super-angry vibe.

Astley seems oblivious, still leaning against the car. He directs his gaze and his words directly at me as if nobody else is even there. "I feel responsible for what happened."

I huff out air. It's so cold that my breath makes a little fog cloud in the air. "It wasn't your fault."

"I disagree," Devyn says as a Dead River oil truck rumbles by. Its tires spit up slush.

Astley ignores him. "I am so sorry, Zara. And I have no word on my mother."

"You've got to stop ignoring my friends." I move forward and grasp his arm. My voice is calm but serious and hopefully will have the right impact.

"It's not nice," Issie adds. She pulls on her fuzzy pink mittens. "And if you want us to believe pixies are capable of being fun, happy goody-goodies, you might want to recognize our existence when we talk. Right, Zara?"

She doesn't wait for me to answer. Instead she charges on, pointing at Astley with her fuzzy hand. "And ignoring Devyn is totally uncool, because he is the smartest, coolest, brilliantest—oh, not a word!—most brilliant guy there is. He hacked into the Department of Motor Vehicle records looking for your mother! That's how awesome he is."

Devyn starts blushing and mutters, "Is, that's illegal. We aren't supposed to tell anyone that, especially a pixie."

For a second it looks as if Astley might implode. A muscle on his cheek twitches.

"I apologize," he finally says. "It is not the easiest thing to do when you all cling to preconceived notions of what it is to be of my kind. Plus, the were constantly glares and he enunciates the word 'pixie' as if it were a curse. However, you are correct. It was rude of me to ignore you."

"Okay, good!" Issie chirps.

Then nobody says anything. Two little twin boys get out of a minivan that's parked in front of the MINI. Their mother hustles them onto the sidewalk, bending down to hold their hands. A tall man with Clark Kent glasses fast-walks up to us, carrying a stack of *Solidarity Now* newspapers.

"Want one?" he asks. "They're free."

"Um . . ." Cassidy's lip goes over to the side. She sticks out her hand. "Sure."

The man passes one paper out to each of us and then heads toward the Maine Grind.

"Random," Issie says under her breath. She tucks the paper under her arm.

Cassidy looks like she wants to use her copy to swat Astley. Instead, she picks up the conversation again. "Do you know why they tried to trick you? Or what that wolf means?"

Astley shakes his head. He finally stops leaning on the back of Nick's car. There's a bit of gold dust left behind, mixing now with the snow. It sparkles. I resist the urge to touch it. It used to scare me before I turned. It scared me when I knew it meant my father was around, but Astley's doesn't scare me at all.

"The wolf is a sign of the coming war. They tried to trick us because they wanted one of us or both of us dead. It is a thirst for power. It happens," he says, his voice both tired and patient.

It's almost like I can feel his emotions now, like they come off him in waves of scent and color. Right now he's agitated about things, and that agitation smells like Brussels sprouts and its color is yellow. Weird.

"You have to believe me that I would never put you in harm's way intentionally, Zara," he says.

Devyn snorts. "He says this after he turned her into a pixie."

"You must believe me," Astley says desperately. I've *never* seen him like this. I can't help but give in.

"They'll believe you. Eventually." I take him by the arm and pace away from the rest, just bringing him a few steps down the sidewalk. This causes Devyn to glower at me, and Cassidy starts clucking nervously.

"Bye, guys!" I wave super big and they get the point. Dev and Is pile into her car while Cassidy walks around the corner.

"Are you okay?" I whisper to Astley as I watch Issie buckle up.

"My mother . . ." He seems to struggle for the words and then starts over again. "My mother is a difficult woman to find, and I feel like such a failure because I cannot find her for you."

I ignore that and ask, "Any attacks? Any Frank sightings? Did you tell the council of pixie people what happened in Iceland? Was Vander a rogue or working for someone else?"

He gives me the lowdown on what happened while we were gone. His people stopped several attacks from the rogue pixies that belonged to my father as well as those that follow Frank. Two died. Three pledged their allegiance to him. It's got to be hard to deal with all that drama and responsibility. Maybe that's why there are wrinkles of fatigue all around his eyes. And to make matters worse, a girl was attacked. It's almost always boys. This chills me. Astley has a call in to the council and they are "pondering" what he reported about Iceland and our quest for Valhalla.

"Pondering?" I ask.

"Pondering," he repeats with disdain. "They tend to 'ponder.'"

I get into the MINI. He pats my hand, which is on the window frame.

"We shall find my mother, Zara," he says. "And then we shall find your wolf."

He looks so broken and sad. I pause for a second and then just say it: "You know, life fractures all of us into little pieces. It harms us, but it's how we glue those fractures back together that makes us stronger."

The air stills between us, his hand still resting on my hand. "Where did that piece of wisdom come from?"

"Inside of me." I give him an eyebrow raise to push my point a little further. "Even if you're a pixie king, it's okay to occasionally admit to the world that there have been fractures and that there is glue."

"Even to his queen?"

I nod. "Especially."

Astley leaves and I just sit in the MINI for a minute, trying to process everything that's going on. Cassidy comes running down the sidewalk, her eyes frantic big. Her braids have morphed into dreads this last week, and the effect has made her prettier, but right now she looks like some sort of frazzled animal. She yanks on the passenger door, but it's locked.

"Let me in," she demands.

I push up on the unlock button in the center console under

the radio and grab the sword I've stuck in the backseat in case of attacks. She slams into the passenger seat and shuts the door.

"Are they after you?" I ask. My fingers tighten around the sword's hilt.

She looks confused for a second. "What . . . ? No! No, I found something."

"You aren't in mortal danger?" I use the phrase because it's so corny and I'm trying to ease the tension. It works. She laughs. I push the red button to turn the heat up a little bit because she's shivering. I can't tell if it's from cold or excitement.

"Look at this!" She waves the paper under my nose.

I take the paper. There's an article on health-care reform, a couple ads. I don't get it. "What is it?"

She taps her finger on an ad for a party at a bar. "This. Right here!"

She's so excited all her words just rush out, but she's not really saying anything—or I'm not really getting it. "I'm sorry . . . a costume party at a bar on Mount Desert Island? That's forty minutes away and we are way too young to get into a bar."

"Look at the entertainer," she insists.

I scan the tiny print. "It's a fiddler?"

She takes the paper back and folds it neatly in her lap with the ad facing up. She smooths her hand over it and pulls in a few breaths, trying to calm herself down.

"Cass?"

She smiles serenely. "Sorry. Just trying to get a way to tell you. Okay . . . Every year my mom brings me to the Common Ground Fair, which is this big-time organic fair in Unity, right?"

"Unity?"

"It's a town in the middle of the state." She waves her hand dismissively. "It doesn't matter. To get to the main part of the fair, you have to walk through this sweet trail that curves through these tall spruce trees. So, right in front of me was this guy. He had a weird vibe. He was wearing all corduroy—blazer, pants. And sticking out from his blazer was this long taillike appendage that was wrapped in different-colored earth-toned cloth. I guess he could tell I was checking him out, because he turned his head and looked at me. His eye was this startling silver color. How startling? So startling that I actually gasped and got creeped out."

"Was he a pixie?" I ask.

"Yeah. His glamour wasn't so good either, but I didn't even know there were pixies back then." She sighs. "I just knew that there were people who weren't actually people, you know?"

"So what's that got to do with the ad?" I ask.

Her eyes sparkle, she's so psyched. She jabs the picture of the fiddler with her finger. "This is that guy—the guy I saw at the fair."

"Cool . . ." I wait a second for some kind of big realization to hit. Maybe it's because I'm so tired, but it doesn't. "I still don't get it. We've located a pixie, yeah. We'll go get him."

"No! That's not it. Look at his name, Zara."

I read the ad. "BiForst?"

"As in 'shimmering path'?" She pokes me in the thigh with her finger.

"I still don't get it."

"As in the way to get to Asgard, where Valhalla is."

"But that's a bridge, not a person." The world suddenly feels full of light. "But it could be a clue . . . He could know . . . Oh, man . . ."

She grabs my hand in hers and our fingers intertwine. "Don't hyperventilate, Zara."

I push my free hand against my heart.

"I am, aren't I? Oh my gosh, Cassidy. What if he knows some-thing?" I grab the paper from her. "This party is tomorrow night. *Tomorrow night!*"

We both do this tiny squee thing and hug each other, reach-ing over the shift and emergency brake. We separate after several seconds of this. I swear I would happy-dance all around the MINI if there was enough room to actually stand up.

"You know what this means, don't you?" I raise my hand for a fist bump.

"Road trip!" she sings out.

"Road trip," I agree, my whole body screaming out happy, hopeful thoughts as I hug Cassidy again. Inside my head, I whis-per to Nick, who can't hear me, I know, but I totally don't care. "You hold on, baby. I'm coming to find you. I am."

Thomas Steffan Waiting for someone else to disappear. Better not be me this time. Or any of my homies. Got that, serial killer? —STATUS UPDATE

Things don't go quite as smoothly as I expect. First, due to the Iceland debacle, I can't even tell Betty about the bar thing without risking a full-blown scene. But then Devyn's parents sequester him at their house because they are working like mad on a vial of my blood, trying to make a pixie toxin, and need all the help they can get. And Issie is still grounded.

"Even on the weekends?" I whine. We're talking on our phones. Is has to whisper because she's not even supposed to use her phone.

"The quote-unquote danger is even greater on the weekends, according to my mom. You're lucky I got out to go to the coffee house," she says. "I had to totally lie and say I was doing a community service project with Key Club and that I'd come right home afterward. My mom is totally paranoid. She's all, 'A serial killer is loose out there!'"

"Can't you lie again?"

There's a silence. I plop down on my pillows, stare up at the Amnesty poster on my ceiling.

"It's okay, Is—," I start to say.

She interrupts me. "No. I have an idea. I'll say I'm going to church group. We have church group tomorrow night. I just can't be super late. And I have to moan a lot about going, because I always do, or else she'll suspect something is up."

I hop out of the bed. "Issie, I love you! I would hug you right now if you were here."

"Well," she whispers. "Just let me live with you when my mom kicks me out, or rescue me from heaven when she kills me. Okay?"

Laughing, I clutch my pillow. "Okay."

Issie picks up Cassidy and me. We cram into her car. It's full of steak knives, which Issie's mom insisted she take for protection. There's also an emergency whistle hanging from a necklace chain. I'm in Devyn's shotgun spot, mostly because Is won't stop worrying about Devyn not being here, and I think it's driving Cassidy crazy.

"We will be *fine* without him," Issie says for the hundred millionth time as we drive onto Route 3. "Right? So it is all girl power tonight. Girl power! Yee haw!"

She raises her hand for a fist bump, but her voice rises up at the end of the sentence the way it always does when she's stressed. Cassidy bumps it. I'm too busy trying to deal with the pounding pain rushing through my head.

"I think you need one of those deal-with-iron pills Astley gave you," Is says. "You have one?"

I try to nod, but the movement breaks off because my head is basically exploding.

"Look in her purse," Is orders Cassidy.

Cassidy reaches up to my lap and yanks my purse into the backseat with her. She pulls out a little plastic bag of pills. "These look so illegal."

"Oh my gosh, Zara," Issie chimes in. "They totally do. What if they are illegal? What if they count as drugs? That's an automatic suspension from school, plus I think they give you a juvie record and everything if they think you are selling them. You can't just carry them around in your purse like that or you will totally get arrested, and you can't get arrested because do you know what they do to cute girls like you in jail? I mean, I know you're a pixie, but they could still do that to you and—"

"Issie," Cassidy interrupts, opening up the baggie and giving me one of the big blue pills. "Honey, you need to breathe."

"Okay, yeah, right, breathing . . . ," Issie says and hauls in a couple big, hard breaths. "I'm just so nervous."

"Thank you," I say, and it's just a whisper. I swallow the pill down and wait. It takes about a minute, but it works.

"Better?" Is asks.

"Yeah. Sorry. Pixie side effect," I explain, trying to organize the steak knives.

"It's not all glittery dust and Peter Pan love, huh?" Is teases. Then she reverts to stressed-out Issie, worrying about going to a bar without Devyn and without telling Betty. Cassidy and I spend most of the car ride reassuring her that we will be beyond fine. My entire body hums with excitement as we drive down Route 3, the two-lane road that goes through Trenton, past a shut-down water place and touristy lobster restaurants and an IGA, and then over the bridge onto Mount Desert Island. There are no street-lights and just occasionally houses before Bar Harbor. There's so much darkness out there, and it's strange how it's people who light it up, giving us glimpses into their lives via their living room windows.

"Zara, you're shaking the entire car, you're fidgeting so much," Cassidy says from the backseat as we pull into the parking lot.

"I can't help it," I say, unclicking my seat belt.

"You can't click until we've stopped. You are so impatient!" Issie pulls into a parking spot. "That's okay, but don't get your hopes up, sweetie. You don't want to—"

"Be disappointed," I finish for her. "I know! But I'm not going to be. I can feel it. We are totally going to get Nick back. We are taking the first big step right now. Right now! Girl power, babies. Girl power."

Cassidy rolls her eyes because I am just a little bit too much PG-13 cheerleading movie for her. We get out of the car, and as Issie locks it we all stand there together, staring at the bar building, which is low, one-story, and has dark smudge marks on the white walls.

"Even the snow can't hide the ugly," Cassidy mutters as we hustle across the parking lot, our feet making tracks in the snow.

We pause outside. The bar is set up along one side of the public parking lot in Bar Harbor. The town is a wicked tourist place in the summer but pretty much abandoned in the winter. Almost all the stores on Cottage and Main streets are boarded up with signs that say BE BACK IN MAY.

"It's so deserted feeling," Cassidy whispers.

We've stopped our power walk and now we're half crawling, half tiptoeing toward the building, which has two entrances. One is on Cottage and the other faces the parking lot.

"Mmm-hmm," says Issie. "I know I'm the one who is always

freaking out about getting suspended and arrested and grounded and everything, so I should probably not mention how worried I am about getting carded."

"We aren't even going to buy beer," I say, trying to sound logical and reassuring even though I'm pretty worried about this too.

"Some places card at the door," Issie retorts.

"And you know this how?" I ask. "Because last I knew, you weren't a big barhopper."

"I download things, that's how I know," she says, embarrassment raising her voice up an octave.

"Issie's right," Cassidy insists. "Some places do card at the door."

"Well . . . um . . ." I don't know what to say. I scuff my heels in the snow.

Issie perks up. "Maybe you can do one of those freaking mind-control things, now that you're all pixie. You know, like the Jedi in *Star Wars* . . . ?"

I grab her mittened hand in my own. "I don't think I could do that, but it's okay . . . We will deal with this. Together."

I push open the steel door, and there's no bouncer, no guy checking IDs. It's actually so crowded nobody even notices us. I'm totally sure our costumes make us look older anyway. Still, something is wrong about the bar, and all my internal danger alarms are screaming at me to turn around and walk away, to go home. It's not just that Issie, Cassidy, and I are totally underage and it's illegal for us to even step inside the bar out of the cold. It's not that the outside of the place looks like an overgrown trailer or that the inside, with all its folding metal chairs and sticky floor, isn't much better. It's something much worse than that. The wrong of it pushes against my skin, twists my stomach into braided knots, but I can't figure out exactly what that wrong is.

"Eww, it totally stinks in here," Issie says, wrinkling her nose. She hugs her arms around her coat like she's trying to warm herself up. "We aren't going to get arrested, are we?"

I give her a patented Zara White eyebrow raise. "We aren't drinking, Is."

"No, seriously. I know that's wimpy to ask with everything else going on, but if we live through this, I want to go to college and I don't want a record," she whispers as people jostle us farther inside. I'm too short to see over people's heads.

"You can leave, Issie," Cassidy says.

"Nope. Not leaving my friends," she says in a fake brave voice.

The fiddling guy has to be here somewhere, but I can't find him. All I can see are backs, so I ask our tall friend, "Can you see him, Cassidy?"

"Not yet." Her eyes flit around, taking in the scene. She's cautious even when she looks. She lifts one of her long hands up to her dreadlock braids. She snarls at a big guy dressed up like a werewolf who has elbowed Is in the back. She puts her arm protectively around Issie's shoulder. "Nobody will be mad at you if you leave."

Issie shakes her head so violently that her rainbow knit hat falls off. "No way. I'm not going out there without Zara to protect me. Are you nuts? It's night and a steak knife is so not going to hold back a pixie attack."

I scoop her hat up off the beer-stained floor and hand it to her. "It'll be okay, Issie. I'll keep us safe."

Although how can I do that? I'm not so sure. There's only one of me and there's a ton of . . . of . . . everybody else. I try to exhale, calm down, remember my purpose for being here, and take in the entire scene.

Then I see him—a strange guy fiddling over in the corner of

the bar. When I say strange, I really mean bizarre more than just plain old everyday strange. He has way too much hair and fake horns sprouting up out of the top of his head. Still, he isn't the weirdest person in here, not by a long shot. The bar is packed with people, most of them human. Some of them are dressed up like vampires with over-the-top black capes and plastic fangs. Some of the girls are supposed to be fae. They have sparkling wings and tiny tutu dresses. They all look clueless and drunk, which makes them look absolutely nothing like the real pixies and fairies they are supposed to be resembling.

"Spotted him," I say and point. "I think . . ."

"Where?" Issie asks.

Listening, I take in snippets of people's conversations.

No. I swear. I heard someone whisper my name when I was walking into the house. It was coming from the woods.

Dude. Get your hand off my—

It's creepy. That whole freaking town is creepy.

Why does it never stop snowing! It's so $#%& cold.

Baby girl, I'll keep you warm.

Eww. Look at his sideburns.

I hop up on a chair so I can get away from all those voices and see around all the tall men who don't seem to want to sit down. My heart stops as I look at him. He's so off, so menacing. "Is that him?"

Cassidy jumps on the chair with me. "Yep, it's the guy from the fair."

"Look," Issie says, elbowing me in the thigh and pointing at one girl who has fake pixie wings and cleavage showing down to her belly button. "It's like a sexified version of you."

"You mean Tinker Bell," I disagree.

"No. You. You're the real pixie here, Zara," she whispers. Her big eyes get even bigger. The standard black witch hat perches over her reddish hair. She's placed her rainbow hat into the pocket of her coat, which she still hasn't taken off to reveal the rest of her witchy ensemble.

"Don't remind me." I push my back up against the wall made of wooden planks. The roughness of it scratches against my skin. I'm dressed up like a fairy too. Only I don't need to pretend to be otherworldly. I *am* otherworldly. I wonder if the fiddler guy is too.

Cassidy leans toward me. Her braids swing with the movement as she ducks her head a bit. She's so much taller than I am that she always bends when she talks to me, like I couldn't possibly hear her from her height even with my new ultra-strong hearing. Her voice is gravelly as she says, "You look pretty human for a pixie."

"You're one to talk, Elf Girl," I say and tap her long swirly skirt with my finger. She's dressed up like a demon, all leather and horns. "We've got to talk to him, not scare him off . . . We've got to—"

The fiddling guy abruptly stops playing and points at me with his bow. People turn to stare.

"You," he says into his microphone.

I tap my finger on my chest. "Me?"

"Yes, you, sweet thing. Come up here," he orders.

I hop off the chair. Issie grabs my arm as I start to move forward. "He's so icky, Zara."

"Stay by the door in case we have to run, okay?" I say. All my pixie senses are on full alert, telling me *Danger, danger* with every goose bump. Still, this is the lead I've been waiting for—this man could be the key.

Issie keeps her tiny fingers clutched around my bicep. I could break free pretty easily—but I don't because it's rude and, truthfully, because I am a bit freaked out.

BiForst points again. "I said to come here, sweet thing."

His voice is staccato and rough and almost irresistible.

Cassidy leans forward. "I don't like his energy. He's hostile."

"Duh," Issie murmurs. "I'm *human* and I can tell that."

Instead of getting annoyed, Cassidy just smiles. "That's because you are an exceptional human."

Issie loosens her hold with the compliment and I move forward as the music starts back up. I push through the crowd, turning sideways to get through the narrow spaces between the chairs and brown circular tables, making my way toward the fiddling man. Some people grunt while others just keep swigging down their beers and munching on their chili cheese fries. The smells are overpowering and diverse: sweat from bodies, yeast from beer, Scotch, rum mixed with Coke, perfume, breath, shampoo, lemony floor cleaner. If I were claustrophobic, I'd pass out from all the closeness.

I have no fear of closed-in spaces, though.

My only fear right now? Failure.

So I push on through and get to where the guy on the stage is perched on his rickety metal stool with his fiddle. It's an electric fiddle. All I can think of is this old country song about how the devil went to Georgia looking to steal somebody's soul and he got in some fiddling contest. That song always freaked me out when I was little.

The guy sneers down at me. He keeps playing. There's some chili in his brown curly beard. I look away from it because I will vomit, and instead I force myself to stare into his eyes. One is silver. The other is the blue of Siberian huskies. I shudder. He sees and smiles. There are more chili remnants in his teeth.

Focus on his eyes, I tell myself. *Do not vomit. Do. Not. Vomit.*

He pushes the microphone aside. "Well, sweet thing, aren't you a little young to be in bars?"

I cross my arms in front of my chest and stare up at him, at his brown cord pants and green corduroy shirt. He's wearing red suspenders. It's not the best ensemble. I sniff. He's pixie too, I think, but his smell is off a little bit.

"No point trying to figure me out," he says. "You don't have the brains for that or the experience."

I bristle. "Tell me how to get to Valhalla."

"Not even a please?" he taunts.

"Just tell me." I take a step forward.

He raises his bow and starts playing again. "Sorry. No can do."

"Please." I say the word through gritted teeth and he laughs.

"Sweet thing, I'm a dead end for you. In more ways than one. Whoever told you to come here steered you wrong." He leans toward me. "Who *did* tell you to come here?"

"I refuse to say."

"Was it maybe the Internet?" He chuckles like this is some five-star joke.

I uncross my arms and hop up on the stage with him. I hunker in close and whisper in his ear, "Don't play games with me."

"You don't scare me, sweet thing. You and your boy king are harmless. True power doesn't lie on your side." He snarls at me but keeps playing, fiddle tucked beneath his chin, fingers moving as fast as they possibly can. "True power never lies on the side of weaklings and do-gooders, afraid of change, making sure they play by the rules. Now run along before I'm forced to kill you."

I decide to call his bluff. "You're so tough? Why don't you kill me now then?"

He lifts his right foot and motions toward the crowd in front of us, dancing, drinking, eating, looking for each other's tonsils, all while dressed up like us, like the fae. "Not in front of the humans, dear. So much cleanup to do afterward."

I let that sink in for a second, assess his strength. Power pretty much ripples off him in waves, but I don't step back. I don't step forward either. I'm smarter than that, I hope. Instead I just repeat what I want. "Tell me how to get to Valhalla."

He smiles a slow, deliberate smile while his hands keep up the frantic playing. "Why don't you tell me who you lost?"

"Like you don't know."

"I don't."

"Then how do you know I lost someone at all?"

"Sweet thing, nobody wants Valhalla unless they've lost a warrior. Tell me who your warrior was."

There are some windows along the right side wall. If I look past the heads and costumes and beer signs, I can see out and it makes me feel better. The outside always makes me feel better now that I've changed. It's snowing.

Behind me I can smell Issie and Cassidy getting closer. Issie is lilac. Cassidy is that kind of incense you always find in New Age stores. I forget what that's called. It doesn't matter. What matters is getting the information.

Focusing on him, I try to make myself seem more powerful, tougher, to project the image of a pixie you do not want to cross. "Just tell me how to get there."

"Are you gritting your teeth?" He laughs. "You don't want to do that. It files them down. Pixies need sharp teeth."

"Just tell me," I insist, and add for good measure, "please."

"What will you give me in return?"

"Anything," I blurt.

He lifts an eyebrow and I swallow down regret.

"Anything," he repeats. "Any*thing* . . . I'll have to think about that."

I wait and he finishes his tune. People clap. Someone hoots and yells for more. He smiles, waves his bow at them, and then turns his attention to me. "How about I give you a tidbit now?"

Hope surges in me. "Okay."

"The queen you replace has returned to the apple. Does that help?" He slaps his thigh like he's so funny and clever and he starts playing again. The queen I replace has to mean Astley's mother. But what does the apple mean? Before I can ask, the pixie clears his throat and says, "A word of advice, newbie. We aren't all on your little star king's side. Got it? Nope. Some of us are in it for ourselves, and some of us—like that one in the corner there—are just in it for evil."

"What do you mean by 'the apple'?" I ask as I eye the woman in the corner. She's not glamoured. Instead her real self shows. Her teeth fang out of her mouth. Her blue skin clashes with her sequined red dress. She has her hand wrapped around a mummy's waist. The mummy is human, male, and probably about to die. I can't let that happen, so I start heading toward her but stop midway and yell back to the fiddler, "And how about you? Who are you in it for?"

"Me. I am in it for me." He lifts an eyebrow and adds, "Same as you."

We eyeball each other for a second. The world seems to still, go slow motion, as we try to sniff out each other's intentions. His pupils flare for a second. It's almost like he's trying to hypnotize me, but he can't. I am not so weak. For a second I wonder if I could do that to him, break his will, but that is not what I do. I may be pixie, but I am still good.

Right?

I am still good.

"What do you mean by 'the apple'?" I ask again.

"*Zara!*" Issie's shrill scream breaks through the crowd. Pivoting back toward her, I take in the scene in an instant: the unglamoured pixie has Issie's head in the crook of her elbow, ready to snap Issie's fragile neck in two.

Boys in Bedford, Maine, are going missing. Yet the freaking town is acting like everything is all hunky-dory. It's like the whole place has its head in the sand—or rather the snow. From what I hear, it's been snowing for three weeks straight. Folks are looking for a serial killer, but I say that the perps are from out of this world. Best be looking for mutilated cows and crop circles, folks, 'cause you got aliens there. —THE CONSPIRACY BLOG

While Issie's trapped in the headlock, the pixie's mummy companion points a gun toward Cassidy's side, just barely hidden from everyone's eyes, thanks to the dangling costume bandages. Cassidy gasps and becomes unnaturally still. Shock and terror elongate her beautiful face.

A growl rumbles through the bar, low and fierce and primal, like a wild animal cornered and ready to fight for her life. That growl comes from me, I realize as I leap over tables and land in front of the pixie. Someone yells, "Girl fight!" and people nearby scatter as I wrench Issie free with one move and fling her behind me. She must land on someone, because there's an *oomph* and an apology. I can't look. I have to focus on Cassidy and the pixie.

"Stand down or I'll kill her," the mummy says. His voice is low, cowboylike. He's thin. He's human. I could break him in a second, but I don't because I am not evil or soulless. I realize right then: I am still me.

"Let her go or I'll kill *you*," I say. My fingers are claws. How? They curl toward him.

"Iron bullets, pixie." He sneers at me while he speaks. The pixie with him doesn't say anything. She just smiles and it is so creepy.

My eyes meet Cassidy's eyes. She's trying to look brave even though her long skinny fingers are shaking by her sides. I love her for that, for trying to be brave.

"You hurt her, I'll kill you before you get a chance to breathe," I threaten. I take a step closer. His finger twitches on the trigger. His pixie companion steps forward.

"Wow. That costume is awesome," some random woman says. "Hey! Does he have a gun?"

People have started to notice something bigger than a girl fight is going on. They're gathering around. Some guy yells, "Cool! Entertainment."

The mummy looks away. It's the break I need. I lunge forward before either of us can think, which, I have to say, isn't always the best move when fighting.

My stepdad always said my biggest problem was a failure to look before I leap. I have to say, he might be right, because I bash into the mummy hard without really thinking about what might happen. The guy's head knocks against the wall below a Budweiser mirror, but he keeps his grip on the gun. Right away, Cassidy's body twists as she tries to yank herself free from him, but it seems like she's moving slowly, way too slowly.

Issie screeches and I yell for Cassidy to hurry as I wrench the guy's thick arm. At the same time, his pixie companion reaches for me, her claws slashing my cheek. Pain scissors through my skin.

"That better not scar," I'm saying as the gun fires. The boom of it echoes throughout the entire room. People scream and scurry backward. It's like dynamite has gone off next to me. My whole body wrenches away from Mr. Mummy Guy, but I don't let go of his arm and instead try to kick toward the pixie and scream, "*No!*"

Simultaneously, I look up at Cassidy. Her face is twisted and terrified. She starts forward toward me, her arms reaching out, and I shout to warn her off. That is when the pain hits. It's like something has exploded into the side of my chest. My legs lose their purpose and I fall to the floor. Waves of tingling rush through me and the world suddenly goes into super-slow motion.

Cassidy's mouth is screaming, "Get away from her!"

The mummy raises his gun again, and this time it's Cassidy who blindside tackles him. The gun flies through the air. I don't know where it goes. I can't see it land. Instead I'm focused on the waves of tingling, the bomblike pain centered inside of me. Some random man with a wicked Maine accent yells, "I've got the gun. Get on the floor. Now! On the floor!"

But instead the pixie girl snarls, wraps her arm around the mummy, lifts him from the ground, and leaps out the window. Glass shatters as snow and cold burst inside, but it's like a whole separate me is noticing even that. The main me is focused on breathing, because my right lung suddenly feels deflated. My breaths are short and sharp and hard. Another part of me is floating above it all, just watching.

I come to. Cassidy's face is over mine. Her eyes are insistent and watery. "You are not allowed to die! Do not die!"

My vision starts to go. It's like a giant white board is shifting in front of my eyes.

"Nick," I gasp, but Nick is still gone. That's why I'm here in the first place, right? Nick. I don't even know if he's alive. I just know he was taken to Valhalla . . . Valhalla? Wait, what is that? Okay . . . okay . . . Right . . . Nick's face swims in front of me and the whiteness fades away. There are laugh crinkles by his dark brown eyes. He starts to smile his boyish smile, the one where it starts really slow and—

"Zara! Stay with us!" Issie grabs my hand and yells, "We have to stop the bleeding."

Then someone presses something into my side.

"You hang on, Zare Bear," she insists. "Call Betty! Get her cell, Cassidy. It'll be on speed dial."

Someone starts rummaging in my pocket. Calling Betty is a good idea. She's an emergency medical technician . . . technologist? . . . No, a paramedic . . . No, an EMT . . . Are those the same? She's going to be so mad I'm shot and that I went in a bar and that I . . . that I still want to find him. She will kill me if I die. Oh, that doesn't make sense! I start to giggle. It's more like a gurgle.

"She's losing it!" some guy yells.

"The phone's all bloody," Cassidy says.

I try to focus, find her face in all the whiteness.

"Astley," I manage. "Find Astley."

"Who is Astley?" some guy asks. "Rick Astley? The singer? Is he listed? I've called 9-1-1."

"He's—he's—" Issie doesn't know how to answer, I guess.

I rasp in a breath. My chest squeezes tighter.

"Her boyfriend," Cassidy lies.

He's not, though. He's not my boyfriend. That is Nick—*was* Nick. He is not my boyfriend because he's dead. I'm going to be dead . . . Focus, Zara . . . Focus . . . Who is Astley? My brain struggles to remember. The apple. The queen I replace is in the apple.

I lift up my head as much as I can and say, "Issie . . . Valkyries?"

"None." She shakes her head.

I am not enough of a warrior, I guess. That's why the Valkyrie took Nick. He was a warrior and a werewolf who was dying. Me? I don't make the cut, I guess. They'd take Astley. Astley. I want him here. I wheeze again. I think I groan. The world has gone completely light.

"She's lost so much blood," Issie whines. "Where the hell is the ambulance?"

"The queen I replace is in the apple," I manage. I clutch at someone's wrist. I think it's Cassidy's. "The queen I replace is in the apple."

"What's she talking about?" Issie shrieks.

Cassidy's eyes meet mine. Oh, she looks so sad. She looks like she thinks I'm going to . . .

"Can't die." My lips move. "Astley needs me."

But a hand presses into my face and his voice is there, right there, as he says, "Hush, Zara. I am already here."

When consciousness finds me again I am sideways in the back-seat of some really fast car. Issie is driving and I'm lying across Astley's lap. Cassidy is murmuring something in the passenger seat and there's a funky goldish glow everywhere that's not coming from the interior lights. Astley's got his hand pressed against my side and he's kind of rocking me back and forth.

"Betty! We have pressure on it!" Issie's yelling into the phone. "Where are you?"

Astley notices I'm conscious, I guess, because he leans closer. His blond hair is caked with blood. I have to assume that's mine. There's a smudge on his cheek. He has nice cheeks.

"Zara . . ." His voice trails off.

"Hard. To. Breathe," I tell him, which is a total understatement, because my lungs are fragments of fire.

"I know. We think it collapsed your lung," he explains. His lips turn in toward his mouth.

"Blood. Your. Car."

"That is the least of our worries. I can dispose of the car, but not you." His eyes narrow and he holds a free finger to my lips. "Cassidy is attempting some magic to slow your blood loss, but she is not full blooded and she has never attempted this previously. She says that she has read about it online."

I would nod but I can't muster up the energy. Whiteness threatens to take over again. I try to hold on. "I'm going to die."

"No, you will not." Astley keeps talking. "Issie has connected with your grandmother, who is on some other call halfway across the county, it appears. Why this godforsaken place has only one ambulance is absolutely beyond me. We will either meet the ambulance or we will get you to the hospital. Either way, you should have medical attention in ten minutes or less."

That's a long time and I don't think I'll make it. I lose my vision again. The whiteness descends down on me. Struggling, I try to focus on his voice and I manage to whisper out, "He said . . . in the apple. Like a worm. Your mother is . . . No sense . . . You . . . save him. Bring him back . . . The apple . . ."

He murmurs a swear and Issie shouts, "She's unconscious again! What do we do? What do we do?"

"Issie, breathe," he commands. "Relay to the grandmother

what is occurring and drive faster. This is a Koenigsegg. She can handle it, but she's full of power. Do not spin out. Cassidy? Are you praying? Focus on your crystals. The elves I have seen connect with them."

He is almost as bossy as Nick. I manage to lift up my hand. He grabs it with his own free hand. Fingers touch warm fingers. The world smells suddenly like the forest in spring, new wet moss, pine needles.

"How . . . did . . . you . . . know?" I wheeze out. It is a hoarse whisper. It is all I can manage.

"Where you were or that you were injured?" he asks.

The car hits a pothole. We bump up and down. I scream. At least I think it's me screaming. The pain spirals through my whole body, even my brain. Cassidy chants more loudly and Issie murmurs a stream of worries and pleas and a lot of swearing. The goldish glowing light is incredibly bright, filling the car.

Astley's fingers let go of my hand and join his other hand, fixing something on my side, adding more pressure. That's when I notice how pale he is—like he is injured too. His voice whispers out, "I knew because you are my queen, Zara. We are connected and it is my duty to know when you are hurt, where you are, all of those things. It is my sacred duty and I swear upon all that I am that I will not let you die. Do you believe me?"

I think about how we're bonded together now, how our lives are interwoven like the branches he showed me in the hotel room after I changed.

"Do you believe me, Zara?" he asks again.

I try to answer, but I am spiraling down, down, down.

The fear of death is thanatophobia.

I will not be afraid of death.

I will not be . . .

"Zara," he insists. "Do you believe?"

I open my mouth, but I'm not sure if any words actually verbalize. Instead I grit my teeth and buck up, then fold into myself.

I am so afraid.

"What is it?" Issie screeches.

Astley's hand lifts up something small and shiny. A bug?

"The bullet came back out," he said. "At least the iron won't poison her any longer. Thank you, elf."

Cassidy just keeps chanting.

"So she'll live?" Issie asks.

"She has lost blood, much blood," he practically hisses. "She would already be dead if she had not just taken that pill. You are sure she took it, correct?"

"She did!" Issie answers. Her voice is drifting away. Issie . . .

Astley's bloody hand rests on my forehead. "Fight, Zara. Fight for us."

I am. I am . . .

When my eyes open again the next time, I'm in Astley's arms and he's carrying me under the bright fluorescent lights of the hospital's emergency room entrance. The world is so white and cold and the lights are so horribly bright. Sliding metal doors open and attendants race out with a gurney.

"How long?" one asks.

The gurney is hard and cold against my back. I try to reach out for Issie or Astley or anyone. It's Astley that grabs my hand while barking at the attendant, "Twenty minutes."

The world whites again before I have a chance to ask him not to leave me. Everyone always leaves and I really don't want to be alone, especially if I'm going to die. I don't want to die alone.

I wake up again, but just for a moment. Betty's commanding scent is right near me.

"Grammy . . ." I struggle to say her name. I can't quite open my eyes.

Her smell comes closer; her voice is a distant echo in my ear. "They are stabilizing you. You hang on, you hear? You hang on, because when you wake up again, I am going to murder you with my own two hands."

When I manage to make it to a semiconsciousness that lasts more than two seconds and the massive pain isn't rippling through me, I run through what happened: gunshot . . . fiddling . . . apple . . . Astley . . . hospital . . . It wasn't in that order, though. I straighten it out, and when I open my eyes, I'm in an ICU room. It's bigger than your average hospital room and there are all sorts of tubes and things attached to my arms, monitors that are bleeping. Someone is here with me. I move my mouth, but no words come out.

"You're awake." Astley's face hovers above mine. He still has my blood on his cheek and in his blond hair. He kisses my forehead with soft, cool lips. "Do. Not. Worry. You are all stabilized. Your grandmother is arguing with the doctors. They say only two visitors allowed at one time in ICU. They want to transfer you to Bangor, because your blood pressure is so low and some of your readings are not typical."

"I . . ." Trying to sit up is so hard, and Astley gently leans me back down. His arm goes behind my shoulders. His hand cradles my head.

"I thought . . . I . . ." I don't know why I didn't tell him where we were going. I don't really know why I didn't tell Betty either. I guess I thought I could do it without them. I guess I worried that they would stop me. "I'm sorry."

"There is no need for sorries," he says. "But let me help you. You need to let me help you, Zara. We are on the same side."

I try to answer, but I can't stay awake.

The next time I open my eyes, Devyn leans into view. His nose is red at the tip. His eyes are tired and the pupils are too big. "Hi," he says.

I open my mouth again to ask about Betty. Still no words come out.

"Betty?" Devyn guesses. "She's okay. She's not mad. She's not happy about things or that the pixie boy is here, but she's not mad at you."

"Are you?" I ask.

"Why would I be?" He shakes his head. His hands are fists. "I'm just mad that I wasn't there."

"Issie?"

He frowns. "Let's just say the grounding has been extended until she is fifty. And her mother wants her to duct tape knives to her skin."

I groan and clear my throat. My voice is whisper weak. "We can't give up."

The world slips sideways as a nurse comes in, but before she shoos Devyn away, he whispers in my ear, "We won't, Zara. He's my best friend too."

MDI police responded to a bar fight tonight. Details are sketchy, but it appears a local teen was shot and is in critical condition. The police stress that the shooting is in no way related to the rash of disappearances in the nearby town that's been plagued . . . —NEWS CHANNEL 8

Days pass where I'm in and out of consciousness. Someone tells me my mother is stuck in Europe because of some airline strike. I didn't even know she was in Europe. Slowly, my body heals. Cassidy's been helping too somehow, using herbs and praying. Sometimes I see her in the corner of my room, her eyes closed and hands together. Betty tells me I'm lucky I'm pixie now, because if I were human, things would be really bad.

"Weeks," she says. "Weeks in a hospital."

I wake up again and there's an Amnesty International poster above me. It's thumbtacked to the ceiling. It takes me a second of staring at the image of a candle wrapped in barbed wire before I really make the connection: I'm home. The information processes a little slowly, and for a second I almost think I'm back in Charleston, where life was warm and full of flowers, where my stepdad was still alive, where I didn't know pixies existed, where I was human.

That tiny hope is snatched away quickly when I turn my head to look out the window. It's still snowing, lightly now, but persistent. The light of the snow fills my room with a cold brightness, but it's nothing like the light in Charleston. There are branches of trees in each corner of my room. I think they are aspen. I don't know how they got there. Cassidy maybe? There are camellias scattered around as well, white and pink balls of petals. And there's some sort of incense burning. The scent is so strong it feels like the inside of my nose is being rubbed by a bristle brush.

I groan. Not from that, but because just moving my head makes it throb. I reach beneath the covers and touch my side, which is all bandaged up. That's when I remember: I was shot. I was in the hospital. Everyone was there, coming in and out of my room one at a time, blurs of memory and action and words that I can't really grab on to.

Now?

Now I'm alone.

I check out my arms, still pale human skin. At least I haven't lost my glamour. I guess you have to consciously make it go away or else it just stays working, just like when I sleep. A twig hits my window, scratching against the pane. My entire body is stiff, but I force it to slowly sit up. Then I swing my legs off the edge of the bed and pull back the comforter. It's bright yellow and sunny. My socks touch the floor. Someone changed me into pajamas and Christmas socks with little snowmen on them. I hope it was Betty and not some horrible group effort. If I had the energy to blush, I would, but just sitting up is a chore. I push my body straight. Pain throbs across my chest. Ignoring it, I shuffle across the floor, grabbing on to the bedpost for a little support. Then, once I get far enough, I lunge forward and grab the wall and the doorknob. I turn it and shuffle into the hall like I'm a hundred and four years old and have lost my walker somewhere in the nursing home.

There are voices coming from downstairs.

"There is no way I will let her know this. You know what she'll do." It's Betty's voice, and it drops off into the nothingness.

"But we have to . . . Nick . . ." Issie's voice is high and she's speaking in sentence fragments, which is never a good sign. My heart hitches a little bit and I move as quickly as I can toward the stairs.

Issie, Cassidy, Devyn, and Mrs. Nix are all sitting in the living room. Betty is pacing back and forth, and Astley stands outside the door. Pixies aren't allowed inside. House rule. Also, they can't actually come inside unless invited in, like that old saying about vampires. And all tied up next to Astley on the porch is BiForst. There are chains around his hands and feet. It's a safe bet that they are iron.

"What's going on?" I say from the stairs. They all look up. Issie's mouth drops into an O and she and Cassidy both jump up like they've been caught doing something really naughty.

Betty, however, has the opposite reaction. She roars at me like I'm the one screwing up. "What are you doing out of bed?"

I swallow hard. She starts up the stairs and stops halfway. Her nostrils flare.

"I didn't know I wasn't allowed out," I say, trying to solid myself up so I don't seem frail.

"You just got back from the hospital. Of course you aren't allowed out." She scowls at me and then bounds up the rest of the stairs. She puts her arm around my shoulder and starts to pivot me around. "Now let's get you back to bed."

My hand grips the banister. "Tell me what you all are talking about."

She stops tugging on me. Nobody says anything. The air is still and cold and heavy. The furnace kicks on, a big rumbling monster. Issie jumps.

"Sorry." She blushes. "Jumpy."

"Well, it's not easy when there are two pixies on the front porch." Devyn mollifies her and puts an arm around her shoulder. For a second, jealousy rips through me. Nick would have done that for me, tried to make me feel better. I honestly don't know if he'll ever be able to do that again.

Everyone looks at each other. Tension makes the air prickle.

"What? Let me in on the secret," I persist.

"Okay . . . the thing is . . . ," Issie starts. She clears her throat nervously, takes a step toward me, and stops. "You need to be calm about this, honey, okay?"

Not a good sentence. She used the words "calm" and "honey." The world hazes around me, but I fight the dizziness even as Betty's hand tightens on my shoulder.

"What is it?" I ask.

Once again they all exchange a look. Cassidy clears her throat. Mrs. Nix stands up out of her chair slowly, but Astley, still outside, is the only one brave enough to just say it.

"There is a time constraint about getting Nick," he says, nodding toward BiForst. "Our lovely associate here has told us that if the warrior is not retrieved from Valhalla within a month, he may never return at all."

"What?" I make a quick calculation of how much time has already gone by and start stumbling down the stairs. Betty must not have expected me to move, because she doesn't stop me as I stagger-walk down the stairs and toward the front door. I step outside, ignoring Issie and Betty and everyone else, focusing only on Astley. "We don't even know how to get there. We don't know how long it takes. We don't—"

I stagger in the thin layer of snow that covers the wood boards of the porch. Astley, who has been crouching by BiForst, reaches up and grabs me by my arms. I can't read his eyes. The cold soaks into my snowmen socks, sharp and raw.

"Zara," he says, staring into me, "we can do this. We will do this."

I cringe. The snow falls around us. BiForst rolls his eyes as if Astley is too smarmy for words. I don't know what's going on in the house behind me as I scan the woods for other pixies. It seems clear for now. I swallow hard again. It's so hard to even swallow, let alone stand.

"We have to get him," I whisper, and I'm whispering it only to Astley. "We can't just leave him there. He'll think we abandoned him. We need him here to fight."

"It is okay." A pulse shows on a vein in his neck. His eyes meet mine.

I have thought about Nick's death for so many hours and days, twisted in my head with moments of every day and night, that the entire memory is solid with echoes. It is like I can touch it, hold it to my chest and squeeze it. The only thing that was letting me continue was the knowledge that I had a chance to save him. Now there's a time constraint?

"Did he tell you what he told me? In the bar?" I gesture toward BiForst. "He was all cryptic and said the queen I replace is in the apple."

"That's why she kept talking about the apple!" Devyn says to everyone in the house.

"We thought you were delirious," Mrs. Nix clarifies. She

breathes deeply and tilts her head just the tiniest of bits. Kindness emanates from her.

"So my mother is back in the city?" Astley asks BiForst, anger rippling out of him. "And you didn't tell me this because . . . ?"

"You didn't ask," BiForst snorts.

I stare at Astley. "New York?"

"The Big Apple," Astley explains.

I feel suddenly very stupid. How could I not have figured that out? My whole body aches from tiredness and cold. I sway a little bit and a soft voice comes from behind me. "Come inside, Zara."

I turn around slowly, because it's all I can manage. Mrs. Nix's round face looks down on me. Her big brown eyes are kind. She's wearing her sweatshirt with the Christmas tree embossed on it.

She tucks a piece of my dirty hair behind an ear. "Now come away from these pixies and into the house with us and get warm. We still have to figure out who is setting these traps for you and why. You were almost killed in Iceland. You were shot in the bar. We've got a cage almost finished in the basement. We're going to keep that pixie there until he talks some more."

I turn my head to check to see if Astley is okay with keeping BiForst trapped, since I know he disapproved when we trapped my father's people. He nods, but then stops midmotion, listening to something. I hear it too—a motor. No, a car. It's coming down our driveway.

"Someone's coming," I say.

The rest of them come to the door just as a silver sedan rolls into sight. The driver cuts the engine and leaps out of the car, her short legs rushing across the snow, her brown hair flying behind her.

I gasp. "Mom!"

The Bedford teen who was shot at a local bar has been released from the hospital and is said to be recovering at home. Police are still looking for the perpetrators as yet another boy goes missing. Unverified reports say his name is Thomas Steffan, a high school freshman . . . —NEWS CHANNEL 8

Wow. Okay. My mom is here. It takes me a second to actually accept this as reality, but I do as my mom quickly checks the perimeter of the woods. It's so obvious she's dealt with pixies before.

As I watch her half run, half power-walk toward the house, I wish I could make everything in our lives completely different, wish that this crazy epic that we're living in never started, that my pixie king father never fell for her, that we never had to stare at the woods and wonder if danger was lurking in it, that the responsibility of knowledge was not ours, that we knew nothing, that we could live happy, peaceful normal lives.

That's selfish, though.

And it's too late for that to happen.

And if it did, I may have never met Nick.

It's all pointless thinking.

I start to sway as my mother bounds up the steps. Astley's arm goes around me, supporting me, keeping me upright a little bit better. Despite the cold, I think I've started to sweat from exertion. My mom eyes us and keeps coming. Her skirt flutters in the wind. She's wearing a big red ski parka that looks like it's left over from the 1980s. She must have dug it out of the closet. Her dark hair lifts from her face, revealing worried, narrowed eyes.

"Don't you touch her," she snaps at Astley. She points a long finger in his face. She has perfect fingernails. Today they are red like blood. She looks like she might scratch him. "I know who you are."

"Mom, it's—," I start, but she yanks me into a huge hug. All I breathe in is parka and her coffee smell. For the tiniest moment I let myself just lean into her, like I used to do when I was little and needed her so much. Sometimes I'd be so tired after a day at kindergarten or nursery school that she'd come into the school and pick me up. I wouldn't even be able to stand straight anymore because I'd be so worn out from a day full of kissing tag and coloring and those singsong finger games that the teachers always led. On those days, I'd just lean into her and she'd take my pink Hello Kitty backpack, hold it in one hand, and wrap her other arm around me. Sometimes she'd just carry me right out the door and into the car. That's what this reminds me of right now when I lean into her: being little and not being responsible and just being able to let go, to be tired, to be scared, to just *be* . . .

"Oh, Zare Bear," she murmurs into the hair by my ear. "You poor honey. What have these things done to you?"

Things. I am one of "these things."

I force myself to move away enough so that I can look at her. She has more white hairs mixed in with all the brown. The skin under her eyes has little lines in it and her chin seems older too somehow, like it's sagging maybe? I don't know.

"I'm okay, Mom," I say as she shakes her head. Tears collect in her eyes. She hasn't seen me since I've changed into a pixie. And now she sees me like this—weak, injured, tired. Her lip curls up a bit and she steps away from me almost like I'm poisonous.

"My feet are kind of cold, though," I say. I'd really like some shoes, actually.

Her eyes narrow and she whirls on Astley and the fiddler pixie guy, who really looks pretty casual for someone tied up on a porch. For a second she just stares at them. I sway backward once she lets go of me, and faster than humanly possible Astley moves to my side to catch the back of my head with his hand before it hits the cedar shingles of the house. My mother loses it.

"Don't you touch her!" she says again. Her hands move into fists.

"It's a little late to play the protective mother now," he lashes back.

"What?" She spits the word at him.

"From what I have heard, you sent her up here into the heart of danger because you were too frightened to protect her yourself." Anger boils up in him like I have never seen it before. I don't know where that anger is coming from, but it rushes through the air, awkward and hard and surprising. I can feel it.

"Astley." I say his name to try to get him to stop, but my voice comes out so weak that even I am not impressed.

He obviously isn't either, because he just keeps going. "From what I have heard, you only come when it is convenient for you, too busy with your corporate job and life to take care of your own blood, instead entrusting her safety to elderly weres who—"

"Astley!" I yell his name this time. Why is he doing this? I think that maybe he's not just mad at my mother but at all mothers. He stops, swallows, but does not apologize.

Crows alight from an oak tree near the corner of the porch. They caw as they flap away.

My mom steps forward. "How dare you!"

He opens his mouth again but is cut off by Betty, who is suddenly on the porch with us. She glares at Astley, probably because she's not too cool with being called elderly by a pixie king, and roars out, "I think you should go."

I sway, my body overwhelmed by everything. Astley lifts me into his arms. I'm too tired to protest much, but I manage to say, "I'm fine."

"Let me bring her inside," he says.

"You're not stepping one foot into this house," Betty says. "This is my house. You are not coming in. Give her to me."

He hesitates. I nod slightly and he flinches, but leans me into Betty's arms. I've got to say one thing for my grandmother: she is strong. My mother reaches out and moves the hair out of my face.

Astley stands in front of the door for a moment. His voice is soft and calm. "We are all on the same side here."

"You turned my daughter into a monster," my mother says. Her glare would kill lesser guys. "We are not on the same side."

Something inside me breaks open and it hurts way more than my gunshot wound.

"She asked me to," he replies, not backing down. The wind blows his hair back from his forehead. "We are not monsters."

My mother doesn't back down either. "You took advantage of her."

He inhales deeply and steps away so that Betty can bring me across the threshold of the house.

"Maybe," he says slowly, as if each word is an effort, "*she* took advantage of *me*."

State police have confirmed that the latest missing Bedford boy is indeed Thomas Steffan and report the grisly recovery of the body of another missing youngster. The police are not releasing details. —NEWS CHANNEL 8

.

My mother is the only one in our family who cries when she's frustrated or mad, and there is something both annoying and endearing about this. Once we're inside the house, she slams the door, shutting out both BiForst and Astley. Tears well up in her eyes and she pushes her back against the wall. She closes her eyes as she whispers, "I hate pixies. I just *hate* them."

I don't say anything, but my wounds suddenly seem a lot deeper as Betty places me on the sofa. Issie and Devyn move so that there's room for me. My mother crumples in the corner of the room.

"Zara really should be up in her bedroom," Cassidy says. "All the healing things are there."

"Cassidy has been working on you," Issie says, fingering the whistle hanging from her neck. She looks proud of Cassidy and happy that conflict time is over. "That's why she's so pale and dead looking and why you're healing so fast, even for a pixie."

"Thanks, Is." Cassidy smiles. Dark circles frame her eyes. She does look dead.

"I didn't mean it in a bad way!" Issie blusters. "You're a total hero."

They are all sitting and standing throughout the living room. Mugs and glasses litter the coffee table and the end table. Issie and Cassidy aren't wearing any shoes. They have the look of being camped out here for a while, and Cassidy isn't the only one who looks tired. Both Mrs. Nix and my mom seem to need a good nap. I tell them it's rude to leave Astley outside, but they all ignore me and chatter on about things. I can't quite follow it all, because my head is foggy and I'm too busy wondering if they all think I'm a monster, if I'd be better off out on the porch with the others.

I clear my throat to get everyone's attention. "The BiForst guy told you that there is only a certain amount of time to get Nick, right?"

They explain that he said they had to hurry or there would be no point. They don't actually know how to get to Valhalla.

"But it's not as if we can trust him," Betty announces.

Mrs. Nix comes to the couch and squats in front of me. Her two hands touch the sides of my face. "He did tell us where Astley's mother is, so that's a good thing. Don't worry, Zara. We will figure this out."

Her eyes are brown and big and soft. She is a bear. She can fight, but she is so peaceful. She isn't meant to be a warrior. None of us are meant to be warriors. Something inside of me hitches and threatens to break. I wipe at my eyes.

"Zara . . ." Both my mom and Issie say my name, but it is Issie, not my mother, who pats my back. My mother has moved far away from me, all the way across the room, and this entire time she hasn't looked at me, not once, even though I've been shot and we haven't seen each other in forever. She hates me now. I can feel her anger and sorrow just like I felt Astley's. Cringing, I watch as she moves even farther away, pushing a chair to the edge of the wall, folding her arms across her chest when normally she'd still be hugging me so hard I couldn't breathe.

I look at all their faces. My voice cracks before I even start to talk. "I changed so I could—we could . . . save him. I changed. I am not human, but I'm not—I'm not . . . bad."

If I were bad, I'd want to attack.

If I were bad, I'd want to kill.

"I'm bringing you upstairs." Betty announces this and swoops me into her arms. I don't resist. "You are overwrought."

She puts me on my bed and pulls the covers up to my chin. She smoothes the hair away from my face and smiles softly at me. Her eyes crinkle in the corners. She starts obsessively tucking the blankets around me again.

"She doesn't love me anymore," I whisper.

Betty stills. She knows who I am talking about.

The candles flicker, cast shadows against the walls.

"Of course she—," Betty starts.

"Don't lie to me," I interrupt. "You aren't supposed to lie. That's not you."

She swallows hard, looks away, but then must think better of it and meets my eyes.

"I am so sorry that you're hurt," she says.

And we both know that she's not talking about the gunshot wound.

I wake up to a knocking noise. Groaning, I shift my weight on the bed and try to figure out what happened. I must have fallen asleep. Cassidy's obviously been back in my room, because there are new candles.

The knocking sounds again. It's coming from my window. I stretch and swing my legs to the side of my bed. My muscles creak and moan. Pain ripples through my chest, but it isn't as horrible as it was before. I stagger toward the window and peek around the shade, pulling it out just enough.

"Let me in, Zara."

It's Astley. He's hovering there, which is super creepy.

"I can't."

"You still do not trust me?" His face is a broken branch.

"Of course I trust you, but I— Betty wouldn't like it," I say honestly as I struggle to open the window.

He smiles a little sheepishly and lifts it for me, saying, "She would not like it that you are even talking to me, would she?"

That's true. My mother would like it even less. Still, I let him perch on the windowsill. His feet dangle into the open air. The cold rushes in and we talk in whispers. He tells me everyone is still downstairs trying to figure out exactly how to convince BiForst to tell them how to get to Valhalla, but he thinks it's pointless.

"There is no need to interrogate him. My mother knows. Now that we know where she is, I shall go talk to her. I can go alone," he says.

But that's not going to happen. I pick at the edge of my comforter. It's frayed a little bit, but the yellow looks so happy and hopeful.

"I'm coming with you," I say.

He knows me well enough to know he can't talk me out of it, but I also think he doesn't want to talk me out of it. Something

calm passes between us. For a second I contemplate telling everyone downstairs about what's going on, especially after Iceland, but
this is Astley's mother and New York is where he grew up. It will be
totally safe. And anyway, I know without a doubt that nobody
would let me go.

All he says is, "You will tell me if your injuries become too
much."

I agree and then make him turn around while I change into
regular clothes and shoes. When I'm done, he motions for me
to join him on the windowsill. He wraps his arms around me.

"My car is parked out on the road," he explains. "I am going
to jump off the window and fly you to it. Trust me?"

"I do." I lean my head against his shoulder because it is too
hard to hold it up anymore. He breathes in and jumps, bringing
both of us into the dark, snow-filled night.

We travel in silence for a while. Astley gives me another iron pill
even though his car is so high end and pricey special that it
doesn't have much iron in it. He's cleaned out the blood—or had
someone clean it for him, would be a better way to phrase it, actually. We travel down the dark Maine highway, adding mile after
mile of solitude and dark night. We get to Augusta and the traffic
picks up a tiny bit. We see an occasional Hannaford grocery truck
or an oil truck. It isn't until we get to Portland that there is any
real traffic. We drive farther and farther away from Betty and Issie
and my mom and home. Each mile makes me a little more worried about the choice I made to just leave them.

"They treat me like a child," I say into the darkness.

Astley doesn't answer.

"They try to take all my decisions away from me," I add.

"Are you cold?" he asks after a ridiculously awkward silence. "I can turn up the heat. How are you feeling?"

"I'm fine." I wait another mile. It passes quickly. "Do you know what I mean?"

"I do." He breathes into the air, shifts the car into a faster gear. "Are you certain about this, Zara? I would like for this to be your choice."

I am sure. Every mile brings me closer to Nick.

At an emergency community meeting, the Bedford police chief threw up his hands. "I don't know what to tell you all," he said. "Short of closing down the entire town, I don't know how to keep people safe. . . . I just don't know."
— *THE BEDFORD AMERICAN*

Normally, it takes eight and a half hours to drive straight from Bedford to New York City, but Astley does not drive like a normal person, and even though we leave at about seven thirty p.m., we get there just a little after midnight. I sleep for most of the trip, and before I know it we're heading into the city and I'm jonesing for a piece of gum to get rid of my stale sleep breath. The light of Manhattan is hazy and orange from the streetlamps and the signs on shops, which are mostly closed because of the time. Astley maneuvers the car through taxis and late-night delivery trucks like a pro. There are menorahs in some windows, wreaths on some doors. Even through the windshield wipers the city looks magical—like anything could happen here.

"It's so different from Maine," I murmur.

His hands loosen on the steering wheel. "I thought you were still asleep."

We park on a residential street, and Astley shuts off the

engine. All my muscles ache from being stuck in the car for so long, but we're here now, and how awesome is that?

"Did you magically conjure that parking space?" I tease as Astley pulls an umbrella out from where it had been hiding near his feet.

He looks at me full on. His face is nervous but kind, shadowed from the night and weary from the driving. "Sometimes if you wish hard enough, things truly do happen for you."

"Is that Disney magic or pixie magic?" I kid as I prepare to get out. My wound stretches and I wince.

His hand touches my shoulder. "It is life magic."

He helps me out of the car, opening my door and half lifting me out. We stand there for a second, close but not touching, and then we start walking. Light shafts around a row of town houses that line the street, illuminating the hazy orange-gray sky above. A cold rain plummets down onto the umbrella that Astley holds above both of our heads, but it still slants under and wets the bottom of my jeans and his dark cords. "Rain" is maybe the wrong word for this kind of precipitation. It is more like icy pellet balls. They ping onto us. Some bounce off the cement sidewalks before creating a slippery glaze. I skid on it a little bit. Astley grabs me before I slip. His fingers press into my side as if it is the most natural thing in the universe for him to touch me.

"I do apologize about the weather," he says, keeping his arm firmly around my waist.

I snap my head up and stare at him, openmouthed. "Astley, why are you apologizing? Can you control the weather too?"

"No," he says forlornly. "I wish we could."

"That would almost make the pixie thing worth it." I sigh before I can stop myself. My breath is irregular and sends rippling pain through my chest. The bandage pricks at my skin like some constant reminder of how horribly wrong things can go.

"I thought getting your wolf back would make it worth it," Astley half asks and half says. It's a probing question.

"It does make it worth it. I mean, it *will* if we can get him back, you know?" I hate the way my voice sounds so doubtful.

"We will." He shifts his weight a bit and his fingers seem to lose some of their chill. "If I *could* control the weather," he adds, "then I would make it warm for you. You miss the warmth, do you not?"

"I do." I pull my coat around me a little tighter. "But at least it's not blizzarding. That's the bright side, right? I am consciously attempting to look on the bright side."

His hand drifts up and pets the back of my hair. It's almost like something a dad would do. His tone is affectionate. "I would say you are always looking on the bright side. If you were not, you would have given up a long time ago."

I shrug. The motion pulls at the stitches. "Maybe."

"It hurts, doesn't it?"

I almost smile. He just said "doesn't" instead of "does not." Maybe I'm rubbing off on him. I say, "A little."

"I despise that you are injured." His sentence comes out like a snarl.

"'Despise'?" Now I do manage to smile a little bit. "Most people would say 'hate.'"

"I am not 'most,' and I am not 'people.'" He hardens up. I can feel his muscles fill with tension, and that tension is reflected in his voice.

We stand there for a second in front of a particularly imposing town house made of white granite. It's five stories high, and the second and third stories bulge out in a sort of half circle. It is embellished with fancy sculpted engravings of ivy and hearts. Three giant windows dominate each level, except for the ground floor, where there are just two barred windows on either side of a dark wooden door. The door looks so heavy I think how Issie (or me in my pre-pixie mode) would never be able to pull it open by herself. The four stairs leading up to the door have black wrought-iron-style railings, only they aren't iron. They are made of wood that has been painted and carved into intricate patterns. It does not fit in with the rest of the brownstones at all. I wonder if Astley feels like that sometimes as a pixie king, like he doesn't fit in.

"Do you ever wish you were human?" I ask.

He doesn't answer, just stares up at the building.

We are at his mother's home. Underneath the regular smell of city sewer and car exhaust is the smell of Dove soap. Even without that smell, which tickles at my nose like an allergy, I can feel that we're here. Still Astley doesn't make a move up the stairs. He is hesitating. It is so obvious, and that hesitation makes me nervous, because he normally seems pretty darn confident, pretty darn unafraid. He is not the type of pixie who hesitates. Actually, none of them are. They are all like Nick, full of action and decision and confidence.

Not now.

"Is she so bad?" I ask as gently as I can, thinking a lot about his reaction to my mom.

He nods and in that nod is all the pain of fractured histories and despair. I know how it feels to nod like that, but I never imagined that *he* would be like this. There are so many layers inside of people, so much soul pain and angsty depth and heart hurt, and some, like Astley, hide all this so well that when it comes out in an action as simple as a nod, your entire world shifts a little bit on its axis.

No words leave Astley's mouth. A taxi driver lays on his horn. The cab is about a block away and the angry sound ripples through the streets. The cold suddenly sinks into my bones and roots around in there.

"She is not a good mother. She is—" Astley breaks off midsentence and instead stares up at the solid wall of granite and window, the intricate details etched against it. Somehow, despite the elaborateness and even despite the way the second and third floors bulge out, the building seems flat. He draws in a large breath. Cars splash by on the street behind us, making their way through the night. Thunder rumbles above us.

"Are you okay?" I ask. I straighten up so that my ribs hurt a little bit less.

He shakes himself almost the way a cat does when she feels contaminated. He gives me a half smile—literally. Only the left side of his lips rises up.

"I exaggerate. All men have problems with their mothers. I am no different." He steps toward the stairs. "I apologize again. It is unfair of me to burden you with my own familial issues."

I move with him, thinking that what he said about all men having problems with their moms is totally not true, but whatever . . . now is not the time to debate. Although I do have to say, "You aren't burdening me. Friends tell each other things."

"Oh, are we friends now?" An eyebrow arches up, a classic bad-boy move, and I'm thinking it's a cover, a mask of braveness, he's putting on for both of us.

I don't answer. I don't know how to answer. I tug on Astley's arm as if I need to get his attention, even though he is always giving me all his attention. "Was that why you were so mean to my mother when she showed up? Was it because you were mad at yours? Was she not there for you when you needed her?"

He turns slowly, very slowly. "I forgot how human you are still, how very young."

"That's not answering the question, Astley."

"I was wrong to do that. I know that you consider it not to be my place, but in my world"—he makes a sweeping motion with his hands to indicate all around us—"in this pixie world, it is very much my place to protect my queen. It is instinctive. I know when you are hurt even in the subtlest of ways, even when you yourself may not realize it, when you may be repressing it."

"My mother is a good mother," I insist.

"I believe you, but to me . . . sending you back to Maine and not accompanying you—"

"Her job keeps her from being there all the time. She still has ten months on her contract."

He eyes me and doesn't answer. I can tell just from how he's looking at me that he thinks it is a pretty bad excuse, but it isn't. There are huge financial penalties if hospital CEOs just up and leave their jobs. It is unfortunate but true. Now that I'm pixie and my father is dead, I don't know if she'll want to come to Maine to stay at all. She might want me to move back to Charleston.

I decide to change the subject. "We've been standing here forever. Are you sure it's okay for us to be here? It's late. Should we wait until morning?"

"Do not worry. I called and she agreed to meet us. She is quite capable of being nice. It will be fine," he says. Even though he says this in Mr. Reassuring voice, it's pretty flat and fake. I mean, seriously? "Quite capable of being nice" is not very reassuring.

I give him my own fake cheery smile. "I know. Don't worry. It will be just fine."

And it's right then that I decide I will make it fine for him. It's the least I can do for someone who has done so much for me, for someone who is helping me get to Nick.

We stand there another moment. I am so antsy and impatient that I just give up waiting and offer, "Do you want me to ring the bell?"

He half gasps, as if realizing he hasn't even rung it, and then he shakes his head, smiling softly. For a moment he looks truly human, regular, like any other guy around seventeen or eighteen years old.

"I shall do it," he says quietly. "I think I am capable of at least that."

He reaches out but hesitates. His face is one big plea for help, and so I just do it, pressing the gold bell button embedded in the exterior wall. A short older man opens the door. He wears a suit coat and a pressed white shirt, and he carries himself with this absolute rigid confidence. He reminds me of someone from an old black-and-white movie about aristocracy, the kind that Betty watches every Saturday night when she's not on shift. Behind the man is an expensively furnished foyer with off-white walls and elaborate gold-frame mirrors that look like they weigh a ton, a dark green velvet sitting couch, and a staircase that winds up to the next floor. Doors lead to other rooms on both sides. The man watches us both. No expression crosses his face. I can't even feel any emotion coming from him at all, which is a first since I've turned pixie.

"Master Astley, we've been expecting you." His accent is British and formal. "This way."

I raise an eyebrow and hope it makes me look all bad girl.

"My mother's butler, Bentley," Astley whispers.

I lower my eyebrow. The house is warm and somewhat stuffy. Dove soap smells fill the air along with roses and lilacs. There's the distant sound of someone walking on the floor above us. Water drips from Astley's umbrella and softly plops on a plush white area carpet, which is partially covering the deep-colored wood floor.

The butler's right ear twitches and he says suddenly, "Oh, sir. I am terribly sorry. Let me take your umbrella."

Before Astley can respond, the Bentley man grabs the umbrella and looks at it as if it is a rat carrying the plague. He thrusts it out and away from him and deposits it in an umbrella stand near the front door. Once he's done with the offending umbrella, he gestures toward a doorway. "After you."

I follow Astley and it is instantly pretty obvious that this is the kind of home where nothing is allowed to be out of place. There will be no dirty spaghetti pots or colanders left in the sink. There will be no crumpled-up tissues hiding beneath the sofa. I wonder if they even have a television or a computer. Somehow it doesn't seem they would.

"Did you live here when you were growing up?" I ask Astley.

"Here and other similar places," he answers.

"It's lovely," I say, trying to be polite as I imagine other similar town houses in other cities. Maybe a condo in a ski resort, a home in the hills, an estate in England. There are so many things I don't know about Astley or about how pixies work and live. I mean, are all pixies wealthy? Or is it just the kings? Do I automatically get some sort of queenly allowance now? Not that it matters.

Astley leads us into a big parlor with one large window. The walls are the same off-white and the fireplace mantel has been painted to match. Afghan rugs rich with color cover the hard-wood floor. Couches and chairs face each other. I stand there as primly as possible with my injury. I feel bad for getting the floor wet and hope that Astley's mother won't hold it against me and not help us find Nick.

"Your mother will be down shortly. Shall I get you anything to take off the chill? Tea? Brandy?" Bentley offers, still standing up as Astley and I settle into a plush velvet couch. My feet can't quite touch the ground when I sit all the way back, so I scoot up and perch on the edge. I won't get the couch as wet that way any-way, right?

"No, thank you," Astley answers for both of us. He's probably noticed my horrified face over the whole brandy offer. I wonder if pixies can get drunk. I should ask that sometime, maybe when things mellow out . . . *if* things ever mellow out.

"As you wish," Bentley says, and does this quiet, gentlemanly bow, bending stiffly from his waist.

I try to imagine Astley growing up here. I bet he had a nanny and a tutor. I bet he wasn't allowed to slide down that big mahog-any banister or spill his milk (or should I say brandy?) or leave his wet towels in a pile on the bedroom floor.

"Was it hard?" I ask him as Bentley leaves the room.

"Was what hard?" His eyes are distracted.

"Growing up here? Wait. Do you live here now?" I ask. "You know . . . when you aren't trying to stop a rogue pixie king in Bed-ford, Maine."

He shudders. "No, I have my own home."

Wow. His own home? That's crazy. Then I remember that I'm actually his queen, which is even weirder. He doesn't answer my original question, which probably means that it *was* terribly difficult to grow up here. Sympathy fills me. We sit there in a companionable sort of silence.

"Are you nervous?" he asks.

I nod.

"She promised to help," he says, taking my hand. "We shall find your wolf, Zara."

Once again, I wonder why he cares so much, but I don't have time to ask, because there is motion on the stairs and the distinct smell of roses. I look up just as a small blond woman flutters into the room. I check for feet because it seems as if she is gliding instead of walking. Feet are definitely there. They are ensconced in glittery silver designer heels.

As she enters, Astley instantly lets go of my hand and leaps up from the couch. He walks toward her and I hang back as he opens his arms. "Mother."

She floats over to him, reminding me of Glinda the Good Witch in *The Wiz* and *Wicked* and *The Wizard of Oz*, and lifts her arms open in a super-melodramatic way.

"Astley." She almost jingles when she says his name. "How good to see you again, my dear, dear son."

The air bristles as they hug. She lets go first and looks around him toward me. Her gold hair ripples in waves. As she smiles her face transforms from something regular into something almost shockingly beautiful. Her nose is a bit long but straight. Her mouth takes up most of the bottom half of her face. She appraises me quickly, bluish silver eyes roaming up and down my body before fixing on my face.

She opens her arms again. "You must be Zara. Our newest queen."

She glides over to me in those shiny heels and her arms

quickly wrap around me in a hug. She's thin and soft. I hug her back. I let go first.

"It's nice to meet you," I say. I don't know what to call her.

It's like she has read my thoughts. "Isla. Call me Isla, sweet girl."

"Isla," I repeat, looking up at Astley. His eyes narrow, watching us. Tension oozes off him and I don't quite understand why. His mother seems so very nice, actually. She's pretty. Her voice is a little high, but that's okay, right? I mean, it's silly to feel put off by someone's voice. It's silly to be put off by something as small and inconsequential as a voice or a smell, and, seriously, who am I to be put off by someone at all? She is so beautiful and lovely and short, and I am sure that she would never, ever do anything even remotely wrong—ever—and she's going to help me find my perfect, amazing Nick, which is a perfect and amazing thing for her to do and I love her for it, and I love how beautiful her eyes are, and they are coming closer to me—those eyes—and they are switching back and forth from blue to silver to blue to silver to blue to—

"Mother!" Astley's voice cuts through the air.

Her voice is sweet, sweet innocence. "What, dear?"

"Let her free," he orders.

She giggles. It is the light, sweet tinkling of bells. It is music to my sad, sad ears. It is a promise of beauty and butterflies and warm Charleston days and—

"Mother! I mean it. As your king I command you!"

She pouts. "Very well then."

The world suddenly shifts and my vision is clearer somehow. I must be staring or something, because her cold hand reaches up and gently pushes on the bottom of my chin.

"Dear girl," she simpers. "Your mouth is hanging open."

Right then, even though I know that she is our best hope for finding Nick, and even though I know she is a pixie queen and Astley's mom, right when she touches my face I want to haul off and smack her. That's not very pacifist of me. I used to be a pacifist. I used to be human. I used to be a lot of things.

I clamp my mouth shut and glare at Astley, who looks aghast.

"Did you do some sort of glamour on me, ma'am?" I ask. My voice drips with Southern charm. I make it that way on purpose. I am accusing her of something, which is totally un-nice, but I will be polite about it.

She bats her eyelashes. "Who, me?"

It starts again. Stars seem to zigzag into my eyes through to my brain. She is suddenly so beautiful and so kind. I want to touch her cheek. I want to . . . I shake my head.

"Mother!" Astley warns and comes to stand in front of me, blocking me from her.

She giggles. Old women should not giggle. "She fought it this time."

"You gave her no warning. It was abominable of you," he counters.

I try to gather my wits. My head still seems foggy. I focus and scoot around Astley so I can face his mother. "What did you do to me?"

"It is called a mystique, not a glamour, little princess," she says. She coos it, really, and then turns to Astley. "Have you taught her anything?"

"He taught me the glamour," I say, bristling. Seriously, I know she's his mother and everything, but that doesn't give her the right to be such a bitch.

"She defends you!" Isla throws up her hands in triumph, making little fists. "How adorable."

"Adorable?" I repeat. Does she mean "adorable" like a kitten or a baby? Does she mean "adorable" as in harmless?

Astley smiles. He actually smiles and says, "Now you have done it, Mother. You have incurred the wrath of Zara."

Isla's petite shoulders move slightly up and down in a tiny shrug. "Oh, she will forgive me. She knows that I only want to ensure that she can deal with the trials that await her if she is to venture on the journey to the gods."

A clock rings in the background. Another sounds a moment after. The entire building seems to vibrate with the sounds as more and more clocks chime. I scan the walls. There are three hanging in this room alone, plus a grandfather clock that stands in the corner. Isla closes her eyes and seems to sway with the noise. It's like dancing, but more primal. Astley meets my gaze and rolls his eyes as if his mother is way too embarrassing for words. He also shifts a little bit closer to me.

The chimes stop. Isla opens her eyes, which have gone black. She blinks hard. They are silvery blue again. The change is so quick that I almost think I imagined it.

"Do you like clocks, Zara?" she asks.

"Yes, ma'am. I do," I answer as she motions for us to sit again. The last thing I want to do is rest on a couch. I feel like pacing, running, screaming, and begging her to tell me where Nick is.

Once again I perch on the end of the velvety couch, trying not to look uncomfortable or show my pain, which isn't the easiest of tasks at the moment. I flinch as my wound stretches. Astley sits in the middle, crossing his legs at his ankles. He gives me a look of concern, but I don't respond, because there are more important things than my personal health right now.

"So, ma'am, I'd really like to know how we can get to Valhalla," I begin.

She raises a hand to stop me. "Are you sure you *truly* want to retrieve your wolf, Zara? It will complicate your relationship with my son, and wolves are so"—she sniffs her nose disdainfully—"furry."

I want to scream out, "What relationship?" but I know that would hurt Astley's feelings. And wolves are messy? What a bigot. Instead of going ballistic on her, I will my fingers to unclench out of super-tight fists and take a deep breath. My lungs burn, angry and still hurt, before I manage to say, "I am sure."

She harrumphs. Her hands smooth down her hair. They are constantly moving. Once she is done with her hair, she fidgets with her hands in her lap. She seems like she'd rather be pacing or running, doing something frantic.

"Mother . . ." Astley uncrosses his legs. He seems to have inherited her impatience. I wonder what else he has inherited from her.

"Please desist from that incessant 'mothering.' *Mother this . . . Mother that . . .*" She flops down in a Queen Anne chair. "Must you always remind me that I am your mother?"

The change in Astley is almost imperceptible, but I can still feel it, because I am his queen, I guess. There's a ripple of sorrow and hurt running through him. I reach out and take his hand in mine. It is strong, but there's a tremble in it. Anger arches through me. If I didn't need her help so badly, I'd yank Astley right out of here. But I do need her help.

"Please tell me how to get to Valhalla," I begin again.

"First let me hear about you." She arranges her tulle skirt

prettily around her legs, smoothing it down. "It isn't every day Astley comes home with a new queen. Did he tell you what happened to the first one?"

Astley stands up. "Enough."

It's like all the clocks on the wall have suddenly stopped, or maybe my heart has just stopped beating. I'm not sure.

"First one?" I manage to whisper.

Astley turns to stare at me. His face is horror stricken. He opens his mouth, but no words come out. His eyes look away, to the side, like facing me is too much.

"He killed that one," she says matter-of-factly.

Something gray and simple settles into my lungs and kidneys, squeezing them into peas. I think it's dread. I think that's what it is, this feeling. Her words echo in my head as I stare up at Astley. He killed that one—not just that she died. He *killed* her?

Astley makes a choking noise. His hands reach up into the air like he wants to hit someone, something. All his emotions seem to swirl in the air around us, volatile, visible like the gold dust trail he leaves. He's about to snap and I'm not exactly sure why, but I know I'm about to snap too.

"You've been lying to me?" I ask in a voice so quiet I can't believe he hears it, but I can tell by how he's flinching that he does hear it. "What else haven't you told me, Astley?"

I'm not sure if I'm trembling from rage or sorrow or what, but I'm trembling.

His mouth opens. No words come out.

"Were you going to ever tell me?" I ask.

He stumbles backward. He looks so wounded. "It is not . . . It is not . . . I didn't . . . I did . . . But I . . . Oh, Zara . . . I cannot stand you looking at me like that."

His eyes clench shut and he whirls around, staggering out of the room.

"Astley!" I yell after him, leaping off the couch. A small and terribly strong hand grabs at my wrist.

"Do not go," Isla says. "Let him be."

"You're a monster and a liar," I say. "I don't know what Astley did, but he would never kill anyone."

She raises an eyebrow and keeps hold of my wrist. "You are truly innocent, Miss Zara White. You even smell innocent. No . . ." Her words trail off as she thinks. "You smell of innocence and *power*, unused power."

"And you smell of roses and mean." I rip my wrist away from her, desperate to find Astley and even more desperate to learn about Nick.

"'Roses and mean.'" She laughs and falls backward into her chair, clutching her stomach. "You talk like the innocent child that you are, Zara White. 'Roses and mean.'"

She reminds me of a nasty girl I used to play with back in first grade. Her name was Stephanie and she'd repeat everything you said like it was the most ridiculous thing she'd ever heard. I knew the names of all the phobias before I knew the alphabet. They fascinated me, and sometimes I'd chant them under my breath at recess. Stephanie tormented me about that, called me Freaky Freak Zara, until I kidnapped her American Girl doll and threatened to throw it into a manhole.

Astley's mother reminds me of that girl. She reminds me of all the bullies and evil people who hurt others around the world. I have had it with those bullies, so I do the best thing I can think of, which is leap toward the wall and rip a clock off the side table. She shrieks.

"Don't hurt it!"

I stare at the device in my hands. Somehow I know that it's worth more to her than her own son, and that just rips through me even if Astley is some sort of weird, murdering liar face. Aren't parents supposed to love their children unconditionally? The clock is French cast with gilt angels on top of a white marble base. It stands about a foot wide and sixteen inches tall. Gilded bronze angels dance on the jug handles.

"That is by Nicolas M. Thorpe," she pants out. Her hand is on her heart and she's flopped back in her chair like some ancient Victorian woman in a Brontë novel.

"It could be by Michel-freaking-angelo," I growl at her. "I could care less. It is a thing. It is a possession, and I am going to destroy it if you keep playing games with me."

She sits up straight, all little-girl pretenses gone. She is predator and queen. "I could tear you apart."

"I doubt it, and even if you could, I'll destroy this first." I raise it above my head, which feels a little bit melodramatic, but the pixies really seem to be into drama. Anyway, the position shows her that I'll smash it to the ground in a second. It works too, because she cringes. I pause and then say calmly, like threatening pixie queens is an everyday thing for me, "Now tell me how to get to Valhalla."

"Then you will hand me my clock?" She simpers and slinks forward another step.

I think about it. "Maybe."

She purses her lips. Her fingers drum against the arms of the chair. The fingernails click against the old wood, once, twice, again. I bet she'd like to use those fingernails on me.

"To get to Valhalla you must find the BiForst Bridge."

"Everyone knows that," I say.

"Yes, but BiForst is not a thing. He is a being, part pixie. He is the bridge to the land. His body acts as a portal, for lack of a better word. There is a ceremony you must perform." She slowly heads to a table.

"You better not be getting a weapon," I say as I try to compute her knowledge. We already *have* BiForst. We already *have* the bridge. Hope starts swooshing up toward my heart.

She moves very slowly, like criminals on cop shows trying to prove they aren't about to pull a weapon. "I am getting a book. It is an ancient book. It has details of the ceremony that must be performed. It is chapter twelve, actually."

She pulls open a drawer and takes out a small red leather-bound book. She holds it toward me.

"Not yet," I say. "Tell me how Astley killed her, killed his—"
I can't say the word.

"His wife? His queen?" she finishes for me. "I do not think you are prepared to know that yet, new one. And why does it concern you? I thought you care only for your wolf."

"I do . . . ," I sputter. "I really do, but Astley is my friend and I thought that—"

"What?" She takes a step closer. She slinks like a cat. "What, new queen? You thought that he was honest with you? That you knew him? Let me give you some advice: trust no one."

I don't say anything and she snorts out a short barklike guffaw. It is very unladylike and very unlike all the cooing, simpering noises she's made so far tonight.

She slips another step closer. I wonder if she thinks I don't notice her moving. She must be underestimating me. People are always underestimating me. It helps me out usually. Although right now I'm not exactly at my strongest. My wound sears like fire, pain spreading through me. It's from holding up the clock, I think. It must be aggravating it somehow. I can feel tiny dots of sweat on my forehead. Great.

"You cannot hold that clock above your head forever." A little smirk plays about her face.

"Of course I can." I am such a total liar. "Now tell me about Astley's queen, the one before me."

She slinks ahead again, just a little closer to me. "Are you aware of the fact that just a moment ago you referred to my son as your friend? Zara, darling, pixies cannot be friends. We are not trustworthy. We do not look out for others' best interests. It is all about us. That is why Astley killed his last queen, and that is why you will likely suffer the same fate. You should not be so wary of me, Zara. I am no more your enemy than he is."

She nods and someone behind me grabs the clock out of my arms. I whirl around to see Bentley. His ghoulish face smiles as he hands the clock to Isla, who has pushed past me. She clutches the gaudy thing to her chest and coos to it. "Oh, my poor, poor baby. Were you scared? I would never let anything hurt you. Oh, no, of course I would not."

"Madame," Bentley interrupts. "What should I do with her?"

She flicks her wrist. "Her? Nothing. Let her go. She is no threat. She has what she wants."

He takes me by the arm. I twist away and grab the red leather book. As he lurches after me I brush him off, heading out into the main hallway area myself. "I'm going, I'm going."

He follows me out and hands me the umbrella. "King Astley left this."

"Thank you." I take the umbrella from him. "Are you a pixie too? You don't smell like one."

"Thank you, miss." He seems to stand up straighter. "I am actually a ghoul. Thank you for noticing."

"Ghoul, huh . . ." I try to size him up. "Are all pixies—are they all so moody?"

"The royals tend to be. Those who have turned either go insane quickly or remain steady emotionally. I don't think your fate will be such as hers. She was born this way. Bad blood." He opens the door for me. "Please give the king my regards. Good luck to you, mistress."

Go insane quickly? Great. I step outside into the cold rain. "Good luck to you too."

Behind him Isla calls out, "Bentley! I need cocoa."

"Thank you." He rolls his eyes. "As you can tell, for the past hundred years I have needed all the luck I can muster."

Before he can go, I call out to him myself, doing the same thing that Isla did, only in a nicer way, I hope. "Bentley, do you know where Astley might have gone?"

He cocks his head slightly, appraising me, I think. He hesitates for the briefest of seconds, and then he must decide I am worthy or trustworthy or something, because he licks his lips just the slightest of bits and says, "When he was young and we were here and they would . . . argue . . . and his father did not intervene, he often ran. I would be sent to find him. Often he would be at the park."

"The park?"

"Central Park."

"Central Park is huge. Where in the park did he go?"

"*Bentley!*" Isla screeches from the other room.

Bentley jerks as if pulled by an invisible chain. He spirals away from me toward the sitting room where we left Isla.

"Please, Bentley, tell me where . . . ," I beg.

He pauses, and it's almost as if there's another chain yanking him toward me. His face clenches up. It's like he is being torn between Isla's wishes and mine.

"Are you okay?" I ask. I cross into the town house again and reach up to him. My fingers graze the fabric sleeve of his suit jacket just as he jerks backward again, backward and away from me.

"Go to Great Hill. There is a meadow, looking toward the Ravine. It will be glamoured, but it is there . . ." He stumbles back.

I want to stop him, to hold him with me and away from her, but he looks as if having us both need him simultaneously could tear him apart.

He whirls away and topples through the doorway to the room where Isla waits.

"Well, that took you far too long. Where is my cocoa?" she demands.

It isn't until I am outside in the rain that I realize:

1. Bentley and Isla must be at least a hundred years old.
2. I have no idea what a ghoul is.
3. I have no idea why Astley flipped out like that and left me alone with his mother.
4. I actually have an idea, a clue—a real lead—on how to get to Nick.

I yank out my phone and send a text message to Betty, Devyn, Issie, and Cassidy: `Have lead. Met ghoul. Astley missing.`

I touch the book. *This* was totally worth the drama. I resist the urge to kiss it, because basically who knows where it's been. I sniff at it while a couple staggers by, arms wrapped around each other's waists, voices high and loud and slurring with booze. The woman keeps singing Adam Sandler's "Chanukah Song" and laughing hysterically. Once they are past, I bring the book out again. It smells like musty basement and leather but also hope. This is how I will get Nick.

I tuck it carefully into the inside pocket of my jacket and smile up into the rain. I forget to put up the umbrella. I forget about wars and torture and pixies. For a moment I forget about everything except my Nick.

And this moment feels so incredibly good.

U.S. federal agents confirm that they have taken over the investigation into the missing Bedford juveniles.
—NEWS CHANNEL 8

I know that I should be thinking about Astley. I know that I should be worrying about how he allegedly killed some other queen, and how he just left me *alone* with his psycho mother, and how he seems to be in a pretty emotionally fragile state, to say the least. Okay, yeah, that's an understatement.

I know all this and yet as I step off the curb and lift up my arm to hail one of those cute yellow cabs that are all over this city, it isn't Astley that I am thinking about. It's Nick. I am really one step closer to finding him, thanks to Astley.

A cab pulls up. The driver doesn't even turn. "Where are you going, miss?"

His accent is so lovely. It isn't Southern like mine. It isn't old-school Maine, where all the *r*'s turn into *yah*'s. It's from an Arabic-speaking country maybe. Closing my eyes for a second, I let homesickness take over. I miss Charleston and how simple life was there. It was warm. I didn't know about pixies or weres. My

stepdad was alive. There was actual ethnic diversity there. However, there was no Nick, no big good-smelling man with the most
beautiful lips and hands in the entire universe.

"Miss?"

The taxi driver's voice nudges me back into real time.

"Central Park. As close to Great Hill as you can get me," I say.

My phone vibrates. I pull it out of my pocket as the cab driver
zips down the street, turning fast and hard around a corner. I
should probably put my seat belt on, but it's got something slimy
on it. I slide across the seat, check the other one, and click it on.
Then I read my text message.

Betty has responded: I can't believe you just left.
Get back here soon and no hero crap. Stay
safe.

Yep.

A heavy sigh escapes me before I can stop it. It's so loud that
even the taxicab driver notices it.

"You okay back there, miss?" he asks.

"Yep."

I start to check out the book. It's heavy for something so
small. The old-fashioned font lies heavy against thick paper that
feels more like parchment than book paper. All the ink is dark,
except for the first page, where it seems to be made out of gold.
The light in the cab is not the greatest. I open up my cell phone
so the light from the screen illuminates the book's title page a
little bit better.

The letters aren't just gold; they glitter like pixie dust. The
words read: *Pixies: The History and Magic Thereof.* It looks like cal-
ligraphy, only not so full of loops.

I flip to chapter twelve. My phone vibrates again. I ignore it.

Chapter 12
Valhalla

All the air inside me whooshes out as I stare at the word: *Valhalla*. There's all this ornate drawing around the border of the page: vines and ivy and trees. My hands shake, I'm so excited. I turn the page and start to read.

It has of late come upon our notice, not without vast hurt to us, that, in a quantity of parts of upper Britain, as well as in the provinces, cities, territories, and regions of Erin, Scot's Land, Iceland, Normandy, and the New Lands, many pictsies of both sexes, unmindful of their own origins and forsaking the courts to which they owe their allegiance, are unaware of the existence of Valhalla, and even if aware are unsure of the process by which, alive and breathing, they may venture to its lofty lands.

It's like reading Latin, only worse.
Sigh.
The phone vibrates again. My mother is calling.
I read on.

We therefore, aspiring, as is our obligation, to eliminate all hindrances in which in any way questors are mired in the exercise of their pursuit of the mythical land, and to avert the failure to even begin such a quest, do herein explicate the procedures by which a hero may enter Valhalla prior to his time.

She wasn't lying. This is really it. I squee, all happy, and punch the ceiling, which makes the taxi guy cranky. I apologize but don't really pay attention, because Astley's face forms itself before me, in my imagination, I guess. His eyes glisten, sad and angry at the same time. His lips move: "Zara."

"What?" I whisper back.

The taxi driver is basically shouting at me. "Miss! We are here. That will be eight fifty."

"Oh! Right!" I was imagining Astley, just imagining him, which basically means I'm losing it. I tuck the book into my coat pocket, where it's safe, and yank out my wallet. I give him eleven dollars. It's been so long since I've been in a city that I'm not sure how much I'm supposed to tip.

"Thanks."

I open up the door and step out onto the wet street. Just standing up hurts me and I hate being so weak—and vulnerable, I realize . . . I am also vulnerable. The taxi zips away and I am alone. There aren't even any cars here. There is just me. The cabbie has let me out on West Ninety-Sixth Street, I think, and I head north, crossing over into the park at West One Hundredth Street. Sniffing the air for threats, I head up the hill. There are signs, which is nice. My breath hitches like I'm really out of shape. The rain turns completely to wet snow as I walk. Giant flakes stick to my hair and jacket.

Scurrying noises lurk off to my right, in some bushes just before the crest of the hill. My skin crawls. Rats. The fear of rats is murophobia. The fear of night is noctiphobia. The fear of snow? Chinophobia. I am a pixie. I shouldn't be afraid of any of these things, but I've got to tell you, rats make me squirmy.

"I am a pixie," I mutter under my breath. "I am a pixie who is going to save her boyfriend and there is nothing to be scared of. *I* am the thing to be scared of."

I wish I could believe this more. Reaching inside my jacket, I touch the book. It makes me feel safer. It is hope.

It's like suddenly being in a nighttime fairy tale. There's this calm, tiny lake surrounded by lawns and trees. At one end are the shadows of a gentle little waterfall. At the other end is another waterfall that sloshes into a loch. I follow the path on the west side and then head up a staircase. There's a garden with winding trails. I basically get lost for a while before I finally stand on the top of Great Hill and I see . . . not much. It's pretty dark. A meadow rests against the earth and there's a dirt running track. It's about one-fifth of a mile and it loops around. It looks like a really nice track, actually, the kind that wouldn't make your knees scream and ache even after you've gone ten miles. There's a restroom with a CLOSED sign. I don't see Astley anywhere. What had Bentley said? Look toward the Ravine? There was a glamour? I don't even know where the Ravine is.

I try to focus, will myself to see the truth beyond the illusion, which is the trick in seeing a glamour. You look for a shadow that doesn't seem like it quite belongs. Sometimes it's not a shadow. Sometimes it is more of a gleam. I search the grass and get nothing. Then I look up at the trees, and that's where I see it, just the faintest kind of shimmer, like the tree is not perfectly in focus.

"Astley?" I call.

There's no answer. I focus hard to make the glamour fade away as I walk closer. The shimmer vanishes and in its place is a house supported in the branches of one of the largest trees. I gasp. The house is made of wood and has a giant window facing outward. Tiny white lights drape all around it and entwine into the branches of the trees. A staircase winds up the trunk of the tree and leads to a porch deck that seems to have roots for railings. It all looks incredibly magical, and I guess it really is, in a pixie way.

I start up the stairs. I have no idea if Astley is actually here, but even if he wasn't, I'd want to explore. Honestly, it might be cooler if he wasn't here, because I have no idea what I'm going to say to him about what just happened at his mother's house and how he abandoned me there, or about what she said. He had another queen and he never told me. Even if he didn't quote-unquote kill her, that's a pretty big lie by omission.

Nick did that too. He lied to me when he didn't tell me that his parents were dead. I never even had a chance to confront him about that. I learned after he was gone.

I pause for a moment, trying to will the pain in my chest to dwindle down, and also so I can think. Why do people and pixies and weres lie so much? Why can't we all just be honest with each other? It would be so easy to just not trust anyone ever, but you can't go through life with a pair of scissors in each hand, snip-snip-snipping away at everything people say or don't say, can you? You have to leave one hand free to catch the truth.

I contemplate my situation for a second. The stairs would normally be easy to climb, but thanks to ye olde gunshot wound they're proving a bit much for me. Still, I start up again, climbing to the level of the house, which is probably thirty feet or so above the meadow. When my feet hit the deck, the world goes a little wiggly and I almost think I'm going to pass out.

"Pixies don't pass out," I mutter. "We are total badasses. We do *not* pass out."

Looking through the giant window, I try to spot Astley inside the house. There are globes of light that seem to float at different levels in the air. They cast a soft and mellow glow, like candles. It is the opposite of how I feel inside. What am I doing?

I'm confronting another pixie killer, and this one happens to be my king. Brilliant. I am brilliant. Obviously I have a thing for drama now too.

There's a door in front of me. It's made of glass and twisted wood that's been sanded soft and smooth. The handle is wood too and has the face of a horse carved into it. My fingertips touch it before I think about it, caressing the horse's nose. It almost feels real. The door opens easily. It's not locked. I step inside and let the door shut behind me, trying to sense if Astley's here. He is. I can feel his sorrow like a paper cut against my heart.

I don't see him, though. I look across the living room I've stepped into. Unlike his mother's house, the furniture is all streamlined and modern. It seems expensive, but a different kind of expensive. It's almost a Japanese feel. I step into the room. My sneaker leaves a wet mark on the floor. There are other wet marks from where Astley must have stepped. I'd follow the glitter trail, but there's glitter all over the shiny wooden floor—it's more like someone shook a carton of it over the floor than there being any one traceable trail.

Bamboo-type mats rest on the floor. Water that has dripped off Astley's clothes darkens the white into gray. I follow the water trail around the squarish white sofa and armchair. He's in the corner, huddled into the fetal position, perched on the balls of his feet and facing away from me so that all I can see is his back.

"Astley?"

When I say his name, his back shivers, even though I know he's not surprised. His senses are amazing. He heard and smelled me way before I came inside, probably before I even climbed the stairs. Still, his back moves as if I've startled him. Nothing else moves, though.

I try again. "Astley?"

Still no answer. Against my better judgment, I reach forward and gently touch his shoulder. It is hard beneath the leather jacket.

He stands up and turns around so slowly. All my skin crawls. A million spiders seem to run up and down the surface of me. I yank my hand back, touch my face, but there's nothing on me. It's him that's making me feel this way. He turns fully around and he doesn't look human at all. The glamour is gone. He is in full pixie mode, all blue skin and teeth, eyes that glint. I shudder even though I know that this is how I look too—like a monster. But it's more than that. He feels like a monster, like some horrible, primal, lethal pixie king instead of the usual calm, slightly troubled Astley.

I back away. I can't help it.

"Stay," he commands.

I can't move. My feet stick to the floor, held by some invisible force that must be coming from him.

"You're scaring me, Astley," I say, but my voice doesn't sound scared. It sounds calm.

"Am I?"

Back in 2004, this forty-nine-year-old guy Ye Guozhu was sentenced to prison in China because he applied to demonstrate against forced evictions. The court said he was "picking quarrels and stirring up trouble." He was upset because people's homes and businesses were being destroyed so that fancy places could be built. His restaurant was one of those buildings. His home was another. The government didn't give the people any money. They just evicted them.

According to Amnesty, he was tortured. The police beat him before his trial, suspended him from the ceiling, hung him by his arms. According to Amnesty, the police used electroshock batons.

These are the sorts of things out-of-control pixies would do, but worse . . . even worse. How can I imagine worse? I don't have to imagine it. I saw it when I rescued Jay Dahlberg from my father's lair. But pixies can do good. Both Astley's dad and mine sacrificed themselves for us, and can there be a higher good than that?

Astley winds around me again in a clockwise circle. His hand lifts up to my cheek. His fingernails are claws. Yes, I am scared, but I'm also not scared, because I know he needs me and he's never been mean to me. But his mother said . . .

"Did you kill her by accident?" I ask.

He stops. His mouth opens, revealing all those sharklike teeth. His eyes close for a second as if he is suddenly very, very weary of it all. "Why would you say that, Zara?"

"Because I can't believe you'd just kill someone."

"You have seen me kill."

"But only to protect others or in self-defense."

His hand loses its tension and his forehead tilts and touches my own, resting there. I still can't move, but I don't feel like I'm in danger anymore.

"I look like a killer, though, am I correct? With all my pointy teeth, the sharp claws?" He whispers this.

"It's not about how people look," I insist. "It's about what's on the inside. It's about our actions."

"But you forget, Zara. We are not people. We are pixies."

"Doesn't matter. The rule still applies."

He laughs a soft, sad laugh. Just as quickly as the laugh enters the air, it is gone. "You believe things so fiercely."

"I believe you aren't evil."

"Then it must be true." He moves his forehead off mine. His hands go to my shoulders. "I apologize."

Just like that, I am no longer restrained. Still, I don't move away. "Tell me what happened with your queen, Astley."

His face crumples. "She died," he whispers. "And it was my fault. I killed her."

His glamour comes back. His eyes implore mine, soft and needy human eyes.

My hands reach up and grab his shoulders. "Just tell me, Astley."

"I didn't want you to ever know," he says. His voice is still quiet, church quiet.

"Why not?"

"I want you to think I am perfect." He closes his eyes as if it's too much to look at me.

Nobody is perfect, though. We all want everyone to think we are, but perfection is some crazy mythical state that we can never achieve. It is a goal beyond our grasp, always shifting and changing and taunting us, because it knows . . . it knows we can never reach it.

His voice breaks as he says, "I wanted you to always feel safe with me."

I bring Astley over to the couch. He sits down, docile and quiet. I groan as I sit down next to him.

"You hurt." He states this as a fact, not a question.

I resist the urge to be all melodramatic and say, "We all hurt." Instead, I just nod.

We sit there for a moment.

"Are you going to tell me?" I ask.

He shakes his head. "It's not as important as finding your wolf."

"Yes," I say. "Yes, it is."

He stares at me for a moment. The tension and pain inside of him is palpable. "My mother was right. I killed her."

Something in my face must show my fear, because he throws up his hand and rails off the side of the couch. He staggers toward me before falling on his knees in front of me.

"Just tell me, Astley," I say. My hand reaches out and touches the top of his head. His hair is thick and soft. His eyes flicker shut like he's trying to keep back tears.

"We had been destined to marry from the time we were babes. Her family was old and powerful, although not royal. I did not care about that. She was beautiful." He keeps his eyes shut as he speaks. The words leave his mouth slowly, making ripples in the air, like hard, heavy rocks dropped into a brook. "She was Amelie's youngest sister. Her name was Sacha."

"Oh." My hand stops its movement in his hair as I try to imagine her—strong, dark, beautiful, brilliant, and focused, if she was anything like Amelie. Something knots in my stomach—it almost feels like jealousy, but it can't be that.

"I had heard about a rogue in my kingdom. Someone was killing other pixies. Amelie, Sacha, and I had worked so hard to root out the problem, but we were always coming to dead ends, and I was so young then. We hadn't, um—we hadn't solidified our relationship in a physical way, just as you and I haven't, and that, coupled with my youth, allowed for rogues to exist without me automatically knowing who they were."

I swallow hard trying to figure out the implications for my relationship with Astley. If we had done the deed, would he have automatically known about Vander? Would my dad not have died? I shake my head and try to focus on what he's saying now, because that line of thought is just not comfortable. He doesn't notice my distraction and keeps blurting out the story in hard phrases. His mother, of all people, had told him where the rogue lay in wait for his or her victims. It was an old cathedral in the lower part of the city. He knew the attacks happened at night and so he waited there with Amelie. They waited for hours, until just before dawn they heard the choked-off scream in the graveyard at the back of the building. They rushed there to find the queen kissing the corpse of a pixie, blood covering her clothes, her mouth, her hands. She had murdered him.

"You have to kill her," Amelie had insisted. "Kill her now."

But he couldn't. He stood there horrified and stunned as his queen turned to look at him. Fear and anger filled her eyes. Still, Astley couldn't move. Amelie rushed forward and snapped her own sister's neck.

"I was too weak," he says. His voice breaks into shards that stab the air with grief. "I could not do it myself."

"You loved her."

"I love all my people," he says, opening his eyes.

Placing my hands on both sides of his face, I urge him to stand up again, and he does. We stand so close that I can feel his chest rise and fall with his breaths.

"She'd been killing," I say. "And you weren't the one who killed her, Astley. Amelie did."

He jerks away. "You do not understand. We found out later that it had not been her. The murderer had actually been the pixie Sacha had found. She had killed him for me. My mother had told her the same information she had told me. She led us both to the same place. She—Amelie—has never been the same."

"Have you?" I ask.

"No." His face breaks in half. "I killed my queen."

I want to say, "Not technically," but I know that wouldn't matter to him.

"She has never helped me, my mother, not ever." He laughs softly under his breath; his eyes lose their tears and glint with pain and anger instead. "Even when she attempts, she just brings death. She said a good king would have known who the rogue was, that a good king just takes what he needs. Why does she never help?"

Before I can show him the book, he starts to rage, leaping off the couch and swearing against her, calling her all sorts of names. As he does, lightning strikes outside, lighting up the park in a vivid, vicious kind of tantrum. The tree limbs sway and rock, battling to stay attached to the trunks. The house itself doesn't sway, though. It is solid. I will myself to be like the house as Astley continues his pacing and fist wagging.

"Astley . . . ," I say, trying to interrupt the tirade. "She didn't tell me, but—"

He paces past me. "I knew she would not! She would never help me. Never do anything that was not selfish, that did not give her gain. I have failed you, Zara. I have failed. I am so sorry. I shall personally go to the high council. I shall—"

"Astley . . ."

He passes by me again, not noticing. I pull the book out of my pocket and wave it in front of his face as he starts the third pass.

He stops.

"She didn't tell me anything," I say, smiling. "But she gave me this."

HatesME: Dude, this place is messed. I am so out of here.

Happyfeet: Then leave already.

HatesME: I should. Rents won't let me.

Happyfeet: Convince them.

HatesME: We r like sitting ducks here.

Mohawk: No, we aren't. We're fighting back.

HatesME: Against what?

Happyfeet: Ducks can fly away.

Mohawk: Against evil.

—BEDFORDAMERICAN.COM CHAT ROOM

As soon as we're out of New York and on the Connecticut interstate, I start reading parts of the book aloud to Astley because all that arcane language is basically gobbledygook to me.

Astley slows down by the exit ramp to a rest stop. "Do you need to get out?"

I tell him I don't.

He nods and speeds the car up again. "Basically, I think what it is telling us is that BiForst is the bridge between here and Valhalla. Reread that last part again."

I begin. "'Where a snake of water that cuts the earth meets the mouth that swallows it and becomes the belly; where the land rises to the Valkyries' flight, the sacred words must be said, the land of gods meets the land of men, make haste and ascend the rainbow.'"

"Exactly. So we need to take BiForst to the place where river meets sea and then land slopes upward. There we light a fire and say the sacred words, and there will be some sort of rainbow or bridge. A portal almost."

"That sounds hokey," I complain.

"Hokey?"

"Cheesy, dorky." I lean farther back into the seat and cross my legs a different way. I am so tired of driving but so excited about the book and the possibility it offers. "It doesn't matter. What matters is that it works."

"Do you know of a place where those conditions are met?"

"Yeah. Down by the town pier the Union River turns into the Union River Bay. There's a conservancy and a big hill there. An eagle nests there. Not Devyn. A regular one." I think a little more as we pass a Saab and a station wagon with bumper stickers about having kids on the honor roll. "That has to be it."

"Read the chapter again. It seems too easy," he suggests.

I read it again. Then I read it another time. I read it as we go from barren trees to snow-covered ones. I read it as we go north and as the sun rises and the snow falls. It's seven thirty a.m. and a whole new day has begun.

"This is all assuming that Bedford is the place that they speak of. The place where the end of the world will begin," he says, then sighs. He brushes hair off his forehead.

"I think that's safe to assume." I laugh and my wound spasms. "Although, maybe not. Maybe there are multiple places where it can happen. I mean, the Vikings came over to the New World, but I think all the Poetic Edda was before that—or maybe not . . . I don't know, but we should try Bedford first, because it's the closest."

I cringe again.

"Are you hurting?"

I lie and tell him no and then riff on how cold Bedford is, how there seems to be a ridiculously large concentration of pixies and weres there, how he himself suggested it a while ago.

I tell him all this stuff and then I fall quickly, promptly, soundly asleep. I dream of sitting in the middle of a road. Nick stands over me. Snowflakes dot his beautiful dark hair. He reaches down and hauls me up as if I weigh nothing, as if I am a body of air and feathers, which I'm not. I'm runner solid, small but muscled. Sort of. It doesn't matter. What matters is that he is in a dangerous place.

"What are you doing?" I demand. "You're not here. You're in Valhalla."

I don't move away, though. I don't move away because his hands are solid against my hips, keeping me standing up. His hands stay there, but then he starts to fade . . . He's fading . . . and I'm grabbing toward him, but there's nothing to grab . . . just air.

"I could hear the danger coming." His voice enters the night. "I can hear it now, Zara. It's coming . . ."

I wake up to the deep, loud horn of a logging truck.

Astley glares at the tail end of the truck, the cutoff trunks of trees, all prone, helpless, and dead. "I could kill him for waking you."

"It's okay." I wave his anger away. It seems too much, too intense. I swallow and attempt normalcy. "I should be keeping you company. Where are we?"

"Maine. Almost to Bangor." He eyes me and swings into the passing lane. "How are you feeling?"

I lift up my hand from where it has been resting against my wound. There is blood on it. "Fine. Psyched about the book still, you know?"

There is a big pause, and then I fill it with, "It's nice that your mother gave us the book."

"You said you had to threaten her."

"True," I say. "But she could have tried to kill me and she didn't, so that's a bonus point for her."

He doesn't answer, just nods and drives. We sit there in a happy sort of silence all the way back to Betty's house. I don't think about my dream once, or about how crazy Astley was back in New York. Okay, that's a lie. But I don't obsess about it, which I think is a positive forward movement in my psychological development.

When we pull up into the driveway, there's just my mom's rental car and Betty's truck waiting for us. I try to shore myself up with a deep breath, but it sends pain through my chest and actually makes me shakier.

Astley studies me before he opens the door. "Are you certain you are prepared for this?"

"Yep."

"And you can face them?"

"Yep."

"I'll walk you to the porch."

"You don't have—"

He jumps out of the car and swings around to my side, opening the door for me before I can protest anymore. We walk across the snowy driveway, leaving a little gold glitter trail behind us. Each step I take is half excited and half worried. Pain ripples through my chest.

"They are going to be so mad at me," I whisper as I slip a bit on the ice.

He grabs my elbow, steadying me. "Most likely."

. . .

It's my mother who throws open the door. She hasn't put on her makeup or done her hair. She's wearing one of Betty's big green fleece jackets that zip up the middle. Her breath hauls in sharply and she shakes her head, tears in her eyes.

"Some days I think I might kill you, Zara White," she sputters. But it's not that much of a threat, because she's crying.

"It's been tried. I'm kind of hard to kill." I gesture toward my gunshot wound.

She gasps/chokes/laughs. She almost hugs me and then stops herself. Something inside of me hitches and breaks.

She doesn't notice. She just says, "Thank God . . . Thank God for that."

Betty comes out of the kitchen carrying an armful of wood. She raises just one eyebrow and half smiles. No lectures from her. She knows that we headstrong types have to be left alone to do what we have to do. Instead she just says, "Well, well, well. How are you feeling, missy?"

"Okay," I say. "Actually, good. Astley and I found out—"

"Zara!" Betty hustles over, dropping her wood on the floor. It bangs and clangs. My mother steps backward. Her hand shakes as she raises it up and covers her mouth.

"What?" I ask, panicked. No one answers. "What?"

I have no idea what's going on. I glance behind me for Astley. He's out on the porch still, looking clueless as well. Maybe I'm blue? Maybe there's a bug on my face? I don't know.

"You're bleeding through," Betty announces, ripping off my jacket. "Sit. Sit!"

I sit on the hardwood floor right by the stairs because she's freaking out so much and I'm too stunned to argue. Cold air comes in. The stairs look high from this angle. The world actually seems a little tilted.

"Get gauze," she orders my mother.

My mother stands there. Then she does a typical my-mother thing. She folds, just crumples to the floor, passing out. Her head hits the coffee table going down. The whack of it rings out.

"Mom!" I lurch toward her, scuttling along the floor.

"You. Stay. Still," Betty orders. She cusses and says through the still-open door, "Pixie, come in! But if you try anything or ever try anything, I swear to whatever gods you cursed things believe in that I will rip you end to end."

He starts but then stops himself just at the threshold. "Are you certain?"

"Yes, damn it, I'm certain. Get your fool self in here and help, but don't make me kill you!"

Astley enters. He shuts the door behind him. He doesn't react to Betty's threat. I guess he is used to threats by now, used to death and pain and terror. He meets her eyes and says, "Where's the gauze?"

"My med kit. By the door." She almost smiles at me. "I'll give him one thing. He moves fast. Calm in a crisis."

"That's two things," I correct as she lifts my bloody shirt.

"Oh, I see you are still your witty self," she says and then directs Astley. He gives her stitching thread and gauze and some sort of tool. He puts ice on my mother's head. Betty explains she'll be fine. It's a slight concussion, not a subdural whatever that is.

"She used to pass out all the time when she was young," Betty says as the needle pierces my skin, pulling my wound together by tension and force. "Can't stand blood. Can't believe she works in a hospital."

I sometimes can't believe that either, but she's an administrator, not a nurse or a doctor or even an X-ray technician. My mother's face is pale and drawn. Creases make homes beneath her eyes.

Just seeing her feels bad to me, makes me ache for a life she could have had—a life without pixies or pain, without a dead husband or a turned daughter.

Astley lifts her up and puts her on the couch. She's groggy but wakes enough so that she can still glare at him and mumble, "Don't touch me, pixie. This is your fault. All of this."

"Mom!" I object. She just closes her eyes again and moans.

Astley backs away. He doesn't say anything to her. Instead he asks Betty, who is still stitching me up, "Can I help in any way?"

She shakes her head. "You might want to hold her hand. This hurts her."

"I'm okay." I grunt—it *does* hurt me. The words don't matter anyway; neither Astley nor my grandmother believes them. Astley grabs my hand. Warmth spreads up my arms from his fingers. I can feel the power of him in my skin, warming it, calming it. We are bonded and this has to be one of the many effects, but it still makes me a tiny bit uneasy because it's so terribly personal. Still, everything we've been sharing is personal. I push my qualms aside and turn up the corners of my mouth, which is as much as I can make of a smile right now.

Betty raises an eyebrow. "So, why don't you tell us why the two of you ran away? Again."

I do.

Tensions in the town of Bedford increase as there is still no news on the latest missing boy and funeral preparations continue for the several dead teens from nearby Sumner High School. "I just want it to stop," one mother said. "I just want us all to be safe again." —*THE BEDFORD AMERICAN*

"More young people have been reported missing in the greater Bedford area," the television announcer blathers on, "which brings the total up to twenty-two. This unprecedented number has some experts talking about runaway plots since most of those missing are young men. However, the Federal Bureau of Investigation has sent in agents to investigate the possibilities of a serial killer or an international child prostitution ring."

The screen switches to a guy who is obviously an FBI agent. He's wearing sunglasses and has short cropped hair. The real tip-off, however, are the yellow letters announcing FBI on his dark blue jacket.

"Currently, we cannot divulge any of the possibilities for the cause of the disappearances," he says in a deep take-no-prisoners voice. "We *do*, however, have leads, and we *are* investigating those leads."

The news anchor returns. "Complicating matters is that some

residents, frightened by events, are simply leaving town on extended vacations, which results in confusion over whether some people are truly missing or just not here."

Mrs. Nix is over and Astley is still here, and we're all crowded into the living room. Betty doesn't ask anyone's permission; she just pushes a button on the remote and the TV clicks off. I pause in the act of bringing my soup spoon to my mouth. My mom made it despite her minor concussion. She always likes to make soup when I'm sick, and she counts a gunshot wound as being sick. Plus, I think she liked being busy so she wouldn't have to look at me.

"Why did you shut it off?" I ask, gesturing to the TV.

"It's not telling us anything we don't already know," Betty says. She puts her hands right above her knees and pushes herself up to a standing position. My mother starts to stand too, but Betty barks at her. "You stay put. I'm just getting some tea."

Betty strides off to the kitchen muttering about being stuck in a house with a gunshot victim, a fainter, and a pixie.

"I'll go help," says Mrs. Nix, smiling. She pets my shoulder. "I'll see if I can calm her down a little bit. You know how she gets."

As Mrs. Nix heads to the kitchen, Astley asks, "How does she get?"

"Cranky," I explain.

Astley's sitting in the red chair, and my mother and I are on the couch. She's clutching one of Issie's steak knives because she thinks he's going to attack any second, despite the fact that only a couple hours ago he took care of her after she'd passed out. My mother has trust issues when it comes to pixie kings, and I can't blame her, really.

"Mom . . ." I try to use her name as a warning, and I think it works, because she leans her head back against the couch, tilts her chin up, and closes her eyes.

Since getting back I've learned that Devyn and Cassidy finished building the cell in the basement for BiForst.

Right now, Issie, Cassidy, and Devyn are off at school, which I am missing thanks to the gunshot thing. Astley and I have gone through the book and even e-mailed a few details to them about what we've learned. Issie responded with a ton of exclamation points and squees. Devyn agreed with our take on things. Now we're just waiting for them to come back from school so we can get on with it.

Betty and Mrs. Nix come back with tea for everyone, even Astley, which seems like a giant step forward.

"Be careful, Zara," Betty says as she puts my mug on the coffee table. "It's hot."

I shoot Astley a look. They're treating me like a baby. I swallow my temper.

"So, we've been talking . . . ," Betty begins. She fixes me with her alpha-dog stare. I swallow but stare back. Something in my stomach drops. "You aren't well enough to go, Zara."

My heart falls out along with my stomach. I start to protest and tell her how I am just a bit achy and that I am totally, perfectly fine to go, which I am, when she silences me with a finger. "Do not argue. We all agree. You have no chance."

"But—"

"No buts, young lady." My mom crosses her arms over her chest. "We'll tie you up if we have to, but you can't do it."

"We can't lose you too," Betty explains.

"You don't all agree. Astley doesn't agree," I respond. Then I close my eyes for a moment, to try to push the pain and despair down.

When I open my eyes, he's moved right in front of me. He's squatting on the floor. His voice is soft and serious. His hands touch the sides of my shins. "I do agree."

The clock ticks on the wall. The refrigerator hums in the other room. All these sounds that show me life is going on, is real, that they are actually saying this to me—even Astley.

"I changed . . . I changed to do this. If I don't get Nick, that means I've changed for nothing." My voice sounds hysterical. I clamp my mouth shut. Tears are popping into my eyes.

"I know, sweetie." Betty pats my arm.

"No, that is incorrect," Astley disagrees. "It is not for nothing. Your change makes me stronger. It brings us stability. When you live with me as queen, we will—"

"Absolutely not," Mom interrupts.

Astley's gaze goes from one to the other of us as he stands up. "That is not the issue at this time. What is important is getting to Valhalla. Who shall go?"

Mrs. Nix puts down her mug. It rests on her big knee. "I will."

"I thought we'd decided that I would," Betty says.

"I am not as needed. You have a family, Betty, medical skills that I just don't have. But I am just as good a warrior as you are and you know it."

Betty nods. "True."

"But you *are* needed," I interrupt, staring at Mrs. Nix's sweet round face. "And you *do* have a family. Everyone at school is your family. We're your family."

She smiles softly at me, this woman who is a bear, and she says, "You are so kind, Zara. Let me do this for you. Let me be the hero this time."

I don't answer. I try to solid up my argument, but I don't know how.

"She has a better chance at success," Betty adds. "If you do it, you're being selfish, Zara. You are lowering the odds of us actually rescuing Nick. Is that what you want?"

I swallow hard. "No."

"Didn't think so," she retorts. "I wonder why only one can go at a time? Where do these ancient rules even come from?"

It is still snowing outside when we leave. It is the kind of snow that seems like it will never stop, maybe because it hasn't for weeks. It isn't too heavy, but it's built up so that there are snow piles where sidewalks should be on Main and High Streets. City public works crews don't seem to ever have a break. They keep hauling it off the streets and parking lots. They dump a lot in the parking lot by the harbor because it's winter and no boaters are out. The town dock is basically a tiny park with a gazebo and a couple of floating docks that are currently hauled up on the parking lot and covered with three huge mountains of snow.

We're all carpooling there. It took a lot of protesting for my mom and Betty to even allow me to come, but I'd gone all the way to New York with Astley, so they could hardly make like a trip across town would be too taxing. I know they are trying to protect me because they love me, but seriously? All the fussing is a little too much, and I've compromised a lot by letting Mrs. Nix go to Valhalla instead of me.

Betty, my mom, Mrs. Nix, and I drive to the harbor in my mom's rental car. Betty and Mrs. Nix sit in the backseat, with Betty giving her pointers nonstop.

"Do *not* trust anyone," she tells her. "Not even the gods."

"Of course," Mrs. Nix says.

"And if you get in a jam, use the lunge—when you rear up you expose your belly to attack."

"Of course."

I turn around and look at them. They are so cute together. "We're here. Are you okay to do this? I can still go."

Mrs. Nix smiles at me and reaches forward to touch the side of my face. "It's my turn to be the hero, Zara. I like it. Plus, I get to reunite true lovers. It's romantic."

Her eyes are soft and sweet but strong too. She drops her hand from my face, and my voice chokes up as I say, "Thank you."

Astley pulls up.

"That car does not fit in here," Betty snarks as she gets out.

This is true. Astley, Amelie, and a tied-up BiForst exit Astley's too-snazzy car as Mrs. Nix exits ours.

I grab the door handle, but my mom stops me. "It's too cold out for you."

I glare at her. "You've got to be kidding."

But she's not. She wants me to stay in the car, just stay here and watch. Everyone else agrees.

"Outvoted," Betty announces, then frowns woefully. "But you have front-row seats."

That does not make it better, but I don't want to make a big scene. I motion for Mrs. Nix to come to the window. She leans in. She smells like cinnamon rolls, like a stereotypical grandmother from the old days, warm and good, full of flour and sugar and love.

"I can't thank you enough," I whisper at her.

A snowflake sticks to her hair. "I am honored to do it."

She starts to move away, but I reach out and grab the fabric of her light blue parka. "Tell him I love him, okay? Tell him . . . I wanted to be the one to save him."

"Zara." She pauses, straightens up. "Nick already knows that, honey. Now, no worries. I'll bring him back soon. You take good care of your old grandma while I'm gone. She's not as tough as she pretends to be and she worries some about you. Deal?"

"Deal."

From my spot in the rental car, which smells of plastic and disinfectant, I watch them walk past the twenty abandoned parking spots in the lot, take a hard right by the shack that passes for a harbormaster's office, and onto the pier, which is part metal and part wood. They are a ragtag group of strange. They stand on the end of the dock. Ice chunks fill the water, looking like tiny dirty icebergs. Mrs. Nix looks like a blue marshmallow in her parka. My mom, Cassidy, and Issie group together like they are searching for strength from one another. Astley callously pushes BiForst in front of the rest. They wear fabric and leather and wool. They wear winter hats and gloves. Some stride (Betty), some saunter (Cassidy), and some seem to waddle (Mrs. Nix), but they are all here for one thing: to get Nick back, and I love them so much for it. I love them so much that it's almost okay that they are making me wait in the car.

What a liar I am.

It is *not* okay at all. They could get hurt. They could need backup. Something could go wrong.

The air starts to shimmer around them. Gasping, I lean forward onto the dashboard to get a better look. A bridge is forming over the river. It's silver and shiny and— It's not a rainbow. Everything I've read has said it would be a rainbow. Maybe "rainbow" is a word that gets lost in translation? I don't know. I want to hope that, but it doesn't feel right. Mrs. Nix steps on it and starts walking. The bridge arches over the river. The snow obscures the end. Mrs. Nix waddles up it, higher and higher.

Everything inside me shudders, and I freeze up. It's not from the cold. It's not from the wound. It's because that BiForst guy is giving off a smell that I catch even from the car. It's an arrogant smell. It's like fire or death or— It's what that Frank pixie smelled like when he killed Nick.

I shove open the car door, ignore the pain, and start to run, but I get only a few steps before the bridge just explodes.

Time stops.

The explosion is so loud it's like it sucks the sound out of everything.

A second passes.

Another.

The smell of burning fur and sulfur rush into the air. Shards of crystals rain through the sky. Someone screams. Black smoke billows across everything, obscures everything.

"Mrs. Nix!" I yell. "Mrs. Nix!"

But I know, even as I yell it, that it's too late.

The silence is huge and horrifying.

It should have been me.

For a moment nobody moves. Then it's all slow motion. Cassidy is screaming. It's inhumanly high and keening, and the air seems to echo with it. My mom moves to stand in front of her. Her hands go to Cassidy's arms. Issie doesn't move. She is shocked still. Devyn pulls her into a hug, protecting her head from falling debris. Astley turns to look at me. His eyes meet my eyes, even though I am still rushing toward them and there is a big distance. He half jumps, half flies to me.

"Are you okay?" he asks. His eyes do a quick once-over, checking for damage.

"Uh-huh. Are you?" I ask this but I can tell that he's got a singed spot on his forehead, a burn mark on his coat, and a cut on his ear. I move him around so I can better inspect.

"I am uninjured," he says. His voice softens with worry.

I blow that lie right off and I raise myself up on tiptoes. There's a shard of a red crystal substance sticking out behind his ear. It's not too big. "Hold still."

Before he can say anything, I wrap my hand around it. It burns because it's so hot. I yank it out anyway, in one quick movement, and drop it on the snowy pavement. Then I press my hand against the wound as the blood spurts.

"She's gone, isn't she?" I whisper.

He nods. "Her essence . . . I cannot . . . She is gone."

A big sob threatens to swallow me up, but I push it down and back. There are things to do. Mrs. Nix would want me to take care of people. Still, my heart pulses slow with loss, feeble and aching. We have lost so many.

What I've learned lately is that people deal with death in all sorts of different ways. Some of us fight against it, doing everything we can to make it not true. Some of us lose ourselves to grief. Some of us lose ourselves to anger.

A roar fills the air, shaking through the snowflakes, splintering away from mere sound and into something solid and fierce. Astley grabs my arm, propels me behind him. I push around to see. Betty has turned. Her tiger self stands near my mother and the others. Devyn has moved slightly in front of everyone else, protecting them, I guess, but why would he have to protect anyone from Betty? Amelie is slowly walking backward, like she's afraid she's about to be eaten, but the tiger's focus isn't on them. Then I understand. Even from over here, Betty's anger and desire to kill form one solid, twisted force.

The tiger takes two steps and leaps up, her mouth open and ready. The front half of her torso elongates and her front two paws stretch out, claws unleashed. She swats one across BiForst, knocking him to the ground. The other paw follows, ripping into his flesh. She falls on top of him, snarling. Issie gasps. I can do nothing. It's too late. My grip on Astley's arm tightens as BiForst stops moving.

Done with him, the tiger turns and looks at me, blood in her mouth. Her eyes are wild with grief and rage. She takes one step toward us. Astley's muscles tense, bracing for an attack. Then the tiger wails, turns, and bounds away across the snow, toward the gazebo in the little harbor park, then up to the trees that border between the houses and the park. And she is gone.

"She killed BiForst." I stagger backward to Betty's truck. The world reels.

Astley touches my cheek with the heel of his hand, and I let him. I do not jump away. There is sorrow in his eyes too, just like mine, maybe not so much for Mrs. Nix, but for his other losses.

I swallow hard, try to push that sorrow into a small place—maybe behind my appendix or something—put it somewhere contained for a while so that I can function. Then I yell for everyone to come back here, to back away from the carnage and destruction so I can take care of them and we can regroup.

Just as I do, a burned piece of fabric flutters down from the sky. It's part of Mrs. Nix's pine green sweatshirt. There's the eye of a reindeer on it. She was so excited about Christmas. She'd already decorated her office with little reindeer, which may be breaking those rules about separation of church and state, but I don't think she cared. Trembling, I scoop down, pick it up, and put it in my pocket. Why? I don't know. Just because. Just because she was a hero and I need something to remember her by, and if that has to be a burned piece of her sweatshirt, so be it. Just so be it . . .

We walk to our cars, wounded and zombielike. I know we have to get out of here before the police come. Someone must have heard or smelled something. Astley and Amelie, however, put a glamour on the area, trying to make it look like it did before. They stand together and a hum fills the air. I do triage, trying to bandage up everyone's wounds before we get out of here. I use the med kit Betty keeps in the metal locker in the bed of her truck but that she'd shoved into the car at the last minute. "Just in case," she had said.

Issie has rips in her puffy pink coat and she's softly crying. Devyn's mouth is a grim line. He's bleeding from the neck and forehead.

"Let me bandage that," I tell him. We are barely moving. Shock numbs us into half of our selves.

"Issie first," he insists. They sit on the back of the truck, feet dangling.

"Issie isn't hurt as badly," I say.

"Issie first."

"You okay with that, Is?" I ask.

She nods, but she doesn't say anything. She hasn't spoken a word the entire time. It's like she's lost her voice. Her eyes are hollow, full of tears. I never even asked her how she got out of her house arrest to come with us. I'm a horrible friend, putting her in danger over and over again, putting all of them in danger. The guilt of it flips my stomach. I take care of Issie quickly and move on to Devyn and then my mother, while Astley cares for Amelie despite his own injuries. Cassidy seems to be healing on her own, thanks to her special blood. She checks on Issie and Devyn, murmuring magic words, hiccupping softly with tears as she works.

"We will be okay," my mother insists.

I work on her hands, applying burn cream. It globs out of the tube. She cringes.

"We will be okay," she repeats.

But I don't know how we will. I look up at Astley. He meets my gaze, and it's then that I notice. His eyes are full of tears, and they glisten, goldish. I wonder if my eyes look like that too. I wonder if we will ever find Nick. I wonder if we will ever stop losing people we love. I wonder and wonder as I work on my mother's hands, but I get no answers. I get nothing but the feeling of loss.

My mother uses the burned palms of her hands to grab my own, stopping me as I roll out the gauze. "We are done with this, Zara. You hear me? No more Valhalla. No more fighting. I forbid you. We are done."

"But Nick—"

"No boy is worth this."

Everyone stops what they are doing and watches us. My mouth has dropped open. I clamp it shut and then open it again, measuring my words, but no words come.

Her pupils flare. "I forbid you."

That tone. It used to make me do anything she wanted. It sent me to my room when I was being a brat. It made me do dishes or get to school on time. But not anymore.

"You can't forbid me anymore, Mom. You can't stop me," I say.

Her hands twitch beneath my fingers. "You used to be so human, Zara, but now . . . but now . . ."

I pull out of her grasp easily. Then I slowly and methodically continue working on her burns. Nobody else says anything. They look away like nothing has happened, but something *has* happened, something big. I feel it inside of me, and that knowledge aches, bitter and hard like death.

Recent sightings of large cat prints have stumped local officials, but some residents are now wondering if the cause of the missing youths isn't a human predator at all.
—NEWS CHANNEL 8

Astley makes phone calls and some of his pixies come to dispose of BiForst's body. Betty hasn't come back. Two days pass and we all mourn. It's a double mourning, for both Mrs. Nix and Nick, because it seems like we've lost all chance of finding him. It's a triple mourning almost, because it feels like Betty will never return. To make it worse, she isn't being careful. There are news sightings of big cats, and one television report showed a man pointing at Betty's massive paw prints in the snow.

The days stretch into grayness, bleak and horrible. Mrs. Nix was one of the kindest people in the universe and now she's gone. Mrs. Nix's disappearance does not go unnoticed at school, nor does Betty's. My mom substitutes for Mrs. Nix, but there's nobody to fill Betty's shoes. On Friday an FBI agent stops me and Cassidy in the school parking lot and asks us questions. We answer the best we can: *We don't know about Mrs. Nix. Betty went to visit a sick friend in New Hampshire.* We give him Betty's cell phone number.

"Aren't you worried about things?" he asks us. "So many missing. I'd think you kids wouldn't even be walking in parking lots alone."

Cassidy pulls her arm through mine. "We aren't alone."

"Oh, you have each other, right?" he snarks.

"You're alone," I say.

"Yes, but I have this." He pats the side of his belt where his gun is. That's not tacky or over-the-top macho or anything.

Later the same day, Astley and I meet at the grocery store since my mother refuses to allow him anywhere near the house. We roam up and down the aisles, carrying little baskets but not really buying anything. Eventually, I grab some mushroom ravioli just as an excuse to actually be here.

He walks me to the car. My hat is lopsided, so I fix it. Astley tucks my scarf more securely around my neck, then asks, "You have given up hope, haven't you?"

I shrug, even though I know it's a pathetic body gesture.

His hands go to the side of my face. "It hurts me to see you like this."

"I am okay," I say. "I—I've dealt with loss before."

He leans closer. The smell of him overwhelms everything else, makes the snow falling behind him in the white sea of the parking lot vanish. It's just him and me here, just us with our grief.

"I would take it all away if I could," he says.

"Why?"

It's his turn to shrug. "I just would."

My butt rests against the MINI. I reach out and wipe the snow off his shoulders. "I wish you could."

His fingers curl around my wrists, wrapping the ends of my mittens with warmth.

"Zara?" His voice is hoarse and aching.

I tilt my head and before I know it I'm clinging on to him, like he's some magic tether that keeps me from sinking under with grief and pain and loss. His head dips down and our lips touch just the faintest of whispers, and then they mold right into each other, aching for life and comfort, longing to know that we aren't alone. The world shimmers. He clutches me closer, and it's just the two of us standing in the snowflakes, air swirling around us, the world spinning on its axis, time slowly clicking forward. It's like the world has wrapped us up in old blankets, warming us with passion and need and . . .

I break away first. My hand flutters to cover my lips. "Oh . . . Oh . . ."

Someone starts a car in the next aisle and pulls out of the space. I try to figure out what to say, what to feel. Astley kissed me. And it was nice. It was more than nice. I can't—

Astley interrupts my thoughts. His face is suddenly hard, lined. "It was all a trap. My mother set us up. She hoped to kill you at the bar, but she had a backup plan. Vander must have been beholden to her, in league with her. It's rare, but it can happen, because she was the queen and I am not as strong as I should be."

Shock ripples through me. "Why? Why would she want to kill me?"

"She is the widow of a king. If I died, she could choose her own king and rule through him, but now that you're alive, you have that power instead of her."

I try to process that. If Astley died, I'd have to find another king. And if we both died, she'd get to rule again. "That's horrible. She meant to kill me? And you?"

"She killed my last queen, I think, through treachery. And Iceland— She— It was her. I am sure of it."

Concentrating on his face, I try to push the anger out of my gut and focus on him and his hurt, his loss. I don't know what it could possibly be like to have a mother like that. How alone he must feel. As I watch his lips, my stomach hitches up. I kissed him. We kissed each other. We . . .

He swallows so hard that I can hear it. "I shall find him."

"What?" Shaking my head, I try to clear my brain. "What do you mean?"

"I will find your wolf. I want you to want me because you want me, not because of grief, not because he is not here. I want you to love me for me. I want you to kiss me first and not because you need me to help you, but because you need to kiss *me*." He lifts his eyebrows just a little bit and his lips open. I drop my hand, reach for him, but he steps back and whisks away, dodging behind cars, before I have a chance to say that I don't want to lose him too.

I see Astley the next day after school. He meets me in the parking lot and we stand by the MINI. His eyes are soft but wary—he's watching the perimeter of the woods while we talk instead of making eye contact, which I understand because I do it too. We can't let our guard down.

"I need to ask a favor of you, Zara," he says.

I nod. I'm cool with that.

"I have arranged a meeting of our pixies so that—"

"In the graveyard again?" I interrupt.

"No. I think that was a bit—"

"Emo? Melodramatic?" I suggest.

Tilting his head, he smirks at me and makes eye contact. "As a species we have a weakness for drama. Thank you for reminding me," he teases. "But no. It is actually in a conference room at a hotel. Many of our pixies are posing as reporters and are at the

Holiday Inn. We've rented a room and pumped in a feed so that everyone in the kingdom, even those who are not here, can watch."

That's smart. But then I think, why?

"I want to tell them all about what happened in Iceland and with Mrs. Nix. I need to reveal my mother's treachery." His Adam's apple moves down in his throat and he rubs a hand through his hair. "It will not be fun."

It isn't. We spend an hour in the conference room with its puke pink walls and old coffee smell. The whole time I remember how I ran at the cemetery, and the shame of it burns my cheeks. They've made such sacrifices being here, to protect the town, the people, my friends, me. They deserve more. Throughout the meeting, Astley stands at a podium and talks and talks, fielding questions from the two hundred or so pixies sitting at tables. The questions are respectful, and from the way that Amelie glares at anyone who asks anything, I'm sure everyone is afraid she'd rip their head off if they were even the slightest bit rude. Astley explains how his mother is basically trying to assassinate us. He also mentions that we saw Fenrir, the wolf who heralds the Ragnarok, the end of our world.

Finally Becca, a pixie who has chewed gum the entire time, raises her hand and asks, "So, you've been trying to find Valhalla to rescue the were who at one point tied you to a tree?"

"Yes," Astley says.

Amelie paces along the perimeter of the room, feral almost. I try to imagine how hard it must be for her, having killed her sister and now having to see me as Astley's new queen.

Becca ignores Amelie and continues on. "And he is the boy-friend of the queen?"

Astley nods.

"And the queen has killed others because of this wish? Exploited it?"

"Yes," Astley says, looking at me. I think we're both hoping that Becca will get to the point.

"Look," Becca continues, "I'm cool with trying to save anyone who can help us kick Frank's ass, but what I'm wondering is, why don't you just ask the council how to get to Valhalla?" She stares me down, but her eyes aren't unkind, just tough.

"I have via phone and I am going there to ask personally after the meeting. As of yet they have not responded," Astley says. He looks around the room to see if there are any more questions.

"Does the queen have anything to say?" Becca asks. She smiles at me. She's so pretty when she smiles. Her parents are from Hong Kong, Amelie told me. "She has been so quiet."

The energy in the room changes. I know they're all remembering how I ran off, how I was weak and scared. That's not what they need right now. I can tell from the feeling in the room that all of them are nervous, on edge about the treachery and the attacks they've been dealing with here.

"This is not about Zara," Astley says, but then he looks at me and adds, "but if you would like to say something, you most certainly can."

My knees shake a tiny bit as I stand up and move toward the podium. I adjust the microphone down. It's beyond awkward up here. Wishing that I'd taken speech or debate or something, I force a slow deep breath through my lungs and out.

"I am honored to be your queen. Every day I become more and more honored by what you all risk just by being here. You know what Frank's pixies do: they torment, they torture innocent people, they drain their souls, rip their skin, ravage their minds. They do this as pixies. When they do this they ruin who we are. Show the world, show me, show your king, and most importantly show yourselves that you are better than that, that you are *not* that. Continue to protect the people of this town. Use your power for good. Be proud to be on the side of good. Be proud of your king and yourselves. I know that I am, and I am so thankful for all of you."

Sitting back down, I start smiling, because I know—without the smallest of doubts—that if my dad—the one who raised me, my stepdad—were here, he'd be really, *really* proud.

After the meeting, Astley drives me home and we stand on the front porch talking for a minute.

"You did a very good job," he says.

"Was it too rah-rah?" I ask.

"No, not at all."

"You did a good job too," I say, deliberately avoiding looking at his lips. We have said nothing more about the kiss.

As soon as we are out of the car, my mother opens the house door and snaps, "What are you doing here?"

"Discussing," Astley says.

She raises her eyebrows and tells us in no uncertain terms that Astley needs to leave.

"Give us a minute, Mom," I beg.

She crosses her arms over her chest and doesn't budge, except for her foot, which is tapping her anger into the floorboards of the porch.

"A minute alone," I add.

"Lovely. Love pixies. Love 'em." She moves toward the door.

"Mom, I'm a pixie."

"You don't count." She says this, but I know I do.

When I turn back to him, Astley gives me sympathetic eyes but kindly doesn't say anything about the exchange. "I should go," I say.

"Okay."

As we stand there another minute, everything becomes quiet and awkward between us. Finally I clear my throat and say, "Stay safe, okay?"

He reaches up his hand, touches my arm. "You as well."

And then he goes.

The rest of us, the ones left behind, spend the days trying to carry on, remembering goofy things about Mrs. Nix, planning how to defend people from Frank and his pixies, trying to figure out how to keep people from killing me, trying to figure out a way to get Betty to come home. None of it seems good enough. None of it seems to avenge the deaths, the injuries. I do homework and go to track, even though I can't run. Only four people show up for our Key Club meeting; only five show up for AFS.

Cassidy works on all of us and we heal much more quickly than we would normally. All the exertion tires her out. Blue smudges rim her eyes. Her hair gets so limp that no amount of teasing or conditioner gives her braids bounce. Her hands shake from simple tasks.

Issie doesn't talk for three days. When she finally does, it is only to Devyn, but then she slowly starts talking to all of us again. First, it's just a word or two, and then it's whole sentences.

I don't even tell Issie about what happened between Astley and me. People are dying. I can't think about kisses.

And then Astley comes back one night when I've just finished patrolling with Devyn. My mom and I are sitting on the couch watching bad reality television when he knocks on the front door. When I open it, he smiles at me. It's a small, hesitant smile. The cold air rushes inside our warm house. He smells of wool and outside. My heart freezes midbeat.

"May I come in?" he asks.

"Of course," I say as my mother spits out, "No."

He had started to step inside, but he pauses. I grab his arm and yank him in, shutting the door behind him, ignoring my mom's protests. He stomps the snow off his boots on the plastic pad Betty put by the door.

My mother harrumphs.

"What did they say?" I try to take his coat, but he won't let me. "Are you hungry? Can I get you anything?"

"No, but thank you." Astley clears his throat awkwardly. His eyes are shiny, excited. "I found out how to get there, Zara. I went to the council. I made our case. I cited my mother's deception, Frank's renegade thwarting of all our rules, and his attacks on this kingdom. I explained that I could not create stability in the region without my queen's happiness, which is dependent upon the return of her wolf."

A silence pulls at both of us until I finally say, "He's not my possession."

"Yes. Right," he sputters. He doesn't unbutton his coat or take off his boots. "Anyway, it is a ceremony. It requires a lot of magic and some special guests, but we can do it."

For a moment I let that register. We can do it.

"Really?" My voice is a tiny squeak. I study his face.

He nods and I fling myself at him. His arms wrap around me in a super hug. We can do it.

"How do you know it's not a trick?" I ask into his coat.

"The council itself told me, Zara. It is no deception. I just wish they could have told us earlier and saved all this heartbreak, but the way is a much-guarded secret."

He steps backward, breaks the hug, but keeps his hands on my arms. His smile lights up the entire room. I bet I have a smile that almost matches it.

"Can all of us go?" I ask.

He shakes his head. "Just one."

My mother's voice comes from behind me. She's gotten off the couch and stands near the white leather chair, her arms still crossed in front of her chest. "Nobody is going anywhere."

"What?" I step toward her. "How can you say that? We can get Nick."

"Nobody is going and that's final." She shakes her head at me. "You are being unbearably selfish, Zara. How many people are you willing to lose? How many people are you going to let die just so you can get back this one boy?"

"That's not how it is," I say.

"That's exactly how it is." She points her finger at me. I back up and accidentally bump Astley with my hip. "You are willing to sacrifice all of us to get Nick back."

"That's not true." Rage and guilt and sorrow hiccup inside my throat, making it hard to breathe. "That's not true. Mrs. Nix insisted. You all insisted that I not go."

"We had no choice. You would have died even if it hadn't been a trap; you were so weak." Her face is a mixture of sorrow and rage.

I stagger backward away from her. Astley steadies me.

"You need to stop." He directs this to my mother and speaks with utter calm mixed with absolute authority.

She whirls on him. "How dare you say that to me! How dare you?"

She raises her hand to strike him, but he doesn't move, even though I know he could. Instead I jump between them. Her hand hits the top of my head, I guess because she'd been aiming for his face. Her mouth drops into a shocked O. For a second there's hesitation, or regret, but then it's gone and she says, "Get out, pixie. Zara, to your room."

"No," I say.

"I should leave," Astley says calmly. He opens the door and gives me a look that is easy for me to understand.

I head up the stairs as he shuts the door.

My mother's voice calls up after me. "You will thank me for this someday, young lady."

Yeah. Right.

Less than a minute later I'm opening up my window and Astley is climbing through. His long legs bend at the knee and remind me of a grasshopper. He shuts the window behind him. I sit on the floor, back against my bed, and pat the space beside me. He pretty much collapses into it. I've never seen him so tired. He wipes at his eyes with the back of his hand and then asks, "Her slap did not hurt you, did it?"

"Not physically. Not really." We are whispering so she doesn't hear us over the music.

"Good. It was intended for me."

"I know."

He sighs out for a second, then unzips his jacket. "My boots are leaking on your carpet."

"Not a problem."

There's another pause. It's all I can do not to beg him for details about the meeting, all I can do not to ask him about our kiss, but I am trying to learn patience. After a second he says, "Mothers do not seem to like me."

"It's the circumstances with mine. I'm sure she would if you weren't a pixie." Now it's my turn to sigh. I pull my leg up close to me and fiddle with my slipper. "My father didn't treat her well and—"

"You do not need to explain, Zara."

I stop fiddling and look at him, really look at him. He's still so young. He's handsome as a human. He looks like the kind of guy who would be a hero in a war movie, some sort of captain. He's this weird mix of wounded and confident, kind and bossy. But right now the vibe he's giving out is wounded, and I'm so worried that it isn't just about our mothers, that it isn't even about our kiss, but that it's something more.

I eye Astley. "They didn't just tell you how for free, did they?"

"I did not have to pay them with money." He breathes slow and deep. His knuckles are scraped.

"But you did have to pay them? With what?"

He doesn't answer. He refuses to answer and I doubt I will ever get him to answer, ever get him to tell me what he's done. Something in my heart cracks a little bit, another sliver of pain. "You do so much for me, Astley. I—I don't know how to thank you."

He smiles this sad, sweet smile. "I am aware of that and you do not need to thank me."

I touch his sleeve quickly and then rub my hands together. "So, tell me what we have to do."

After he tells me everything he knows about the ceremony, Astley and I escape out my window again. Someday I hope we can just use the door. He brings me to Issie's house as we discuss the preparations.

The moment we get there I realize that I don't want him to go, that I want him to come inside with me, that I'm scared and it's easier to be surrounded by people that you know have your back.

"I'll wait for you. It will all be ready," he says. His hand touches my cheek for the briefest of seconds. "Be careful."

"You too."

He shoots into the sky before I can thank him again or worry with him or make him wait. So I turn around and I ring the front doorbell. Issie's mom comes to the door. She's a short, hyper woman who dresses in swishy skirts and men's dress socks that are pulled up to her knees. They sometimes fall down at grocery stores, according to Issie. Anyway, she throws the door open, steak knife in hand. "Zara! Come in! Come in! Get out of the cold! Did you see anyone out there? Anyone lurking? I can't believe Betty lets you out alone like this!"

She hustles me into the house, which smells like gingerbread and chocolate cookies.

"I am baking for the holidays," she explains, stashing her knife and brushing flour off of her too-large navy blue cashmere V-neck sweater, which looks like it belongs to Issie's dad. There's an ax by the door. "Issie and Devyn are upstairs in her room—with the door open, I might add, so don't worry! Just go on up."

She shoves a cookie at me. It's chocolate chip and delicious. Nick used to make me cookies.

"It's so good. Thanks!" I say, chomping down.

"Oh, I'm so glad you like it," she says as I slip off my wet shoes and head up the stairs. I've made it up two before she calls my name. I stop, half turn. In a much quieter voice she says, "Do you think Issie is okay?"

I cock my head, feign ignorance. "Why?"

"The past few days, she's barely been talking. She's getting better now, but . . ." Her face is a scrunched-up ball of worry.

"She's upset about all the people who have gone missing," I say, telling a part of the truth. "She's so sensitive and she's so worried about everyone, you know? And she has a hard time being grounded."

"I know, but it's for her own protection." Her lips turn inward the way mine do when I try not to cry. "She's such a good girl."

"She is," I say. "She is made of awesome sauce."

"Awesome sauce . . . Zara White, you are so silly." She slaps her thigh. "You come down if you need another cookie. They have a plate up there, but if you need more . . ."

"Thanks," I say and hustle up the stairs as quickly as I can without being rude—I really like Issie's mom and she's like Issie: nobody should ever be rude to her.

Issie's room is crowded with stuffed animals and lit by one of those electric window candles. It takes me a second to see her and Devyn cuddled on the bed, totally making out.

I clear my throat. They both jump.

"Oh my gosh! I thought you were my mom." Issie smooths her hair. "Sorry."

She makes room for me on the bed by moving some stuffed animals around.

Devyn lifts an eyebrow. "Something happened?"

Issie gasps and clutches his arm. "Not Cassidy? Something hasn't happened to her? Or Callie?"

I shake my head and sit on the cleared-off bed space by Devyn's feet. His socks smell pretty rank actually. I try to focus on the other smells. "No, it's good. I mean, I think it's good. You guys . . . ? I don't know."

Devyn cocks his head slightly. "You have another lead on Valhalla."

"It's not just a lead," I say, and then I gush out all

the information I have: how Astley appealed to the pixie council people, how we need to have one of each species of fae and human there, how I need my friends to help but only if they want to, because I can't possibly put them in danger again—not after what happened with Mrs. Nix.

"Do you really trust him, Zara?" Issie finally asks when I'm done.

I think about all we've been through: Iceland, gunshot wounds, Mrs. Nix, our kiss . . . "I do. If it's another trap, he's not the one setting it."

Devyn is silent, staring out the window. Finally, he turns and says to Issie, his voice crusting over with emotion, "What do you think, Is?"

She sniffs and stands up, clutching a stuffed bunny to her chest. "Nick would never give up on us."

"No," I say, my chest tightening. "He wouldn't."

"Then we don't give up on him, and I honestly think that Mrs. Nix wouldn't want us to give up on him either," she says. "But no dying, Zara. No explosions, no gunshots or injuries or stab wounds. Okay?"

Her lips tremble a little; she's trying so hard to be brave. It's the most words she's said in a long time.

"I'll do my best," I promise her.

I hug her and her bunny as Devyn leans back against the wall, shaking his head. Finally, I can't stand it anymore and ask what's been bothering me since my father died in Iceland. "Do you think it's selfish of me?"

"What?" Devyn asks.

I let go of Issie and cross my arms over my chest. "To keep trying to get Nick back."

"If there's a chance that we can, I think we have a moral obligation to rescue him, not just because he's our friend and not even because he'll help us deal with the pixies, but because he is a person. How can we not try to rescue a person?" Devyn asks honestly. "You're the one who fights for people all around the world. Would you call off a rescue mission for a tortured monk because military personnel might die?"

"No," I say honestly. "But they chose the risk. They know they might die."

"And so do we," Issie says. Her eyes are big and scared but solid tough.

"If you're selfish, then we all are," Devyn says, standing up straight. "Okay?"

When I nod, he reaches out and grabs my hand, shaking it the way he used to shake Nick's, some kind of guy bonding thing. He smiles and says, "Let's go."

$\mathcal{D}$ude, sometimes I think my whole town is a horror movie set. I heard screams in the woods. **#Bedford**, less than 5 seconds ago

We say good-bye to Issie's mom and make up an excuse about going to a study session at the high school, which is allowable under the grounding rules, especially since we're traveling as a group. We grab some cookies and steak knives to go. Once we're out the door there's no time for talking. Danger waits in the trees; I can smell it. I push Devyn and Issie ahead of me and whip out a knife, ready to strike, trying to provide them cover if any bad pixies attack.

"Issie," something whispers from the woods. "Come to me."

"Ignore it. It's not the king."

The whisper comes again. "Issie."

"Leave my girlfriend alone!" Devyn yells, stiffening up as tall as he can. His hands are fists. It's really sweet, actually, but I am in charge here now.

"Get in the car, guys," I order.

"I think being a pixie brings out a previously suppressed

controlling aspect of your personality," Devyn mutters as he crawls into the back of the car.

We head to our prearranged meeting place, the Brown House, which is this old brick Georgian manor built by some log magnate guy back in the early 1800s. It's up on this great sledding hill. There's a museum inside and a trail for running behind it. A couple other cars are here, including Astley's. Relief and nervous excitement flood through me.

Issie parks in the little rectangular dirt parking lot behind a big barn that used to hold horses. The paint peels from the sides.

She's shaking still. "You can't die, Zara."

"I won't."

She keeps nodding. Her fingers squeeze mine. "Zare. It's just— First Nick, then Mrs. Nix, and you all pixified and Betty missing. It's all so much to handle. I'm just human, remember?"

"Adorably human," I correct her. "Strongly and smartly human."

We let go of each other's hands. I open the door just as Astley strides over to us. Glitter sparkles in the snow.

Devyn flies out of the car. He perches on the roof and gives an angry eagle screech. "Devyn, be good," I order.

"Take this sword," Astley says to me, sounding terribly formal and regal. He fastens it on my belt with the giant peace buckle, which just seems wildly inappropriate. "The ceremony will be in the woods."

He starts walking on the snow that's been trampled down by cross-country skiers and dogs and runners like me.

Issie doesn't follow. "Is it safe?" she asks me. "Are there bad pixies here?"

"Not at the moment," Astley answers. "We will protect you with our lives, Issie. I promise you."

Issie looks up at me out of the corner of her eyes and grabs my hand again. Just then Cassidy's car comes screaming into the parking lot. She flings herself out of it and runs to us. Vaulting into Issie and me, she wraps us both in a hug.

"I'm so scared," she says. "Are you scared? Don't answer that."

We walk together following Astley, with Devyn swooping above. We follow him into the woods. The knots in the tree trunks look like wide, stunned eyes blackened with pain. Boulders hunch on the side of the trail, waiting for whatever will happen.

"There is only one way to cross from the realm of man to the realm of the gods. This is called BiForst. It is a bridge made of a rainbow. It is not a pixie," Astley tells us. "We'll be opening it up here during the ceremony. It is hard magic. According to the council, only kings and queens can do it, and only rarely."

"Like your mother," I prompt.

"Yes. She came for her brother, the council said."

"She has a brother?"

"I never knew, but yes. She has a brother. A pixie named Frank. He has other names, but that is the one he currently uses."

We stop walking. Astley's eyes move back and forth, surveying the land as he hustles back to us and takes my other hand. "I know. It is a lot to comprehend. I swear to you I did not know before now. It kills me that he is my uncle, that my mother—that she did all this to you, to us, that they are aligned somehow."

I swallow hard and squeeze his hand. It's so different from Issie's, broad and solid. "It doesn't matter now."

All five of us seem more connected than ever. Issie says, "You can't blame yourself for your relatives. We'd all hate Zara if you could, but we love her. It's okay, Astley. Zara trusts you. Cassidy trusts you. And I trust you. You're one of us now."

For a moment Astley seems like he might break. His lip

wobbles a little and when he speaks his voice is a humble whisper. "Thank you for that, Issie. You really are outstanding."

She smiles and lightens the mood, tugging us along. "Come on. Tell us what else you learned."

"No matter what, do not step on the red. It's fire, an insanely hot fire," Astley commands. He drops my hand and starts long power-striding across the snow again. "And just follow my lead during the ceremony. All of you."

Cass leans in. "I like him, but he's even bossier than Nick."

"I know!" I whisper back. "I didn't think that was possible."

He calls over his shoulder, amusement in his voice, "I can hear you."

Devyn squawks unhappily as we step into a patch of woods surrounded by giant hemlock trees. There are seven other people there. All wear long brown robes with hoods that cover their faces. The sky seems low, heavy, weighed down with snow, touching the tops of the trees. The people stand motionless as we come toward them. I grip Issie's hand fiercely, like I can somehow hold on enough to keep them safe, to make this all go right.

"They look like monks," Issie whispers. "The robes are so brown and I can't see anyone's face."

"Stand here." Astley points to a spot in the middle of the trees. "Issie, please stand near the back with the others."

Issie squeezes my hand. It is one of the hardest things I'll ever do, but I manage to let go of her fingers, and she moves to a position where she makes a circle with the robed people. One of them hands Issie a robe, and when she moves, I can see that it's Becca. Her face glows brightly. The one on the other side of Issie nods as she and Cass put on the robes. He is tall, slim. His ears are slightly pointed, but he looks human. He must be some sort of fae too.

At the perimeter of the woods are my pixies. They step into the light so I can see them. They are tall and short, strong every one. They bow as I glance at them. I want to promise them that we will make it through this and be stronger for it.

"Zara, I need you in the center," Astley reminds me.

I look back over my shoulder at Issie. She's shivering and her eyes are wide open, which is how she looks when she's scared. Devyn perches on a tree branch just above her head. He's a big bird, but he looks so small, dwarfed by the trees and the events. I want to protect them both somehow, but if Mrs. Nix taught me anything, it's that I can never totally protect anyone. Danger can just explode without warning and take us away.

Astley hands me a spear that's longer than my body. "It's iron tipped," he says. "Hold it in your right hand. Let the butt rest on the ground."

We wait. I count my heartbeats. I get to thirty. Astley lifts his arms out in some sort of salute. The others do the same. His eyes get deadly serious. He stands in front of me and starts chanting. "*With this ceremony we position our traveler one footstep nearer to Odin.*"

The robed fae and Issie join hands and move in closer. I shudder nervously. They circle around us, hands clasped, and are chanting words that I can't quite make out, but I don't think it's the same thing that Astley's saying. I look up at Astley. He nods at me like he's trying to be reassuring, but it's not really working. I flash back to Mrs. Nix climbing that silver bridge, exploding. I tucked the charred piece of her sweatshirt I had recovered into the back pocket of my jeans. I am glad she is with me now. Nick's anklet touches my skin. He is here too.

"*One heartbeat nearer to Valhalla,*" Astley chants. "*One march nearer to all that is accepted.*"

The earth seems to shake a little. Glitter swirls up out of his hands and around us. At the same time a funky force-field type thing forms around Astley and me. Opaque and massive, it buffers out the noise, the shiver of the trees, the murmurs of the pixies, the frantic breaths of Is. I cannot believe this. The force field curves around us, reaching high into the sky. A shield.

I catch Issie's eye. She makes herself smile. It's pretty obvious that it's hard for her. She's probably remembering Mrs. Nix too. The glitter swirls around Astley and me. It's like we're in a snow globe, and it's so strange but so beautiful. I reach out my fingers to touch the glitter. There is the faint sound of softness and magic whirling in the air, and Astley's voice, but that is all I can hear.

"And we plait her into fortune," he says, all focused power. Then he starts the chant over. *"With this ceremony we position our traveler one footstep—"*

Something captures his attention and he falters. The swirling glitter slows. I turn my head to look behind me. More pixies have arrived and it's clear from their look of kill and lack of robes that they aren't ours. They thunder out of the woods, rush-run from between the trunks, claws extended, mouths open.

"Issie!" I turn and rush toward her, hitting the translucent dome that's around us. I bounce off. I whirl around. *"Astley!"*

He's chanting fast and furious. His hands bend into a cup shape. His fingers open. He motions for me to do the same.

I shake my head. "Issie! Cassidy!"

An arrow hits one of our pixies. She falls to the ground in a clump. The others grab hands and fill up her space. Another death . . . another death because of me . . . I fold in half, crumpling as a ball of light appears within Astley's hands. His eyes implore me. I straighten again, copy his motions, and the ball is within mine. It's warm and glows gold like the glitter, like him.

"So if our essence is worthy," he shouts as the wind starts to blow. *"If our essence is worthy, allow this traveling queen to reach your mighty halls, open the BiForst Bridge, and let our queen trod to the noble lands."*

The balls of light whirl in our hands as our eyes meet. The balls leave our fingertips, join, then circle each other. I feel a little shallower somehow, like something is missing from deep inside me.

Another one of our pixies falls. A third is trying to fend off an attack without letting go of Cassidy's hand. I can tell from her mouth shape that she is shrieking and screaming, but I can't hear her. Devyn crashes into the bad pixie's face, talons outstretched.

"We have to get out of here and help!" I yell.

Astley whispers no, then looks upward. Pain and worry stud his face. The ball of light breaks through the force field. It is the first time I have ever heard him swear.

The world shakes a little more. Astley yells to be heard above the roar. *"We gather, all of the Shining, to beg of you to open the path to your realm. Let one of us go and seek what she desires. So be it."*

The glitter falls to the ground. The light flashes so that it's completely blinding and then dims. I blink hard, and then all of a sudden there's a freaking rainbow above my head. It's brilliant. There are only three colors, though, and it's about wide enough for an army tank to cross. The red leaps with heat, but the blue and yellow seem fine to touch, if I could get up there. The snow starts melting beneath my feet.

Sweat drops cover Astley's forehead. "This isn't quite good. It's outside the shield."

"Everyone is outside it!" I yell. "We have to help them!"

Astley grabs my arm. "No! You must go! We cannot do this again."

"But Issie, Cassidy, Dev, your people— I can't even get to the rainbow." My insides tear apart. I can't leave them. I can't just run away when they're being attacked.

"It's the shield," he says, rushing to the edge. He places his hands against the energy. He pushes. It gives a little but doesn't hold. "They are keeping it up by chanting."

"Make them not chant!"

"They must think they are protecting us." He shakes his head and then punches the wall. He races along the perimeter in a sort of Captain Kirk command mode. "They have sworn to protect us because I am their king and you are the queen."

"What are you doing?" I ask, chasing after him.

Issie has let go of the hands next to hers. She's grabbed some sort of dagger and is holding it in front of her. Her back is against the force field. A bad pixie is moving toward her. More pixies are scrambling out of the woods.

"Astley!" I yell. "There are more coming! They're all going to die unless they fight!"

"I know," he growls back. He stops and puts his hand on the dome, staring at Amelie.

"Let it down," he commands her. She shakes her head no, and he points above his own head. "The bridge is outside. It is outside the dome. We cannot get to it."

Amelie's eyes narrow. She stops chanting and lets go of the hands she was holding, whisking out a sword from beneath her robe. She strides toward the evil pixies. A tiger emerges from the woods, silent, stalking from behind. My heart leaps to see her—Betty.

As our people drop hands and fight, the protective bubble around us shudders and the world rushes in. Issie stumbles backward and falls. I rush over to her, gather her into my arms.

"Oh man, Zara," she says, trying to get her footing as a pixie heads toward us. "Oh my freaking—"

"It's okay, Is," I lie, grabbing her and pulling her away from the fight. "We'll be okay. Betty's here. Where's Cassidy? And Devyn?"

An arrow flies toward us through the air. Astley appears out of nowhere, snatches it in his free hand, breaks it with his fingers. His voice is a growl. "I will take care of them."

He yanks his sword out of his belt. His face becomes a mask of determination and strength. "Do not falter now, Zara. Many have already died so you can get your wolf back."

He gestures at the crumpled, unmoving bodies of two of his pixies. Fighting heightens all around us. The world seems so much darker than before. It's like my brain is beginning to focus and dread crawls over my skin, because this is when I get it. Darkness exists. Things in the dark exist. I am one of those things. Me. And it isn't always easy to know what is bad or good, or who to trust and believe, but it is always, *always* easy for me to want to protect my friends.

"I can't leave them," I say. "Not even to save Nick. I just can't. They'll die here."

"Zara," Is protests. She trembles because she's so afraid, but she still wants me to go.

"I will keep them safe." Astley's eyes meet mine.

"Evil pixie approaching. Three o'clock!" Issie interrupts.

Astley spins and flash-flies to our right. He doesn't make any noise as his sword detaches the pixie's head from its body.

"Holy— H-h-holy—," Is stutters as I pull her away, tucking her head into my shoulder.

"Don't look," I tell her. "Just don't look."

Astley resheathes his sword; the soldier strides back over to us. He orders, "You are going, Queen."

His hands grab me around the waist, jerking me from Issie, and he throws me up the twenty feet to the beginning of the bridge. He threw me—just like his father threw him. I land on the yellow. The impact makes yellow dust fly up.

"You have to take care of Issie and Cassidy," I yell again as Devyn swoops over Issie, feigning right and left, talons out-stretched as the dark pixies approach. "Astley! Keep them safe! Please . . . please . . ."

Astley nods. I see his claws sharpen beneath the glamour. He glows and stands taller, shoulders back, and in that moment I realize that he is remarkably beautiful. He is the king. My king?

The light pulls at me. There is the sound of brass horns in the distance, coming from the other end of the rainbow.

"Go, Zara!" he yells. His hands readjust on his sword, sheaths it, pulls out his bow. "I will keep them safe. I promise."

I start to go, then stop. "You better! And you have to stay safe too, Astley. You have to be here. No dying. *No dying!* Okay?"

He lets an arrow fly. Something shrieks. "Just come back to us, Queen. Just come back."

"I will!" I say, because, you know, everyone wants to come back to fighting, carnage, fear of death, right?

But I do.

I want to come back and keep them safe.

I nod fiercely. "I'll bring him back. We'll fight with you, I swear. No more tying you to a tree or anything."

He starts to laugh, bends, and gets me my sword. His voice resonates inside my head, but his mouth doesn't move as he says, *You will be a great queen when you come back, you know. And someday you'll love me the way you love your wolf.*

Local churches in Bedford, Maine, are holding a candle-light vigil for the lost teens, despite the advice of local law enforcement, who say that the vigil would be much safer if performed during the daytime hours. —NEWS CHANNEL 8

I run up the bridge fueled by hope, ignoring the worry and the pain in my chest as the sound of fighting echoes beneath me, growing fainter and fainter the farther I go. The muscles in my quads tense and flex and release as I sprint as fast as I can. I've always been a good runner, but this—this is insane. It's like running on a steeply sloping sand beach. Colored dust flies behind me with every footfall.

Yes, I am running on a rainbow and, yes, I am no longer human, but it doesn't matter. All that matters is getting to Nick. A white bird circles in the sky over my head, leading my way as I leave behind the world of humans, leave behind the world of questions and wiggly lines between good and evil, leave behind all the mistakes I've made.

To my left are mounds of earth that look like fairy tombs; to my right is a meadow on a hill where suddenly it is spring. The air is warm and amazing, smelling of lilacs and thawing ground. On top of the hill wait large standing stones like at Stonehenge. They are in a circle reaching toward the sun.

It is so beautiful here. It is nothing like Maine. No naked tree limbs scratch at the sky. No ice beneath my feet. No snow.

I almost want to slow down, stop, try to figure out how the heck any of this could be real, but I can't because the bridge disappears behind me as I run forward. I'm not sure what would happen if I stopped. Maybe I'd just vanish, caught between the world of fae and the world of human. Would I no longer exist? I'm not sure. I'm not sure about anything except that running forward gets me closer to Nick and farther away from the fighting—and from Issie and Astley and everyone. Worry shatters my happy. How can it be spring here, so peaceful and quiet, when they are in the middle of cold, of death, without me?

My calves burn. It feels like I've been running for freaking ever when finally, I can see the end of the rainbow. There's a building. It's golden and glows in the warm sunlight. There are five different layers of thatched roof and three doors and no windows that I can see. There are two higher rooms that seem to grow out of the roof like mini towers.

"This can't be real," I pant. "How can this be real?"

A giant white man explodes out the center door. He carries a horn. He has a Viking-style hat on his head and more horns stick out of the sides above his ears. I think they are ram horns, but honestly, I have no freaking clue.

"*Hold!*" he bellows. "Who are you that cross to the realm of the gods?"

Oh my gosh. Did he just say "hold"? Who says "hold"? Who wears Viking hats? And his teeth? His teeth are gold, like he's gone all rap star and had them capped with precious metal. I stop in front of him, panting, hands on my hips.

"Zara."

I try to say it as bravely as I can. I try to act like all of this is perfectly normal, because if I don't? I will start totally freaking out.

He eyes me and lowers his voice. "I am Heimdall, protector of the gods, guarder of Asgard and Valhalla."

I reach out my hand, hoping my instinct to shake is right and won't make him cut it off with the giant sword sheathed to his hip. "Hello."

His lips edge up a bit. His giant eyebrows rise up toward his hairline. He grabs my hand in his fingers and squeezes. "Pixie?"

I nod. I notice a bunch of sheep grazing by the hall just to my left. They form a perfect circle and are perfectly clean. They are all too ideal, really. My heart skips a beat.

"Queen?" he asks.

"Only just recently," I explain, hoping I don't look as bewildered as I feel.

This time he does smile for real. "I can hear that in your heartbeat and smell it on your breath. Your newness is obvious, Zara White, Pixie Queen."

He lets go of my hand. Resisting the urge to rub my fingers back to life, I take in the scenery. Beyond his hall, woods wait on gently sloping planes. The trees are enormous Christmas trees. Pinecones as big as my head dangle from the limbs. Birds twitter in the air. The lawn I stand on rolls along like a picture-perfect golf course. Giant hydrangea bushes blossom around the foundation of the hall, huge flowers bursting into the air. It's beautiful and magical.

"How do you know my last name?" I ask, eyeing him. He is enormous and just exudes power, way more power than Astley and Nick have ever emanated. His muscles are almost comic book in size, or like a professional wrestler.

"I am Heimdall. I heard your name on the wind. I can hear for a hundred miles." He says this all matter-of-factly, not sounding boastful at all. He shifts his weight on his far-apart feet. He unsheathes his giant sword. It glints in the air. It's nothing like any sword I have ever seen before. It curves and the blade is almost triple, with two arched edges echoing the original blade. "This is my sword. Its name means 'man's head.'"

I don't say anything. I realize I'm shaking. I step back and bump into a peacock. It squawks angrily at me.

"Tell me, Zara White, new pixie queen, former human, why have you come to our realm?" His voice echoes, and even my skin can feel the power beneath each syllable.

"I have an urgent mission," I say, and hit myself in the head with my hand. *Urgent mission?* I sound like a character on a girl-power spy show on a TV channel for little kids.

"Urgent mission?" he asks without any trace of mocking or sarcasm. His expression becomes even more Viking-like, wary and full of pride. He raises his sword.

I lace my hands together, trying to look as meek and unthreatening as possible, and tell him. I don't know why. I just tell him. "Sort of. My boyfriend was taken by this Valkyrie thing named Thruth, and I need him back. And I just left my friends fighting a battle and I want to hurry. No offense. I mean, it's nice talking to you and everything . . ."

"True love's quest?" He turns his head to his side and smiles up at the sun.

"I guess. Yeah. I mean . . . It sounds corny when you say it like that, but we all love him more than anything and we need him back home. He's our warrior, really. He keeps us safe."

Something rustles from under a bush. A bunny hops along

the edge of the lawn right by the hall. Its gray tail bobs up and down.

Heimdall scrutinizes my face and then leans against the building. His muscles ripple like waves with even the smallest movements. He lowers his sword arm and leans the sword against the tree bark. "There are other warriors, yes?"

"Yes, but—" Something in my chest hitches. "He's Nick."

"And there's only one Nick?" he asks kindly.

I nod hard my agreement because I can't trust my voice.

"Do you vow that you are not a minion of the Frost Giants or their like, that you do not enter Asgard in an attempt to do harm to Odin or the rest of us old gods?" His voice booms. He towers above me, with shoulders that are easily three times as big as mine. He leans forward so that his nose is an inch away from mine.

"I promise," I say.

He cocks his head. His lips part. His teeth? They gleam. "Are your promises good, Zara White, new queen of pixies?"

"Yes," I whisper. "I hope they are. I promised Nick I would take care of him. He didn't actually hear me because he was unconscious at the time, but—"

His voice stops my sentence as he stands up straight, hands on his hips. "You will have to convince Odin, young queen, but they keep the pixie warriors at Freya's, and that is to the—"

"Oh, he's not a pixie. He's a wolf," I interrupt.

Those massive hairy eyebrows rise up again. "Oh. A pixie and a were in love." Something shifts again in his eyes and his whole body changes. He suddenly seems to respect me more. A peacock struts across the lawn, followed by three little gray peahens.

"Is that—" I stop myself midquestion. Maybe I don't want to know.

"Impossible? It is unusual." He reaches out a hand and

ruffles up my hair. I resist the urge to woof like a puppy. "But love makes all possible."

My stomach settles a little. It's still possible.

"Still, it seems your heart is divided, Zara. Is there another?"

My mouth opens, but no words come out.

"No matter . . . No matter . . . Would you like to come inside? Are you hungry? You must be—I have been watching you run." He smiles at me. His smile is dazzling and congenial. The air here is warm, so I pull off my jacket and tie it around my waist. Sweat has wet the back of my neck. My throat is parched and longs for water.

"I'm starving, but I really have to go. I'm sorry. I mean, if I am allowed to go." I look up the hill. There are other amber-colored halls beyond us. The sunlight makes rainbows that gleam off the windows, off his sword, off everything. Birds sing in the distance. Trees in full bloom are scattered along the landscape. Everything looks so inviting. I rub my hands along my hair and fix my ponytail.

"I believe your quest is worthy, Zara White, new queen of pixies." He opens his arms. "It is love which made all this. War which protects it. With love comes responsibility and possibility, fear and hope, quests and suffering. I am not talking merely of romantic love, but the love of warriors and friends and family. You understand this?"

"I think so." I swallow hard. "And me getting him back? And bringing him home? Do you think that is possible?"

"You will have to convince Odin," he says. His hand stops rustling and rests simply on my head. "Odin can be a hard man to convince, but only sometimes, and your wolf must want to return. Many come here and have no desire to go back to the realm of man."

"It's so beautiful and peaceful it's easy to see why," I say.

"Your sigh smells like sorrow." He takes his hand off my head and puts it beneath my chin so I lift my head up. Our eyes meet. He reminds me of Santa Claus, all *ho-ho-ho* kindness, only with no pillow belly and gold teeth instead of cookie breath.

"I'm a little afraid," I admit.

"All warriors are afraid."

The peacock twitters and spreads his tail feathers, which is what they do when they want to mate. The peahen activity gets a little frantic. They start pacing back and forth in little movements, changing directions every few seconds.

Heimdall laughs, amused at the birds, I think, and says, "You are not like the peahen."

"I'm not?"

"No. You know where you need to go." He points to the left at a large hall that peeks out above the canopy of lush green trees. "You have a direction. Odin's hall, Valhalla. It is a quick ride. I shall get a horse. Have you ridden before?"

"A little. At camp."

"An easy mare then." He whistles and a golden horse trots from around the edge of the building.

"She's so beautiful." I sigh the words out, press my hand against the horse's soft, strong flank.

"Yes, she is." He laughs again and puts his hands out for me to step up. I could probably just jump, now that I'm all super pixie, but I take the hand up. The horse doesn't even stir as I fix my sword and make myself comfortable. He rubs his hand across her side and says appreciatively, "Good girl."

I bite my lip.

"You are very nice," I say, because he is. Now that I'm on the horse, I'm more at his level. I have to resist the urge to look away.

Who am I to be talking to him? Who am I to be in this crazy, weird place? I clear my throat. "Thank you. Do you think . . . ?"

His hand slides across the horse's flank and he simply smiles.

"I owe you," I say quietly, but he hears me.

He taps the horse with his hand. There are scars crisscrossing the skin. "Then fight on our side when I blow my horn and the war comes."

War.

"I promise."

"Good!" Heimdall laughs. "And go get your wolf, Queen. Bring him home."

Bedford police responded to reports of screaming at the Brown House tonight. Eyewitnesses stated there were howls and moans, shrill inhuman cries, and a giant rainbow that reached into the sky. While police do say that evidence in the area pointed to a crime, no bodies or body parts were found. They are investigating. —NEWS CHANNEL 8

Philophobia is the fear of being in love. I've never had this fear, not really, but right now I am scared not only of failing to get Nick out of here, but also that he might not want to leave, might not want to come home with me, not want to love me anymore because I'm no longer Human Zara. Human Zara wouldn't even have been able to be here. I doubt Human Zara would have ever kissed Astley a second time. It's got me wondering if I'm even the same soul that Nick used to love. I already know people can still love me. Issie does. Betty does. And I also know that some people can't see beyond the pixie, people like my mom. Which will Nick be?

I keep blinking as I ride through the woods. It's so different from home. The trees are lush and in full bloom. Everything feels enchanted and full of possibility. The air is sweet with the smell of growth and moisture and warmth. The horse exudes a happy heat as she gallops through the spruce and pine trees. Every one of them looks like a Christmas tree waiting to happen.

I am heading to Nick.

I am heading to Nick!

My little flame of hope has become an action. My little want might become a have. Everything inside of me shivers in a good way, grows like a bunch of secret black-capped mushrooms in a fern grove. I can feel all my darkest worries fade away and become something cool, something real, something good.

I may be a pixie now, but I can still feel love and hope. I can still worry and care. I was so afraid that I would lose those things I think of as "human" that I wouldn't even let myself contemplate it before I changed. I just rushed in and did it. I won't regret my decision no matter the consequences, not if I can get Nick back. I won't regret it at all, not even if it means my own mother can't bear to look at me.

The thought of Astley and all my friends and my pixies fighting back behind the Brown House worries my stomach, erodes my happiness. So I turn my face up toward the sunlight shafting through the green tree leaves. I focus on remembering Nick's face, its angles and crinkles.

Something in the woods calls out a low hoot. Another hoot answers in return. It's meant to sound like an animal, but it is not an animal. Beside us, maybe two hundred feet to our left but on a parallel course, are men running through the trees. They wear some sort of brown pants, no shirts, helmets that obscure their facial features. Their chests are broad and full of muscles. They remind me of those evil Orcs running through the *Lord of the Rings* movies, pounding strength and terror in each footfall.

"I hope they are on our side," I murmur and put my heels into the horse, pushing her faster. "Can we hurry?"

The horse and I break out of the woods and into a clearing.

She stops. This building is even bigger than Heimdall's. It's tall and the roof looks as if it's made of shields. The metal glints in the sun. The door is this massive, heavy timber-framed monstrosity covered in hammered metal. It looks like it would take ten men to open it.

My fear is not a phobia I can name. I don't know how to describe it even. What if I repel Nick now? If he doesn't even want to see me?

There is a thundering noise to the right of me. I turn the horse to face whatever it is and watch as the warrior men pound out of the woods, muscles rippling with strength and power. They are heading right for me.

"Crud," I curse out, trying to figure out how to back up a horse who doesn't seem to be freaking out at all like I am. She just holds steady, waiting.

They run in two lines, which I didn't realize before. Most of their hair is plaited and hangs down. They have boots on and no weapons, which is good news. I pull out my sword and hold it in front of me, but there's no way I could possibly battle them. No way at all. So I sheath it again, just as the men in the front reach us. I press my lips together, waiting for the inevitable words of threat, the hands yanking me off the horse, the questions about what I'm doing here, but none of this happens. The men divide around the horse, rush forward and past me. They smell of sweat and wood smoke and beer. They don't make eye contact, don't say a single word.

I pivot the horse around once I have enough room to move her, which isn't until the last men are past us, and that's when I see them entering the hall. They thunder inside and the door slams shut behind them. I can't believe it.

"I am an idiot," I tell the horse. "We could have slipped right in there with them."

She neighs and I swear there's a hint of amusement in that horsey neigh.

"I guess I have to knock, huh?"

I hop off her back, keeping a hand on her side. Her fur is so warm and rough and comforting. My old wound tweaks a little bit from the movement, but not too terribly much. I've healed so quickly. The horse bumps her muzzle into my shoulder and huffs out her nostrils. I reach up and scratch her.

"Thank you," I murmur. "I suppose you can't go inside with me?"

She tosses her head back. Her eyes roll so that whites appear. Then she trots off without even saying good-bye. She breaks into a gallop, enters the woods, and is gone. It's just me now.

I knock.

There's the sound of rope and pulley working together as the door slowly opens. There's no sign of the warriors at all. A relatively small hunched-over man dressed like Heimdall, only with dirtier clothes, steps to the center of the doorway and nods at me. A broach near the base of his neck features the image of a wolf, which hitches my breath.

"Hello," I manage to say.

"Hello." He nods again and waits.

"I'm looking for Nick Colt," I explain.

"The warrior recovers in a room on the western corridor." He points to the left.

The warrior recovers.

"The warrior recovers" means he is alive. He is alive and this all . . . this all wasn't for nothing.

He recovers.

A clasping knife seems to be working its way through my insides, cleaning them out, taking away the dead, dried-up pieces.

"H-how—how do I get there?" I ask.

The door guard's face is as pale as Betty's winter feet. He shakes his head as if he's disgusted by my lack of motion, by the look of crazy that I know must be plastered on my face. His voice is annoyed as he says, "Go through the door at the far end of the hall. His room is the last."

I wait, expecting more, like maybe I have to pass a test or a trial or something.

He waits too. He has two large swords on either side of his belt. People just wear swords here? Does he want to cleave me in half?

"Um, I can just go?" I ask. My voice squeaks. "You don't need to know who I am?"

"You can just go, Zara," he says much more casually, as if he's given up pretending to be formal. "Odin has been expecting your arrival."

"Okay." I hop on my toes and then enter the hall cautiously. "Thanks."

I enter a room that's built of giant stone blocks with tall, thick pillars that support the roof. The pillars look like they're made of the biggest trees, the kind that do not exist anymore. Giant spears line the walls like bamboo shutters. There are different levels of stone blocks all set so that each level is offset from the next, forming a shallow shelf. These shelves are lined with white, flesh-bare human skulls.

It is shudder worthy. I race through it as quickly as I can. My shoes echo on the wooden floor. I rush by long wooden tables and toward the door. It leads to a hallway. The hallway is long and dark. There are closed wooden doors on the sides. Nick is behind one of these doors! I start full-out running. There's a door cracked open at the end. I stop outside it.

"Breathe," I tell myself. "Breathe."

But it's hard to breathe. It's hard to think. Nick is there, my Nick, behind the wall, in that room. Emotion threatens to explode inside me. I hiccup and then I reach out to push open the door.

How many people do we have to lose before this stops?" one protestor outside Bedford City Hall asked this morning. "Someone has declared war on the youth of Bedford, and it's about time we take up arms and strike back."
—CNNS NIGHTLY NEWS BREAK

My hand spreads across the wood of the door, small and pale. I put a little weight into the push. There's a motion behind me. A clawed, long-fingered hand grabs my wrist and snatches it away. I whirl around, yanking my hand free.

It's Thruth, the Valkyrie, who has shown up at the door, all stealthy and beautiful in her scary way. She motions for me to be quiet and yanks me forward.

"What are you doing?" I growl.

"You are not to see him now," she says.

"Like hell I'm not."

She doesn't let go of my wrist and she's so much stronger than anyone I've ever met, stronger than Nick or Betty even. "If you wish to see the wolf, you must obey the rules of this land."

Frustration cuts a hole inside my stomach, but I follow her a few paces down the hallway. The moment she lets go of my wrist, my hand goes to the sword on my hip. I know she can outfight me, but I won't make it easy for her.

"He's granted you an audience," she whispers, fast-walking down the hallway back in the direction of the big room. "He is too kind, the kindest of all the gods."

It's pretty obvious from her grumpy face and stick-straight body language that she is not cool with his decision. She's no longer in her warrior garb; instead wearing this Viking-style women's outfit, a long skirt, a cape-type thing attached with clamps that hang right above the center of her breasts. Her wings must be folded and hidden beneath the cloak. She says nothing else as we make record time down the corridor, and then she steps into the entrance hall. It's full of warriors, men and women with crushed metal armbands and bulging muscles. They are wearing these bright-colored ornate jackets over hose. It wasn't what I was expecting. Their buttons glint and reflect the colors of the fires in the big hearths. I stop walking and just stare for a second.

"Up there," she says, gesturing toward the head table. A lanky-looking man flutters his gray cloak over his shoulder. A staff rests on the wall behind him. A cloth patch hides one of his eyes. He waves for me to come to him.

I cut a path through the tables. The warriors pause in their eating and are silent as I pass. I get to the table and quickly salute him the way Astley taught me.

"Odin," I say. "Thank you for your audience. It is gracious of you."

"How could I not grant an audience to one who has sacrificed so much?" His voice is a deep, kind rumble. He reminds me of Gandalf and Dumbledore and all the wizards in all the books my dad read to me when I was a kid. His eye sparkles.

I can feel the stares of the curious taking in my clothes, my sword, everything. A dark-skinned man smiles at me and nods just a bit. He sits at one of the many tables. Everybody begins eating again, helping themselves to the food and drink, reaching over one another like some big happy family. Manners don't seem to be very important either. I try to ignore their stares and focus just on Odin. My knees, I am ashamed to say, shake, but I can't back down now. Nick is just down the hall, just behind the door, just barely out of my reach. I clear my throat, meet Odin's eye.

He does not blink and asks, "You are here to get your warrior?"

"Yes." I look around again. Everyone is listening. *Focus.* I have to focus. "He is needed in Bedford."

I almost say "on Earth," but we're still on Earth too, aren't we? I don't know.

"Make your case, Zara, new queen of the pixies," he orders.

For a second I am more confused. Make my case? "Oh, you mean tell you why Nick should be released?"

"His role here is vital," a large man yells. "To fight here with us for Odin is to fight for the most lofty of causes, the most vicious of battles, the most valiant of all claims, the most glorious of all—" He seems to lose his train of thought, because he abruptly cuts himself off and then starts again, glaring at me. "You would take him away from his rightful place as a warrior of Odin for a paltry thing such as love?"

"Erik, enough," another man growls. "Let the female speak."

Great. I'm "the female" now. Odin nods at me.

"Nick Colt belongs in Bedford because he is too young to be here," I start.

"Ha! I am four years younger," one warrior bellows.

Odin raises his hand for silence and I begin again, flinching. "He belongs in Bedford because Bedford is weak without him. He is our leader and we face a terrible battle with a band of rogue pixies who are attacking humans."

"Is this true?" the man next to Odin asks. "If so, why does not the pixie council stop this?"

"They are compromised. Traitors in their midst," Odin explains, like this is some everyday occurrence. "They have charged the young king Astley to try to hold peace for that region, first because the other king had been too weakened and compromised, but now he is no more."

The man next to him raises an eyebrow, shakes his head, and downs some ale out of his large silver cup. "That makes no sense. One so young . . ."

I rub my hands against my legs and start again. "The pixie king charged with keeping peace is having difficulties. There are traitors within our own realm."

People begin grumbling.

I continue on. "But it is more than that. Nick is the leader of the non-pixies. We look up to him and he gives everything he can to protect the humans there, and the other weres. He has sacrificed his time, even his life, but we are losing without him. There are murders. There are missing children. The entire world is starting to notice, and Nick—" I hiccup with emotion but fight through it. "We need him. I can't lose him. The world can't lose him . . . not yet."

"Your plea is well thought out, Zara of the Birch and Stars, Zara of the White, but Nicholas Colt is not the leader," Odin pronounces. "You are."

I am?

Blood rushes to my head. The smell of roasted meat overwhelms me suddenly.

"But—but—," I protest, and scramble for words that make sense and pretty much fail. "But I'm not even a good fighter."

"Being a leader is not always about being a fighter," Odin says. "A leader inspires and pulls together. A leader's actions transition her people's goals, their wants and dreams, into reality. A leader entices her people to do the right or the wrong thing. *You* are the leader."

The hall is silent. Thruth leans against a far wall, arms across her chest, glowering at me. I glance over the entire crowd of men, trying to look brave and tough and queenly despite a tear that's escaped, dripping out the corner of my eye.

I am a leader. Me.

Thruth harrumphs in the corner as a large hand wraps itself around mine. It is Odin. He pulls me a step closer to him and says, "In order to win back the wolf, you must defeat the one who sent him here."

It takes a second for the words to sink in.

I gasp once I get it. "That pixie king?"

"Beliel." Odin says the name and his face becomes infinitely weary. He drops my hand. "Also known as Frank."

The crowd erupts. I think some people are placing bets. Others are saying things like how unfair it is to put such a puny thing (me) against such a monster (Frank, aka Beliel, also known as Astley's uncle).

"I am not a good fighter," I try to explain again, fingering the edge of my shirt. "I mean, I am really bad at fighting, not as bad as my friend Issie, who is possibly the least fightery person in the world. I mean, I'm getting better, but still . . . I mean— Oh, I'm sorry. I'm babbling."

Odin smiles slightly. He closes his eye for a moment, as if my begging is too much, and then says, "He's already here. We fetched him when Heimdall saw you coming."

At least he is not at the fight in the clearing, but still . . . "You knew?"

"We knew that you would not want to return home without your warrior, so, yes, we knew." He smiles softly. "We are gods after all."

I follow his gaze to Frank, who is standing in the back of the room. He's wearing this ridiculous red outfit. Red leather pants with matching jacket is just not cool unless you're a 1980s pop star. Especially when it comes to the too-tight pants. A giant man with a bright auburn beard and muscles that would make any professional wrestler jealous holds Frank by the arm.

"Thor," Odin says, "would you mind bringing our visitor a bit closer?"

They walk through the tables. Many of the warriors—pixie, were, elf, and fairy—seem to hiss and recoil as the pixie king walks by.

"They all want to attack him. We don't fancy evil in here," Odin explains to me. "But it's necessary."

Beliel or Frank or whatever walks up to us. Thor lets go of the pixie's arm and looks at his own hand.

"I feel like I could drink four kegs of ale," Thor says to me and then turns to Odin. "Or just have a nice beheading." He laughs with a hearty *ho-ho-ho*. There is a piece of fuzz in his beard. I thought gods would have immaculate beards. His good mood seems to shift and his eyes grow softer. He adds, "Good luck, warrior queen. Heimdall sends you luck as well."

It takes me a second to realize that when he said "warrior queen," he meant me. I nod and say, "Thank you, Thor."

Beliel lifts an eyebrow. Just that movement seems deadly.

"You will fight with swords," Odin says.

Swords?

Fight?

"You can't be serious," I say, moving backward. This is the guy who killed Nick. This is the guy who wounded my father. I am so bad at swords. "I can't fight with swords."

Odin's hands spread out flat on the table, framing his plate. His eye does not waver. "I am indeed serious. I am also sorry. Are you sure you want to do this, Zara White, queen of pixies, creator of alliances?"

If I don't, then Nick has to stay here. There's no choice.

"Yes." My voice is hard and strong and confident.

Beliel laughs and actually rubs his hands together.

"Fun," he snarls. I glare at him and he laughs. "Oh . . . scared . . ."

The warriors begin to mutter and talk. It becomes a massive roar in two seconds. Still, I can pick out individual words and sentences in the din.

"She won't last thirty seconds."

"One minute tops."

"I don't think I want to witness this. It is not sport."

Odin raises his hand. Everyone is instantly quiet.

"Move the tables," he orders.

Giant men and a few women leap up and move the tables to the sides. The tables look like they weigh two hundred pounds apiece, but they make easy work of it. Some Valkyries roll out a red mat on the open area. Then the warriors tip the long wooden tables on their sides, making the center matted area more like a pen.

Nerves clench up in my stomach. I am glad Nick is not here. I wouldn't want him to see me get trounced or witness me screwing up his one chance to get back home. No, I will not get trounced. I do not have the luxury of being trounced.

I glance at the pixie king. He smiles. I finally understand the meaning of the expression "wicked grin." It grows larger as Thor tosses him a blade. He catches it in his hand by instinct, it seems, because his eyes never stop staring at me.

"Do you need one or do you want to use your own?" Thor asks.

"My own," I answer.

This gets appreciative muttering. I hope that means I've chosen correctly. I unsheathe my sword, feel the weight of it in my hand. It makes me think of Astley, which braves me up a bit. We step inside the matted area. I'm wondering if this is a fight to the death or not. My head is full of questions. How do I attack the guy who overcame Nick? What kind of chance do I honestly have here?

The pixie king silently nods at me.

I silently nod back.

"You may begin," Odin announces. "Valiant fighting to both."

The pixie king bows and immediately rushes toward me. I wince and duck. The sword soars through the space where my head was a second ago. Crud. He's coming at me again. I roll. A split second later the sword slams into the floor. The entire hall reverberates from the blow. I was just there. He barely missed.

I am still rolling, clutching my sword to my chest. He comes after me. His foot lands on my chest.

"You're not making this much fun, princess," he hisses. The weight of his boot pushes the air out of my rib cage.

"It's *queen* now, thank you," I grunt back.

"You fight like a human."

"And that's an insult, right?"

He grinds the boot in a little deeper. "Right."

For a second neither of us moves. I swear he's gloating.

Someone in the audience yells, "Do not torment her. Get it done and be quick."

I guess that's a supportive comment. Maybe?

He leans closer. That wicked grin spreads further. He lets his glamour go. He is all blue and wildness.

"The goody-goody king has turned you, but he has not achieved his full power, nor have you." He says this low enough that I'm pretty sure I am the only one who can hear it.

"And you know this how?" I try not to get embarrassed, and act tough instead. Only problem? I'm no good at acting.

His nostrils flare. "I can smell it. That means you can still be taken, that your full power can be taken by another."

I get what he means. And I do not like it. My fear, all my fear, suddenly hardens and morphs into something totally different: anger. It burns through my pixie blood. It pulls its way into my organs, feeding me. Anger. Passion. This—this monster pixie man—this so-called king is the one who let my father's pixies loose to ravage our town, the one who killed Nick, the one whose people caused the death of that entire busload of Sumner students, the one whose people might be killing Issie and Devyn and Astley and Cassidy right now.

I smile at him, all Southern charm and sweetness.

His weight shifts. I use his split-second of confusion to thrust my hips up and out. My legs bend so I can use my feet to push up off the ground. The power of it sends him stumbling back.

The crowd roars its approval.

I whirl around, thrust my sword at him. I nick him in the arm. Blood pours out, dark and foreign. It's my blood too, but it's not. We may both be pixies, but we are different, totally different.

"You talk too much," I say. "Why do the bad guys always talk too much?"

"Because we like to prolong the win," he says, slashing his sword toward me. "It's sexier that way."

"Point to remember," I say, "bad guys are never sexy."

He is so much more skilled than I am. He attacks low with a double thrust, but I leap high, turn in midair, and land behind him.

"Nice," he says, whipping around to meet my sword blow with his own. "But not good enough. You're never quite good enough, are you, princess? Always trying to save people—your stepfather, your wolf—but never quite doing it."

"Well, it seems like you aren't either," I huff out, trying to catch my breath. "You tried to kill Astley and me *how* many times? But you keep failing and failing and failing."

"Not this time."

He increases the speed of his attack. His sword flies high and fast. It is all I can do to parry it. I move backward from the force. I have to super-react to every move while he looks as calm as all get-out. It's like he barely has to use his muscles to make the big sword thrust and slash. And me? I am a suck-a-saurus.

A voice fills my brain.

Fly.

It's Astley's voice. It's Astley's voice right in the middle of my brain.

Up.

It's more than his voice, though. It's like his essence, his power is right here. I can feel it bolding up my muscles, my brain, my heart.

Fly up.

Fly up? What is he talking about? I can't fly. Still, I take a risk.

I don't know what else to do. I jump. My free hand grabs the banner that dangles from the ceiling. It doesn't rip. It holds my weight. The warriors laugh below me. Frank/Beliel joins them. He pauses for a second, totally cocky, his free hand resting on his hip.

"Do you forget I am a king? I fly too!" he boasts and leaps into the air. His laughter turns into a snarl and the point of his sword plunges just above my left collarbone. As it twists I feel my flesh open, feel the blood flow out of me. I thrust my own sword up, and his sword rips up and leaves my body. I let go of the banner and drop.

Great idea there, Astley.

Landing in a crouch, I avoid two blows to the left. My gold blade flickers between us. Then I remember what Nick always told Issie and me: "Strike with your feet." I swipe my leg beneath him. His face makes a surprised O and he topples down, dropping his sword. I lunge for him. My body slams into his. I use my knees to keep his arms down. My sword blade thrusts against his neck, but I do not pierce the skin.

I have him. One sharp move from me and his jugular will be severed.

"I defeat you," I hiss. I don't even recognize my voice. It is hard and low and sounds more like Astley than me.

"Then kill me," he snarls back. Sweat glistens on his forehead. His voice is brave but his eyes fill with fear.

My hand twitches. He tries to buck away, but I'm ready for it. He doesn't get anywhere and my sword lightly presses his neck. It's just enough to make tiny beads of blood appear on his awful skin.

I ignore him and yell up to Odin and Thor, "Do I win?"

"Damn straight!" Thor yells, sounding more like a surfer than a god. He pounds over to us and snatches up Beliel's sword. "You may arise," he says to me.

I know I should, but something in me doesn't want to. Something in me actually wants to kill the pixie underneath me. I swallow that something down. It is like bile. It burns.

Beliel hisses at me. I shift my weight away, take my sword from his throat, but keep it pointed.

"We have it from here, warrior," Thor says. Three other men grab Beliel and yank him out of the hall, through the open door, and into the springtime air. The others start stomping their feet on the floor and clapping. The entire hall shakes from the vibrations and the sudden loud warrior-man cheers. I blush. They are cheering for me.

Trying to catch my breath, I stand up straight and face Odin. He smiles down upon me. Astley is next to him. I can't catch my breath at all. He looks so alive and so beautiful. But his face . . . I can't read his face. Where did he come from?

"Do I win?" I ask Odin. I know what Thor said, but Odin is the decider here.

"You win." His one eye blinks. "You win, Zara, Queen of the Star Pixies. You win and you win with honor."

It's all I can do not to jump up and down and scream. My eyes meet Astley's eyes. He smiles and everything in my body explodes in a burst of happy. Without thinking about it, I leap over the table and into his arms.

The warriors start whistling and banging the table, the strength of their fists thundering their approval and applause.

"You are amazing," Astley yells into my ear.

I wrap my arms around him and hug him back. "You were in my head. I could hear you, and your support made me stronger, Astley. I'm so glad you're here."

He starts laughing. "I was so worried, but I knew it. I knew you could do it!"

I lean away to study his face. "Wait. How are you here?"

"Odin had them bring me when they brought Frank."

I break away. "The battle? Issie and Cassidy and Dev? Our pixies?"

"We won, mostly thanks to your grandmother. Your friends and our pixies are safe," he says as he separates from me even more. We are an arm's length apart and the distance feels like a cavern. "Now go get your wolf, Zara. I will be waiting for you in Bedford when you return."

High school officials report that all after-school activities have been canceled pending further notice. In addition, the town's curfew has been changed from dusk to three p.m.
—NEWS CHANNEL 8

The warriors insist on dressing my wound and finally tell me I can visit Nick. As I stand up to go, Astley waves good-bye. I mouth *Thank you* and rush down the hall and this time I don't hesitate—I throw open the door. The light coming out of the room is bright, clean. It seems otherworldly and not like the rest of the rugged hall at all. I peer inside. There's just a bed with solid wood posters and white, white sheets. There's a body in the bed. My stomach clenches. A body.

"Nick?" I whisper.

He sits up. His eyes squint like he's just woken up and is trying to focus. I remember that squint from when he woke up at Betty's, groggy and sleep brained on the couch. Everything inside me stops the moment I see him. There's stubble all over his cheeks. His eyes widen.

It *is* him. He exists and moves and breathes and lives. He lives. His eyebrows are so beautifully messy and big and his eyes are open and he's breathing and . . . I swear I can taste my happiness. This can't be, but it is. He's here. He really is.

I take a step into the room and get ready to vault myself into his arms. "Nick!"

"Zara?" His voice sounds strong. It sounds alive and real. *He* is alive and real.

My voice explodes in happiness. "Nick!"

He leaps up out of the bed growling and lands a few feet in front of me, massive and angry. The room suddenly seems much darker than it did a moment ago.

"Someone has . . . has *turned* you," he roars. "Who? Was it the same guy who killed me?"

I crawl backward, stagger to the doorway. Moss crawls over my heart, sinking its tiny tendrils into me. I knew it—I knew he'd hate me. His face is lined with anger and maybe age. He looks older and angry and alive, really and truly alive.

"You aren't dead," I sputter. Tears threaten to leave my eyes. "So he didn't kill you?"

"He did kill me. They brought me back," he corrects. He tilts his head. His hands reach for me and then clench into fists, as if touching me is too horrible to imagine. He jerks them back to his sides. "I swear, Zara, I'll avenge you. I'll find some way to make this right. Maybe there's a way to reverse it. Maybe Devyn's parents can—"

I hold out my hand as he steps closer. "It was my decision."

He stops. His face twists. He pivots away and stands by a massive window. He leans forward, hands outstretched on the cold wood sill. His shoulders shake with emotion. "What?"

"I chose to turn." My words are quiet knife wounds to his heart. I know that, but I can't change it.

"What are you saying? What . . . ?" His hands go into his hair, rubbing it into crazy spikes.

"Our lives are bigger now," I try to explain as my heart breaks. "We have responsibilities to protect people, to protect each other."

"Zara? What . . . what are you talking about? We always have," he insists. "That doesn't mean you had to change. What the hell have you done?"

"But now I can help for real. Now that I've become a pixie—"

He shudders when I say the word, but I keep talking. "I'm much stronger; I can do so much more now. I couldn't even get here, couldn't come bring you back, if I stayed human. I could only come if I was fae." And a queen, but I don't say that.

He whirls around. "Then you should have stayed there. You should have stayed human."

"Without you?" My stomach twists. I press my hand into it. My voice is a plea. "I had to find you. We need you. Issie and Devyn and—everyone. We need you. It's gone crazy. There are two other kings around; my dad's dead. The town is in total chaos. There are FBI agents there. More than twenty people are gone."

"So you need me to fight." He snorts. "That's why they want me here too. Because I'm supposedly such a great warrior."

"You are."

"If I was, I wouldn't have died, would I? If I was, I wouldn't be here and you wouldn't have turned pixie to save me. I'd be back in Bedford protecting you from them, and now—ah—now you are one of them." He cringes and backs up against the wall, his arms wrapping around his trunk. "Oh God, Zara . . . I can't believe you did this. You aren't even human anymore. You aren't you."

"I am me. I am still me." I step toward him. My voice is a quiet want. "I did it for you."

He shakes his head and closes his eyes.

I give up. I rush over to him and take his forearms in my hands and try to pull them down so I can reach in and hug him, press my head against his chest like I always used to when I was human. He cringes again.

"I. Am. Still. Zara," I insist. I wrap my arms around him, press as close to him as I can. "Please, *please*, believe me."

He tightens up, but he doesn't push me away. Every fear I've ever had is nothing—nothing—compared to this. This horror of him not loving me, of not hugging me back when I hug him, of not wanting me near him.

"It doesn't matter," I whisper.

After a second he goes, "What?"

I don't answer.

"What doesn't matter, Zara?" he asks.

"That you don't love me. That you hate me now. What matters is that you can come back home. You hating me is just—it's just— I can be okay with that as long as you are there." I gasp out the words and let go of him, rush-turning away, but he grabs me by the arms and pulls me back to him.

His deep brown eyes stare into mine. His lips move. "I love you."

"What?"

I don't think I got it.

"I still love you, Amnesty," he says. He swallows hard. "I love you so much. It just—it just kills me that you changed to save me. I don't know . . ."

For a moment I cannot speak. Wiping my cheeks dry, I try to push the feelings of hurt out of me, try to be the leader I'm supposed to be, and say, "I'm taking you home with me."

A woman's voice comes from the doorway. "Like Loki you are."

Nick stiffens and I turn around, even though I recognize the voice. Thruth, the Valkyrie.

"Oh, not you," I mumble.

Thruth storms into the room. "Yes, me."

"Don't try to intimidate her," Nick scolds the Valkyrie.

"I don't have to try. Even as a queen she's puny and weak," the Valkyrie spits out.

I stomp toward her and point. I've *so* had it with her. "That is *so* not nice."

"You don't even talk like a queen." She glares at me.

Nick raises an eyebrow at me. "You're a *queen*?"

I walk to the edge of the bed, stand just a few inches away from her. Power rolls off her. "Okay, please refrain from your insidious comments, which are obviously geared to inflict harm upon my psyche. I do not appreciate it."

Nick cracks up. "Well, you *are* the same Zara."

I turn to smile at him and reach out my hand. He takes it. His fingers in mine are easily the best, most amazing-feeling fingers ever.

"I'm taking him home," I announce. "I have come for him and we're leaving."

"You cannot," she blusters. "You can't just leave. Nick must go through a ceremony. His memory must be purged of his stay here. There are certain rules, ways. You can't just expect those to be ignored because of your trivial wishes, your ludicrous love."

Nick loses his smile completely, and for a second I think he's going to let go of my hand. Instead, he pulls me to his side and growls. "Valkyrie. You have no right."

"Don't tell me what rights I do and do not have, wolf." She straightens up even more, looks like she's ready to fight.

"Fine," I cut in.

She taps her long blue fingernails against the bedpost. She looks at Nick. "Do you choose to leave the sacred halls of Valhalla, to renounce your rightful place as a warrior of Odin, and return with her?"

He hesitates. He closes his eyes for a moment and he actually hesitates before his voice comes out gruff and slow. "Yes, I do."

The words seem to hang in the air, powerful. Thruth bristles even more.

"I shall be back for you again, wolf." She fast-turns out of the room and flutters away, all purpose and fury.

"I really can't believe she's on the good side," I say.

Nick groans a little as he moves.

I study him. "Are you still hurt?"

"Not really." He's panting, though, and there are little stress lines around his eyes.

"You are such a bad liar. Sit down." I motion toward the bed.

He resists, but I push his chest gently and he falls back on the sheets. There's a faint shimmer of sweat on his forehead. He's paler than he should be too. I didn't even notice that before. I rest my hand on his forehead. He smiles.

"I can't stand that you're a pixie," he murmurs.

"I know." I close my eyes for just a second. "Most of the time I can't stand it either."

"Most of the time?" His voice cracks and I'm not sure if it's because he's upset or because he's still healing. I don't want to push him too far right now, overload his brain.

I lightly trace his too-big eyebrows and say, "I want you to rest."

"Just for a minute," he agrees. His voice is hoarse and sleep deep.

I keep my hand on his forehead, hoping it will calm him down, make him feel safe. "Mmm-hmm . . ."

In about thirty seconds he falls asleep. I can't resist the urge. I crawl into bed next to him and drape my arm across his chest. There is something so good about this moment. I can hear his breaths. He's alive and he's Nick and he obviously has some issues about me being pixie but he can get over it. I know it.

Still, a tiny bit of fear gnaws away at my stomach. Worry nestles inside my bones.

Because Mrs. Nix is dead and Betty is all feral and Nick is about to lose his memory and I am a pixie and there is war everywhere and danger everywhere and even though we are together and that is so good-good-good, nothing really is the same, and it won't ever be the same again.

And part of me feels like I've betrayed Astley.

I watch Nick sleep for hours, it seems, just thinking, memorizing his face, and eventually I fall asleep too.

They will take all of Nick's memories of being here. It is part of the conditions to getting him home, and while I'm not too cool about that, I guess it's worth it. I get to remember because:

1. I'm a queen and therefore the rules are different for me (this is totally unfair).
2. I was not brought here by a Valkyrie.
3. I did not die.
4. Blah. Blah. Blah.

We follow the bridge back. We ride the horse because Nick isn't fully recovered. The slope is extreme and powdery dust molecules lift into the air as the horse moves slowly and carefully down the yellow part of the rainbow. With each step, Nick grows wearier. He battles to keep his eyes open. Eventually, I have to hold him up so he doesn't fall off the horse. The weight of him is massive.

As we ride I watch him sleep. I press my hand against his face, count his breaths. I trace the line of his ear with my fingertip. Every single inch of him is so precious to me. I want to shackle myself to him, bind our hands together, make it so that he can never be taken from us again. And I think of the other people I love who are gone, like Mrs. Nix and my stepdad, or who are vulnerable, like Issie and Astley, Devyn and Cassidy, my mom. I wish there was some magic way that we could always be together. Losing them would be as horrible as losing Nick.

Mrs. Nix wasn't in Valhalla. Nor either of my dads. I guess not all warriors go there. I wonder if they are in heaven instead.

How much more grief will there be? Odin said there is a war coming, an end-of-the-world kind of war, and we have to keep it from happening somehow. That's going to put *everyone's* lives in jeopardy. My heart thumps hard remembering how the world went still when I lost Nick, when I lost Mrs. Nix, how there's a huge, gaping hole in my chest from their deaths, and my dads' deaths, and from Betty going were and never coming home anymore. Why do we have to hurt so much? Why does life have to be so hard?

The bridge ends just by Betty's house. The snow chugs down all around us and it's freezing cold again. The horse stops at the edge, neighing.

I gently shake Nick's shoulders. "Nick. Can you wake up?"

He groans, and his eyes flutter open a tiny bit. I slide off the horse, keeping my arms up so he doesn't fall off, and then I help him swing his leg over and get down. He sags against me as I pat the horse good-bye.

"Thank you," I tell her, and then I wrap my arm around Nick's waist and jump the eight feet down to the driveway, bringing him with me.

There are lights on in the house. My mom's car is in the drive-way. Casting a glance behind us, I see the bridge is already gone. There is just darkness. We are back in the land of cold and war. I head us toward the light, because really that is the only direction you should ever go.

One missing Bedford boy wandered out of the woods this morning. He has no memory of any events that occurred while he was missing. Police report he is wounded but recovering.
—NEWS CHANNEL 8

My mother throws open the door. Her cheeks are tearstained and her nose is red.

"Where have you been?" she demands. "Where have—?"

"Help me get Nick to the couch," I tell her.

Her mouth drops open, stunned, but she wraps her arm around Nick's waist and takes some of the weight. We hustle him to the couch. Once he's sitting, I yank off his shoes, lift up his feet, and make it so that he lies down. The entire time I'm working my mother is questioning me, demanding to know where I've been, how I got Nick, if I've seen Betty, and so on and so on. I beg off the questions until I get Nick settled. It's only after I've wrapped a blanket around him that I explain, "I saved Nick."

But that's not exactly true, because he didn't really need saving. He wasn't harmed there. He was just . . . in the afterworld?

She falls into the chair by the woodstove, her hand over her mouth. Horror overwhelms her. "I can't believe you did that."

"How long was I gone?"

"A day."

"Just a day."

She closes her eyes. "It felt like forever. It's the solstice today, the shortest day in the year. It's almost Christmas."

I go to her then because she looks so fragile and scared, as if she can't take any more. I go to her because I love her and I say, "I am so sorry, Mom."

"You have nothing to be sorry for." She brushes my words away with her hand. "I do. I was wrong to be so—to be so— I don't have the word for it, Zara, but I should have been better when you changed. I missed you. I missed my Zara."

"I'm right here," I say.

"I know," she says, and opens her arms for a hug.

Nick starts snoring on the couch, long, loud breaths. It makes us laugh.

My mom breaks off the hug first and says, "And I miss Betty. I don't suppose you could find her too?"

"I saw her before I left, taking down some pixies. She's next on the list," I say. "Right along with saving the world from imminent destruction, catching up with homework, and getting into college."

She thinks I'm kidding, but I'm not. While Nick sleeps I call Issie, Devyn, and Cassidy. Issie sneaks out of the house, and despite the curfew they all rush over and crowd into our living room. They stare down at Nick. For a little while it's weird but amazing, like the whole room vibrates with the enormity of what we've done. We brought him back from the dead.

"He still snores," Devyn says after I've briefed them on Valhalla and Nick's memory loss.

"And his feet twitch like a dog's," Issie remarks, leaning into

Devyn, who wraps his arms around her. She looks at Nick again and adds, "That is so sweet! You're positive he's not zombified or anything? Because he did just come back from the dead."

"Positive."

"I feel like we should give him a bone or something," Cassidy says.

"Cassidy!" I punch her in the arm and she giggles.

Issie and my mom start making hot chocolate. Devyn pulls some cheese out of the fridge and puts it on a board. There's eggnog and cookies too. It's a celebration and the guest of honor sleeps right through it. Even with all the happy goings-on, something makes me shiver. For a second I can't figure out what it is, and then I know—the spider feeling that I always used to get when I was human and evil pixies were around.

The doorbell rings.

"They're going to wake up Nick!" Issie shouts as if this would be the end of the world. It's funny because if all our commotion and her shouting don't wake up Nick, I don't think anything will.

I rush to the door, yanking it open. Snow and cold fly in. Astley smiles weakly.

"May I come in?" he asks.

My mom hates him. Nick hates him. I imagine Nick waking up and the first thing he sees being Astley hanging out in the kitchen, so I shake my head sadly. "Let me come out. Hold on."

I slam on my coat and some shoes, taking a second to touch the anklet Nick gave me. It is so fragile, just like all of us, yet it's unbroken, despite all the fights and journeys and deaths. It's unbroken and it is still here. I tuck it safely inside my sock and join Astley on the porch. We don't say anything for a minute. The snow falls down around us.

"Thank you," I say, choking up a little. "I mean, I know I've already thanked you, but . . . you know, you did a lot for me. So much, I can never repay you for keeping everyone safe and helping me get to—"

His finger comes up to my lips. "You don't have to thank me, Zara."

"But it was a big deal."

"That's what kings do. That's what friends do." His voice becomes infinitely sad. He swallows so hard that I can see it. "How is he doing?"

I tell him as quickly as I can about Nick, about Valhalla, about us trying to prevent a war.

"There has been similar talk at the council," he says.

"Odin or Thor said there was a traitor there," I tell him.

He exhales like it's news he expected but didn't want. We are quiet for a moment. The snow trucks down. I can see the inside of my house. Everyone gathered in the kitchen, Nick still sleeping on the couch. Devyn puts his arm around Issie's shoulders. She lifts up and kisses his cheek. Cassidy uses the cheese knife to scratch at her neck. Issie grabs it away from her. My mother stands leaning against the counter, sipping eggnog from a bright yellow mug. It looks so peaceful and warm and good, yet here I am standing outside in the cold night.

"They look so happy," I whisper.

He stands a little closer to me. "What do you think will happen when Nick wakes up?"

He's actually said Nick's name, but I don't comment on that fact. Instead, I tuck my hair into the collar of my coat. "He'll be upset. He won't remember Valhalla, so he won't immediately realize the gravity of what I've done or why I've done it, you know?

And I think I have to be okay with that—with the possibility that things might never be the same between us again—and just be grateful that he is here, alive."

Astley, wisely, doesn't answer. Instead, he takes my hand. I let him. There's comfort there. He is, after all, my king. But more importantly, he is my friend.

"Someday, when we have time and life isn't so dangerous-crazy, let's just hang out, okay?" I stare up into his sad face. "Please . . . Maybe go sledding. I still haven't done that."

He clears his throat. "Anytime."

I start to tug my hand away and then think better of it. My mother smiles at Issie in the kitchen. Nick stirs on the couch, beginning to wake up. I will have to go to him, tell him everything all over again, protect him as he has always protected everyone else.

"Odin said that I am the leader here, not Nick?" I ask. My stomach hardens. "Do you think he's wrong?"

Astley's fingers tighten around mine. "No, but we can pretend that Nick is the leader if it makes it easier on you."

"If he's not the leader, what is he?"

"A man. A warrior. Someone you and your friends love."

Now they are all laughing inside, clanking their mugs and glasses together, toasting something . . . I don't know what. My mother looks out the window again, and behind that smile is the look she has always had, the look I never recognized before—fear.

"We have to figure this out," I say, turning away from the warmth in the house, turning away from the people I have left, and turning toward him, the pixie king with snow in his hair and sorrow in his eyes. "We have to figure out how to keep everyone safe, to stop the war."

His grip tightens. "We will."

Acknowledgments

Pixie kisses (the good kind) to Bruce Barnard, Lew Barnard, Betty Morse, Rena Morse, and Debbie Gelinas for being the best family and the goofiest family ever. Thank you for being made of awesome, Mom.

Thanks to Emily for making it a hard choice between Team Nick and Team Astley. You are amazing. Remember Heppy! I love you. You're the best kid ever. And yes, I know how lucky I am.

Thanks to my own John Wayne. You are the only cowboy I could ever want and the best man in the universe. Thank you for giving me faith in how good men can be.

Thanks to Shaun Farrar for teaching me all about the beauty of chili cheese fries.

The magnificent Jennifer Osborn, Lori Bartlett, Melodye Shore, Kelly Fineman, Steven Wedel, Tami Lewis Brown, Devyn Burton, and Carrie Randall all earn a warrior's place in Valhalla for giving me the confidence to keep writing. Special props go to Steve because he made me fall in love with writing all over again. And then again!

Thanks to Perry Moore for giving me the magical cowboy hat that allowed me to continue to write the series. Honestly, sometimes a writer just needs a magical cowboy hat to keep going.

Thanks to Marie Overlock for giving me the best surprise retro-kitty gift ever and for making me laugh when I'm being a big perfectionist goody-goody tool, and to Shaun Farrar, Amelie Bacon, Jim Willis, Ken Mitchell, Travis Frost, Lorraine Bracey, Leigh Guildford, Kevin Edgecomb, Lori Bartlett, Ryan Lawson, Jack Raymond, Debbie Hogan, Perry Moore, Alice Dow, Callie Cox, Matt Heel, Chad Campbell, Lori Bartlett, Dotty Vachon, Evelyn Foster, Bethany Reynolds, Stephanie Preble Vickburg, Bubba Duncan, Caroline Peters, Belinda Albee, Lea Feldman, Megan Kelley Hall, Rod O'Connor, Will Rice, Dale Jackson, and Karen Heaney. All of you have said something or done something that made this book into what it is and made me into what I am. You probably don't know that though. Shh . . . Don't tell.

To the women of the tollbooth and to Vermont College of Fine Arts: you all are the best, the best ever. Thank you for helping me to be a better writer. Special shout-outs to Tami Brown and Chris Maselli and The Awesome Emily Wing Smith, the Whirligigs, the PWs, and Tamra Wright and Robin MacCready.

There is no person I need to thank more than Edward Necarsulmer. This time it's for being tireless, for letting me almost kill him on a road trip to the Outback, for wearing flannel, for being the best knight/agent a writer could ever want, and for actually being proud enough of me that he bragged to the waitress. You are golden. "Think of me as a place." And to his awesome and amazing coworker/sidekick/human Christa Heschke, who is beyond wonderful.

Strong woman thanks to Michelle Nagler, who is an editor of awesome, for making this a book, a real book with a real structure, and for being delightful in real life. I am insanely jealous of your voice and yet I still adore you.

To the rest of the amazing, stunning, exceptional, and incredibly caring Bloomsbury U.S. crew—Deb Shapiro, Melanie Cecka, Caroline Abbey, Beth Eller, Kate Lied, Katie Fee, and the people I don't actually get names for. You are all so incredible. Thank you for taking such good care of me and my books. I'm sorry if I sometimes make it hard. And thanks to the exceptionally awesome Bloomsbury UK staff as well. But most especially thanks to Deb for guarding my heart.

Special thanks to Nicole Gastonguay who makes covers that are so stunning that people pick up the books. You are an artist. I am in awe.

And thank you to all the people who read the books and love them enough to send me e-mails and message me on Facebook. You all make it worth it every single day.